SECOND CHANCES AT HOLLYHOCK FARM

GEORGINA TROY

Boldwood

First published in Great Britain in 2024 by Boldwood Books Ltd.

Copyright © Georgina Troy, 2024

Cover Design by Lizzie Gardiner

Cover Images: Shutterstock and Adobe Stock

Every effort has been made to obtain the necessary permissions with reference to copyright material, both illustrative and quoted. We apologise for any omissions in this respect and will be pleased to make the appropriate acknowledgements in any future edition.

A CIP catalogue record for this book is available from the British Library.

Paperback ISBN 978-1-78513-768-6

Large Print ISBN 978-1-78513-769-3

Hardback ISBN 978-1-78513-767-9

Ebook ISBN 978-1-78513-770-9

Kindle ISBN 978-1-78513-771-6

Audio CD ISBN 978-1-78513-762-4

MP3 CD ISBN 978-1-78513-763-1

Digital audio download ISBN 978-1-78513-765-5

This book is printed on certified sustainable paper. Boldwood Books is dedicated to putting sustainability at the heart of our business. For more information please visit https://www.boldwoodbooks.com/about-us/sustainability/

Boldwood Books Ltd, 23 Bowerdean Street, London, SW6 3TN
www.boldwoodbooks.com

For my family

1

ZAC

Zac leant on the fence at the bottom of the lower meadow and gazed at the beautiful pink granite farmhouse that had always been his family home. The symmetrical two-storey house had varying shades of hollyhocks growing up on either side of the front door and windows. To its right stood the largest of two barns with a smaller barn next to that and then several other outbuildings graduating down in size.

He smiled, proud of his older sister Lettie and the way she had given up her job in fashion and moved from London back to Jersey to take over the running of the eighty-acre farm when their father had suffered a heart attack earlier in the year. He thought of the contracts he had refused – looking after the sound at various music festivals around the island – to help her and knew he needed to think about returning to work. He might have a good reputation as a sound engineer, but there were other engineers only too willing to step in to cover for him, and the last thing he wanted was to end up not being offered work.

One of the Jersey cows in the upper field mooed. He loved

the sounds of this farm. Even though his father had moved from dairy to growing organic produce over ten years before, Zac couldn't help thinking how typical it was for his father to be unable to part with several of the older cows, insisting they should spend the rest of their days on the farm where they had been born. He looked behind him at the paddock with three alpacas and still found it strange that anyone would bring these beautiful creatures to the island, only for his father to end up giving them a home when the owners moved away and insisted they wouldn't have space for them.

He thought of Brodie, the local vet and his sister's boyfriend, and the dog he had given a home to a couple of months before after Lettie had found it on one of the nearby lanes. He could never understand how anyone could let these lovely animals go.

He heard his sister's anguished shout and, following the direction of her voice, hurried to the kitchen to see what was wrong.

'What's the matter, Letts?'

Lettie's face was flushed with temper. She groaned and held up a letter that looked as if it had been scrunched up before being flattened out again. 'This is so infuriating. The insurance company is refusing to cover the entire cost of the repairs to the barn roof,' she grumbled. 'Apparently our policy hadn't been linked to cost-of-living increases and they're only paying seventy per cent of the cost of repairing the storm damage.'

'What?' He had no idea how much money the work would cost but imagined it wasn't going to be cheap. 'But you need that fixed before winter if the animals are going to stay in there.'

'Exactly.' She folded her arms across her chest. 'We could keep some in the smaller barn, but not the larger animals. I'm so angry about it.'

Upset more like, he thought. 'Sorry, sis. That is a bit of a blow. What can we do about it?'

She shook her head and shrugged. 'I've no idea, but something needs to be sorted out because I can't do without that barn.'

He walked over to her and took the letter, reading it for himself. 'Rotten sods.' This was all Lettie needed. She had bravely taken on the farm but it hadn't proved to be as easy as she expected. 'We'll think of something. Try not to worry.'

She pulled out one of the chairs and sat, resting her elbows on the table before lowering her face into her hands. 'I'm already shattered and this is a problem I hadn't seen coming.' She looked up at him. 'Another thing that shows how inexperienced I am at running a place like this.'

He sat next to her. 'Hey, you're doing brilliantly. You will sort this.'

She turned to him and after a look of disbelief he noticed her expression harden. 'You know what, Zac? You're right. I will sort this. I just need to figure out how.'

'There. I knew you'd fight back.' He stood to go and put the kettle on and make them both a cup of tea. It was the standard reaction to most dramas in their house.

'I know,' Lettie exclaimed. 'We'll raise money by holding a fundraising event.'

'Good idea.'

She gasped. 'It could be a festival. We've got the land. Yes, that's what I'll do – I'll hold a festival here at Hollyhock Farm.'

His interest piqued, he forgot the tea and sat back down again. 'A music festival?' He loved the idea. He was a sound engineer after all and a lot of his job entailed working at festivals. 'That'll be brilliant, Letts.'

She shook her head. 'Sorry, Zac. We can't have loud music

and people singing and making noise around the animals; it would terrify them.'

She had a point. 'I hadn't thought of that.' If she wasn't thinking of a music festival, then what? 'Tell me more.'

'A wellness festival.' She beamed at him, clearly delighted with her idea.

'What?' She went to repeat what she had said, but he stopped her. 'I know wellness is all about looking after yourself, but I don't know what sort of things you'd offer.'

'I've only been to one.'

'So you know what they do at these things?'

She shrugged. 'I can learn. That's what the internet is for, surely.'

He didn't like to argue, not when she was this enthusiastic for an idea. He liked seeing her ready to fight back and had no intention of crushing her excitement.

'From what I remember there were stalls where people sold things like special teas, ideas for better nutrition. Various therapies, like...' she thought for a moment '...crystal therapies, herbal remedies, sound baths. Ooh, and yoga or Pilates classes. People offered courses at the one I attended and gave samples of products and product demonstrations for things like juicers, or whatever.'

It didn't sound like his sort of thing, but he hid his thoughts. This wasn't about what he preferred. His sister needed his support and he intended doing all he could to be there for her.

He wondered how much time she would need to prepare for something like this. 'When do you think you'd want to hold the festival?'

Lettie gave his question some thought. After a while, she shrugged. 'Well, it would need to be before the weather turns but not too soon that we aren't able to make all the arrangements properly. So latest the end of September, I think.'

'I'll help out in any way I can, Letts. So will Brodie, and I'm sure your friends will do all they can to help you too.'

'Thanks, Zac.' She gave him a grateful smile. 'I just hope whatever we do raises enough money to cover the cost of the roof repairs.'

'I'm sure with all of us helping you, we'll do it.'

He heard his name being called and looked up to see his mother hurrying into the kitchen. His parents were due to go on another trip that evening and, not wishing to delay them, Zac ran to see what she wanted from him.

He followed her into the kitchen. 'What is it, Mum?'

'You're not busy, are you?' She looked from him to Lettie.

He'd have to help Lettie bring the animals into the barns before it got dark but that was hours away. 'No, why?'

'I need you to do something for me.' She held out her car keys.

Zac went to take them from her. 'Shopping?' he asked, hoping she would say no. He hated food shopping, unless it was for snacks and beers to watch a rugby match.

'No. I need you to hurry to Rozel, to the campsite there.'

Zac withheld a groan. He tried to think what his mother could possibly need from a campsite on the other side of the island. 'I don't understand.'

'Kathleen, one of my Book Club Girls, has a friend and her granddaughter who need collecting.'

Still none the wiser, he frowned. 'I need to take them somewhere, I assume?' he asked, wishing he had thought to say he was busy.

'They're on the island for a few months and it's only been a week and I think it's been a bit much for Patsy – that's the grandmother.'

Zac thought of all the tents he had slept in: some large and fancy; others tiny, hot and uncomfortable. 'Right, but what do you want me to do with them?'

She rested her hands on her hips and stared at him for a few seconds. 'Sorry, didn't I say?'

He shook his head.

'I need you to bring them here. Lettie has been talking about eco travel.'

He had a vague idea about what that meant but thought he should ask to be certain. 'Which is?'

She stared out of the window thoughtfully for a few seconds. 'If I recall correctly, it's about being aware of the impact our travels have on the environment. On local communities a traveller visits. You know, being mindful about the impact we make when we visit somewhere and how we can go about protecting those places by, among other things, supporting local businesses.' She seemed satisfied with her answer and Zac had to admit he was impressed.

'And Kathleen insisted the ladies would be happy to stay here and help out on the farm for a couple of months, or so. It won't cost your sister anything apart from meals and she might enjoy the company.'

He didn't like to remind his mother that he was also working on the farm. Trying to imagine where the two guests would stay, Zac thought of his mother's craft room that had once been their spare room. He groaned, hoping he wasn't going to be forced to clear out the room to make it up as a bedroom for their guests. 'I know you and Dad are going away, but you'll be back in a couple of weeks so I hardly dare ask, but where will they sleep?'

'There are two perfectly good rooms up in the attic.'

He thought of the rooms she referred to and couldn't recall the last time he had been in there. 'Aren't they full of boxes of junk?'

His mother's expression darkened. 'No. There might be a few things that can be thrown out, but most of it will be fine. There are still beds in there and with a little bit of effort we could make the rooms comfortable for the two women.'

'By "we" I'm assuming you mean me and Lettie?'

'Of course,' she said, looking flustered. 'I have packing to do and your father hasn't even begun to sort out his clothes for our trip to the Mediterranean.' She pointed to the wall clock. 'Forget the rooms for now. You'd better leave to fetch them. Kathleen will have let them know that you're on your way, so they'll probably already be waiting.'

'Fine. I'll see you in a bit.' He went to say something about the festival to his sister.

'Zac Torel, I need you to go straight away,' his mother said before leaving the room.

Lettie widened her eyes, clearly amused.

'I'm going. You're going to need to think of a name for the festival, work out what you think it'll cost and exactly when you'd like to hold it.'

'And we'll need to set up a website,' she replied enthusiastically. 'I'll make some notes and get on with all that.'

'Go, sis! I'll help you later if you want.'

'Sounds amazing,' she said, leaning over to the worktop and grabbing a notepad and pen. 'Thanks, Zac.'

* * *

'Zac Torel, are you still here?' their mother called from somewhere in the hallway.

Zac rolled his eyes.

'You'd better get going.'

It took all Zac's patience to stop letting his frustration with the traffic get the better of his temper as he slowly made his way there. The roads were full of people seemingly out on leisurely drives. Every cyclist on the island also appeared to be out and about and, when he managed to find himself on a clear road, a tractor or some other farm vehicle materialised in front of him, slowing him down again.

He pulled into the campsite car park and realised he had no idea what the two women looked like. He decided that the best thing might be to get out of the car and stand by it, hoping they would think to speak to the person who was clearly waiting for someone.

Eventually two women walked into the car park and seemed to be looking for someone. They had large rucksacks and one seemed older than the other from what he could see of her face under a huge floppy straw hat. It seemed more suited to lying on the beach or on a lounger in the garden than in a campsite.

He stepped forward and raised a hand waving at them. 'Are you looking for me?' he asked cheerily. 'I'm Zac from Hollyhock Farm.'

They both smiled and began walking more quickly towards him.

'Yes, that's right,' the older lady said, leading the way. 'It's jolly kind of you to come all this way to fetch us.'

'It's no problem at all,' he said, realising he wasn't only saying that to be polite when he saw the beautiful girl take off her hat momentarily to reveal her bright pink hair. She pushed her hair back from her face before replacing the hat on her head.

2

MELODY

Melody should have known camping wasn't going to suit her grandmother Patsy's idea of comfort but once Gran made her mind up about something there was little point in arguing. At least they would soon be staying in a farmhouse with, she hoped, real beds. She caught the eye of the handsome, tanned man who had come to fetch them and hoped the rest of the family were as friendly as him.

'Hi, I'm Zac Torel,' he said, shaking her grandmother's hand.

It dawned on her that maybe the Torel family expected them to pitch their tent in one of their fields. She hoped not. Melody was looking forward to sleeping inside again. One week sleeping under the stars was enough for her, especially sharing an airless tent with her gran.

Melody watched her grandmother introduce herself to the man and decided she couldn't love anyone more than she did this caring, protective woman whose zest for life surpassed anyone else's that she knew. It was comforting to know that there was someone who had your back no matter what life threw at you. All it had taken for her gran to insist they come to the island was Melody turning up on her doorstep in floods of tears after the last time her husband Rhys had turned on her.

Melody raised her hand to her right cheek, touching the skin lightly with the tips of her fingers, even though the bruising had now gone. She saw Zac glance at her and pulled her hat down lower. It still shocked her to recollect how volatile Rhys's temper had become since their marriage only two years before. She was embarrassed to think how he had manipulated her to believe she was the cause of so much of his rage. Then he had hit her and she decided that she had endured his jealousy and accusations for long enough. It was time to leave.

'That's it,' Patsy had said after Melody had explained what had caused her sobs. 'You need to get away from that toe rag. I've always wanted to visit the Channel Islands and now there's nothing stopping the pair of us going there. Pack your things.'

Only too happy to agree with Patsy's plan, Melody had waited for Rhys to leave their Edinburgh flat before sneaking in and packing a rucksack of essentials, grabbing her passport and returning to her grandmother's bungalow. All her parents knew of their trip was that she was accompanying Patsy. Her mother and Rhys's mum were best friends and Melody didn't want to cause a rift between them by telling her what had really been going on in her life. Her father would hunt him down and probably resort to hitting him, and she didn't want to be responsible for that happening either, so confiding in her grandmother had been the safest option. And the best, she now realised.

Patsy was still talking to Zac. 'It's very good of your family to offer us somewhere to stay and thank you again for coming to fetch us.'

'May I take your rucksacks for you? They look rather heavy.'

'They are a bit,' her grandmother said, turning to let him lift the heavy weight from her back. 'That's much better.'

Melody bit her lower lip to stop herself from smiling as she saw Zac wince at the unexpected weight of her grandmother's belongings.

'Thank you so much.' She held out her hand and after moving the rucksack from one hand to the other, Zac shook it.

She gave him a knowing smile and he looked embarrassed to realise she had noticed his pained expression.

'I'm Melody,' she said, wanting him to relax with her. 'Patsy's my grandmother. Gran insisted camping would be a good experience for me, but I'm incredibly grateful that your sister invited us to stay in your house.'

He laughed. 'I don't blame you. I like my creature comforts too, despite how untidy I probably look right now.'

He went to take her rucksack but she shook her head. 'I travel much lighter than Gran does,' she said, lowering her voice. 'I'll make it to the car without collapsing.'

Zac laughed. It was a deep, rumbling laugh and didn't go with his slim frame at all.

'I'm not completely deaf yet, Melody,' Patsy said, clearly amused by her comments. 'I must admit that I'm happy to end our camping experience, too. I thought it would be great fun, and to be fair it was for the first week, but I'm glad to call it quits now.'

'My sister will be very pleased.' He opened the boot of the car and heaved Patsy's bag into it, waiting for Melody to load hers in before closing the lid. 'Please, sit where you like. It won't take us too long to get back to the farm. It's not the height of luxury, I'm afraid.' He gestured to the car.

Melody didn't want him to think they cared how old the car

might be. 'I think Gran's happy to get out of the sun and to your farm,' she said, keeping her voice low.

As they drove along the north coast, Melody listened as Zac pointed out the French coast in the distance and Melody realised she was seeing far more of the island in this short trip than they had done over the past few days. 'It's a little wilder on this side with the high cliffs.'

'It is,' he said. 'There are beaches and coves on this side of the island but they're more dramatic to look at, whereas on the east, south and west sides you have the large expanses of beaches where tourists traditionally spend their time sunbathing or surfing.' He changed gear, crunching them noisily. 'Sorry, this is Mum's car. So, is this your first time to Jersey?'

Melody wound down the window and leant her arm on it as she stared out at the deep blue of the sea to their right.

'It is,' Patsy said. 'We've been on a couple of tours and caught the bus a few times, so have seen something of the place, but I hadn't expected there to be so much to visit and we really should have thought about hiring a car.'

'It is easier with one.' He slowed down as the road narrowed and a large tractor and trailer needed to pass from the opposite direction.

'At least the weather is good for your visit,' he added, 'and you can see the island at its best.'

'We've loved it, haven't we, Gran,' Melody said. 'I've always thought about coming here at some point but have mostly travelled further afield. Do you travel much?'

'I travel quite a bit for work, but mostly to the mainland,' he explained. 'My parents want to spend more time travelling, which is probably why my mother was so willing to offer you both somewhere to stay.'

'Yes, Kathleen did mention something about ecotourism.'

Patsy turned slightly in her seat and looked over her shoulder at Melody. 'Is that right?'

Melody nodded. 'It is, Gran.'

'It would be,' Zac said. 'My parents are retiring so my sister, Lettie, is taking over from them and looking for ways to be more sustainable. She's only been doing it for a few months but is keen to implement her ideas to update the running of the farm. She and I are trying to find ways to increase finances for the business.'

Melody tried to picture Zac's sister and parents. She looked at his wavy chestnut hair and tanned arms. He had a laid-back way about him that appealed to her and she sensed she and her gran were going to enjoy helping Lettie and Zac on the farm and getting to know Mr and Mrs Torel.

'I'm still getting used to the idea of my father spending time on a cruise ship instead of wearing his overalls and boots like he's always done. I'm not sure he was too keen to give up work at first, but he had a heart attack.' He turned left and Melody realised they were driving inland. She wondered why he wasn't continuing along the scenic route and wished they still were.

'Oh no,' Patsy said. 'He's all right though?'

'He is, thankfully,' Zac assured them. 'However, my mother decided that enough was enough and had always been eager to spend more time travelling.' Melody could see his eyes crinkle slightly in the rear-view mirror and knew he was smiling. 'She took the opportunity to book their first cruise and they're off again this evening for a couple of weeks.'

'Good for them,' Patsy said.

'I agree,' he continued. 'I'm pleased for them. They've always been so dedicated to running the farm. Lettie and I feel that it's our turn to take over now and keep the place going.'

'I love that your parents are making the most of their opportunities,' Melody admitted, unable to keep a wistful tone out of her voice. She could imagine her mother wanting to do the same thing, but doubted her parents would ever have the spare cash to fund much travelling.

They drove down a long hill with houses on each side and past a built-up area, then turned right onto a road with two lanes. Seconds later she noticed the sea to her right and an impressive building on a rock in the bay.

'Look, Melody,' Gran said, pointing at it.

'I'm looking at it. What's that place over there, Zac?' Melody asked.

'That's Elizabeth Castle. You can visit it if you like because it's open to the public.'

Patsy laughed. 'It's surrounded by sea. I can't picture myself swimming there and would need to find someone with a boat to get there.'

'Ahh, but that's not necessary,' he explained. 'There's the Castle Ferry, an amphibious vehicle that looks like a misshapen tank – or maybe a truck – that takes visitors there and back. They're known locally as Ducks. You can also walk along the causeway when the tide is out.'

'Sounds fascinating,' Melody said, hoping she would be able to see the causeway at some point. 'I presume it has quite a bit of history to it, like the castle in Gorey that we struggle to pronounce the name for.'

'That one is Mont Orgueil, but the locals sometimes refer to it as Gorey Castle, so you can always call it that instead.'

She listened as he explained that the islet they were looking at was a fifteen-acre Elizabethan fortress.

'It dates back to when Sir Walter Raleigh was the governor of Jersey. Did you know that King Charles II was given refuge here during the English Civil War? To say thank you, he gave the island a huge area of land in America.'

'Really?' Patsy gasped.

'Where?' she asked, intrigued.

'Have a guess.'

She thought about it as he continued driving.

'This bay is St Aubin's Bay by the way,' he said. 'Hollyhock Farm is in St Ouen, on the north-west of the island. It should only take us another fifteen minutes to get there because there's not too much traffic at this time of the day.'

He indicated the hamburger stall at the end of the avenue and laughed. 'That's where me and my mates spent many evenings as teenagers eating burgers and chatting before catching buses home.'

She liked hearing about local life on the island, wanting to absorb the sense of what it really felt like to live there.

'Sorry, I never answered your question about the land in the States, did I?' The car slowed as the two lines of traffic filtered into one. 'Any thoughts on where it could be?'

She thought for a moment and, when Patsy didn't say anything, Melody answered. 'I have one suggestion, but it seems too obvious to be right.'

'Give it a go.' He smiled at her in the rear-view mirror. 'Go on.'

'I don't suppose it's New Jersey, is it?'

'It is.'

'No way. That's amazing. And all because the king was allowed to come here.'

'Yes. You see, being welcoming is something that's in our blood. It's nothing new to us locals.'

Melody laughed. 'It must be.'

'Have you never wanted to leave here?' Patsy asked. 'Or maybe you haven't always lived on the island?'

'I worked away until fairly recently, as did Lettie. She was in London working in fashion and I worked all over the place. I'm a sound engineer by trade.'

'Sounds fascinating.' Melody liked that Zac and his sister gave up everything to step in and help keep the family home and business.

'It can be. I've enjoyed my work and being based in London for the past few years, but there comes a time when family needs to come first and this was that time for me. I will have to think about returning to do a few contracts soon though, otherwise they'll forget who I am. How about you?'

'I've done all sorts of things. My mother was a homeopathic practitioner, and I learnt a lot from her, but branched out into other areas, like crystal therapy, colour therapy and aromatherapy, until I began training as a yoga instructor and that's how I mostly earn my living. Gran has always been one to try out new things and I think our interest comes from her initially.'

Patsy laughed. 'Her mother has always blamed me for making her eat what I grew when she was young.'

Melody recalled many amusing conversations when her mother teased her gran about her childhood. 'I think she was more bothered that you always insisted on making all her clothes, Gran.'

Patsy nodded. 'That's true, Zac. I didn't realise until she was in her teens how she was teased at school for my "New Age" ideas.'

Melody thought she should finish telling Zac about her work. 'I've always practised yoga and finally trained as a teacher several years ago. It's these things, especially the yoga, that's helped me pay for my travelling.'

'I see,' Zac said. 'So you work as you move from place to place?'

'I used to.' She decided not to mention her marriage to Rhys because it would probably lead to questions about her relationship and she wasn't anywhere near ready to discuss that with anyone yet. 'Pretty much.'

'And now it's brought you to Jersey.'

'I wanted to visit here,' Patsy said. 'And Melody, um, decided to join me.'

She saw him glance at her in the rear-view mirror. Zac clearly suspected there was more to her story, so she decided to elaborate enough to avoid awkward questions. 'I'm recently out of a long-term relationship and thought it was the perfect time to put some distance between me and my ex.'

It wasn't the whole story but Melody didn't think Zac needed to know that.

'Sounds like a good idea,' he said.

She was enjoying the lack of complication in her life right now. She smiled at him. 'We thought so.'

3

ZAC

As they drove he explained about there being two rooms for them in the attic and his sister's plans to hold a wellness festival and why there was a need to urgently raise money for farm repairs.

'We're looking forward to seeing the farm,' Patsy said, smiling at Zac from the passenger seat. 'And we'll do all we can to help your sister with the wellness festival.'

'I'm sure she'd appreciate any help you can give her. It'll be the first time we've held one and she's bound to be anxious to make it a success.'

Melody leant on the back of Patsy's seat. 'I've been to several wellness events over the years,' she said, before sitting back again.

'I'm interested to become involved and see what it's all about.' Patsy lowered her window. 'This trip is all about experiencing new things, isn't it, Melody?'

'It is, Gran.' She caught Zac's gaze in the rear-view mirror and he was struck by her pale blue, almost aquamarine eyes.

He wasn't sure if it was the light in the vehicle, or if they really were the colour of turquoise.

'Hey, look out,' Patsy snapped.

Immediately turning his attention to the road, Zac had to swerve to miss a granite wall. 'Sorry, I was distracted there for a moment,' he said, mortified. He glanced in the mirror and noticed Melody's amusement. He really needed to pay more attention to what he was doing.

He drove on, telling the women about Derek and Spud – the farm dogs – and wanting to look back at Melody once again. There was something about her. Maybe he was wrong and it was simply her stunning eyes that had made him feel as if he had been hit by a bolt.

'Here we are,' he said, turning into the driveway.

'This is beautiful,' Patsy gasped.

'It really is, Gran,' Melody agreed breathily. 'We've lucked out here, that's for sure.'

Zac felt the cool breeze strengthen as Melody's window lowered further and she leant out. He was used to people being taken aback by the farm on their first visit and even found himself being surprised by its prettiness when he returned after being away for several months.

'You're very lucky living here,' she said.

'I know. Although I've only recently moved back in. I was living away and then in a flat close to town, but with everything we've had going on it made sense to save rent and also be closer to where I'm needed, at least for the summer months.'

They passed through the village where he spotted Callum's pristine Golf parked by the shop and pointed out where Pasty and Melody could buy most things they needed.

'That's the Village Veterinary Practice where my sister's boyfriend Brodie treats the local pets.'

After checking neither of the women needed to stop and buy anything, he continued on to the farm.

Zac turned into the driveway, aware they were both looking out of their windows at the passing fields and paddocks, which although fairly dry and less lush than during rainier seasons were still beautiful. Zac slowed and pointed to fields on either side of the track. 'All this is us, over to the other side of that wooded area over there.'

'It's very pretty,' Melody said.

He slowed down even more as they neared a pretty granite farmhouse surrounded by a wall and what seemed to be two barns and a couple of other smaller outbuildings. The car pulled into the yard.

'Look, Gran. All those hollyhocks and in so many colours too.'

He looked at the mass of his mother's favourite flowers – their pink, yellow, dark purple, white and red colours like gently swaying gems growing up against the house and barn walls.

'It's very beautiful,' Patsy said, the awe clear in her voice. 'I can see why it's called Hollyhock Farm.'

'It is impressive at this time of year, I suppose.'

'It's glorious,' Melody said.

He smiled to himself.

'I love hollyhocks.' Patsy sighed. 'I hadn't realised this place would be so colourful and, well, picture-perfect.'

'It's not at its best at this time of year,' Zac admitted. 'But even I can see why people react like you've both done the first time they see it. I find myself being surprised too some of the times I return after being away for a while.'

Zac saw Melody's hand reach forward and rest on Patsy's shoulder from the corner of his eye. He was glad they were happy and knew his mother and sister would be too. They were both proud of the farm and it was always nice to watch someone seeing the place for the first time. It helped make giving up the past few months of his life to help here all the more worth it, when he witnessed reactions such as these.

He parked the car. 'Shall we go inside? I'm sure my sister will be only too happy to show you both around the place, although it might be better to wait until later when the temperature lowers a bit.'

Lettie appeared from the larger barn, smiling and waving to them.

'Hello. I'm Zac's sister Lettie. I run this place. Or at least I do my best to do that.' She held up her hands. 'I'm a bit mucky from cleaning the barn, so I'm going to have to ask Zac to show you to your rooms. I hope you like them.'

'I'm sure we will,' Patsy assured her.

'I know we will.' Melody laughed.

'I do hope so.' She smiled. 'I'd better carry on here for a bit and then when you've had time to freshen up you can come and find me and I'll show you both around, if you like.'

Spud ran out of the house and immediately started sniffing the women's legs, wagging his tail. Zac saw his mother walk out of the house drying her hands on a tea towel.

'Welcome to Hollyhock Farm,' she said proudly. 'I'm Lindy Torel.' Lindy tucked the cloth under her left arm and reached out to shake their hand. 'It's wonderful to meet you both.'

Zac left his mother chatting to them and lifted both rucksacks from the boot of the car.

'I'm sorry but my husband Gareth and I will be rushing off in a few hours on holiday. I'm sure Zac and Lettie will take good care of you while we're away though.'

'I'm sure they will,' Patsy said. 'We're very grateful to your family for taking us in and look forward to paying our way by helping out in whatever way you need us to on the farm.'

'This is Spud. He's nosy but harmless, unless you decide to steal one of our sheep.' Lindy patted her right thigh. 'Leave her alone, Spud. There's more than enough time to get to know our guests.'

'He's no bother, Mrs Torel. I love dogs.'

'Please, call me Lindy. We can't be formal with each other, especially when we'll all be living under the same roof.' She waved for them to follow her. 'Let's get you inside; it'll be much cooler in there.'

'Thank you, that would be lovely,' Patsy said, taking off her hat and wiping her forehead with the back of her hand.

They followed his mother inside and, as Zac knew it would, the temperature instantly dropped.

'This is lovely.' Melody sighed.

'That's one of the best things about this house,' Lindy said. 'It's always cooler in here. Now, take a seat and I'll pour us all something refreshing.'

When their guests were seated at the table and everyone had a cool drink, she turned to Zac.

He knew that look only too well. 'You have a job for me, don't you?'

Lindy took a sip of her drink and nodded. 'I need you to help your sister finish clearing out the two attic bedrooms for Patsy and Melody.'

'I've done most of the work,' Lettie said, sitting at her usual seat. 'It shouldn't take us too long.'

Zac would have much rather done anything on the farm but clear out two attic rooms, especially on such a hot day. It must be at least thirty degrees, he reasoned. He wondered why his mother was mentioning this chore in front of their guests and then it dawned on him that she did it because he couldn't refuse with Melody and Patsy sitting in front of him.

'Sure.' He drank his cold water.

'Please don't worry about sorting rooms for us,' Melody said. 'I'm sure Gran and I can do it. Just show us the way and let us know where we can find bed linen. You're bound to have more than enough to do today without preparing rooms.'

'Not at all,' Lindy argued. 'We can't expect you to do that.'

'We really wouldn't mind,' Patsy assured her.

Zac wasn't sure who was more determined to get their way, Patsy or his mother. 'Why don't the four of us get them ready,' he suggested. 'It would take half the time and then you can both have the rooms exactly how you think they'll work best for you?'

Patsy finished her drink and stood. 'That's settled then.'

Lindy shrugged. 'Fine by me. I still need to finish the packing for our trip but when I've done that I'll prepare an early supper for us all so we can get to know each other a bit before Gareth and I need to leave for the airport.'

'Great,' Zac said, relieved they had all agreed. 'Shall we go up to the attic then?'

* * *

Zac showed them up to the attic. 'There are quite a few stairs, I'm afraid.'

'Don't worry about us,' Patsy said. 'We're used to stairs. I live in a townhouse and my room is on the third floor so this will be fine. Anyway it's all good exercise. We look forward to helping your sister on the farm, don't we, Melody?'

'Yes, we really do.'

Zac was relieved for his sister that she would have a couple of helpers and wondered what exactly she would be asking them to do.

They reached the top floor and standing in the hallway Zac indicated the two open bedroom doors. 'Take your pick. I hope you'll find them comfortable enough.'

Their guests entered a room each. He saw Melody enter the yellow bedroom and her face light up in a brilliant smile.

'This is gorgeous,' she said, gazing around the room.

'After lying on a camp bed for a week this will be utter heaven.' Patsy sighed, sounding equally delighted.

'There's only a shower on this floor, I'm afraid,' he explained. 'And it's pretty tiny, but there's a loo and basin in there, so I hope it's OK.'

'It'll be fine,' Melody assured him. 'We've been used to an ablution block.' She giggled. 'Or at least that's what Gran's been calling it. I'll be delighted to only have to share with her.'

When the women had chosen their rooms, Zac took each rucksack into the correct one and set it down on the chairs that Lettie had left there for them.

'Towels are there,' he said, pointing to the wooden towel rail underneath the window in Patsy's room, 'and there are extra in the airing cupboard downstairs. Just shout if you need me to find them for you. Um...' He tried to think what else they might need. 'I see my sister has left a tray with a few things on it for you.' He looked at the carafe of water, a glass and a small tin containing, he presumed, some of his mother's freshly baked biscuits. 'I imagine your room has the same set-up,' he said to Melody when he noticed her standing at the door.

'It does. I think they've thought of everything.'

'I feel thoroughly spoilt,' Patsy said looking, Zac thought, extremely happy with the rooms and how they had been set up.

Aware they must want to unpack, Zac went to the door. 'I'll leave you both to settle in and will catch up with you later.'

'Perfect. Thank you, Zac,' Patsy said, unzipping her rucksack. 'This is much more luxurious than we had expected and we're very grateful to you all.'

'We really are.' Melody smiled at him and again he was transfixed by her unusual eyes.

Unable to speak for a moment, Zac cleared his throat and forced his legs to move. 'See you in a bit then.'

4

MELODY

Fifteen minutes later, having helped her grandmother make up her bed, Melody accompanied her downstairs.

'What do you think?'

'I don't care how hard the work is,' Patsy said, keeping her voice low. 'I'm going to make the most of every moment in this idyll.'

So was she, Melody thought, relieved to know that she would be sleeping on a comfortable bed again that night.

* * *

'I hope we haven't kept you waiting,' Melody said, entering the kitchen and seeing Lindy, Lettie and Zac already there.

Lindy turned from where she was standing by the stove. 'Take a seat, both of you, then you can tell me what you fancy to eat.' She held up a wooden spoon. 'I forgot to ask if you have any food preferences, allergies, that sort of thing, so we know.'

'I eat anything,' Patsy said proudly.

Melody smiled. 'I'm a vegetarian.' She hoped that wouldn't

be a problem on the farm. She knew it was an organic business but wasn't sure where the family stood when it came to eating meat. 'But I like most things other than meat or fish and I don't have any allergies that I'm aware of.'

The sound of a noisy engine came from inside one of the barns. 'Useless bloody thing,' a man she presumed must be Mr Torel grumbled as he exited through one of the large double doors. 'It was fine until its last service and I'm not going to fork out for another.' He seemed to notice them all and frowned. 'I didn't realise we had guests.'

'I'm afraid it was all a bit last minute,' Patsy said.

Gareth smiled at her.

'Most things are when my wife is involved,' he joked.

Lindy frowned at him. 'This is my husband. Gareth. And these ladies are Patsy and her granddaughter Melody.'

'I'm very glad to meet you both.' Melody saw him stare at her hair for a couple of seconds before seeming to realise what he was doing. He raised his hands displaying oil on his skin. 'Er, sorry, mucky hands. What do you think of the place, or is it too early to say?'

'We've only seen our rooms so far, but Lettie is going to show us around a bit later.'

'Good. She can introduce you to the animals we have here.'

'We're looking forward to seeing everything,' Patsy said, making him smile.

'They haven't seen anything of the place yet, Dad,' Zac said taking cutlery from the drawer. 'I only brought them here a short while ago.'

'I hadn't realised. Been too busy faffing about with that tractor in the barn to notice much else.'

Melody sensed Gareth's frustration.

Lindy folded her arms across her chest. 'But you've fixed it now, haven't you? Or should I call that nice mechanic to come and help sort it?'

'I'm not paying his exorbitant fees. Anyway it's fine now. I think,' he grumbled. 'I didn't want to leave here with the thing not working and cause Lettie problems. I've spent enough time thinking about that now though, and if it breaks down again, I'll tell her to give the mechanic a call. Do I smell cooking?'

Lindy widened her eyes at Melody. 'Anyone would think I didn't cook his meals every single day,' she said, sarcasm clear in her voice. She cocked her head in her husband's direction and winked. 'Maybe I should start training him, now he's supposed to have retired from farming. I don't want him getting bored.'

'Chance would be a fine thing,' Gareth said.

Lindy smiled and Melody knew she was trying to wind him up.

'If I thought you'd allow me to cook in your precious kitchen,' he said, giving her a peck on the cheek, 'I'd gladly fry us a couple of eggs and some bacon, but you won't hear of it. Don't insinuate to these lovely people that I'm at fault for not having cooked anything for us yet.'

Lindy laughed. 'He's right. I refuse to let him loose in there. He'd only mess the place up and it would take me longer to clear up and put everything back into its rightful place than it does to cook the food.'

Melody already felt comfortable with the Torels. The gentle banter and teasing amused her; they were obviously very close-knit. She caught her gran's eye and exchanged a happy smile. 'I think we're going to be very happy here.'

'I'm very happy to hear it.' Lindy smiled.

'Tea, or coffee?' Zac asked, standing by an open cupboard,

which Melody saw was full of various mismatched cups and mugs.

'Coffee for me, please,' Melody said.

'Ah, a girl after my own heart,' he said. 'I'm a coffee drinker, but the rest of them seem to live off gallons of tea each day.'

'Never mind that,' Lettie said. 'Melody needs to be told more about this place, our plans and what we hope her involvement in it might be.'

This was more like it, Melody thought, smiling. It was exactly what she needed if she didn't want to dwell on Rhys and what had happened between them. 'I can't wait to be shown round the farm and hear more,' she admitted.

'Hurry up and wash your hands,' Lindy said as Gareth made his way over to the sink. When he was seated, she served up a plate of delicious-smelling food and then passed it to Zac who placed it on the table in front of his father.

'We don't usually eat this early but I had already told Gareth what time to come in for his food, and I'm sure you're both hungry. Apologies for serving him first,' Lindy added, 'but I'm determined he's going to finish his packing. Now, what do you fancy eating? We're only having something light, but I can always rustle up a snack later if either of you are hungry.'

Unsure how to answer, Melody glanced at Gareth's plate. 'I'd love some eggs, please.'

'How about some mushrooms, beans and tomatoes to go with them?'

'Yes, to the mushrooms and tomatoes,' she said. 'I'm not too keen on beans though.'

'No problem,' Lindy said, turning back to her cooking.

Melody was aware they hadn't discussed what work Lettie needed her and Gran to help with. 'Gran and I are looking forward to helping on the farm and we're willing to do whatever you need us to.'

'That's so kind of you both,' Lettie said. 'Thank you. I'm pretty used to running this place now, but any extra help harvesting our produce, keeping our honesty box well supplied with fresh stock and feeding and mucking out the animals is mostly what I'll need help with.' She widened her eyes. 'Especially now I've landed us with the wellness festival to plan, set up and host.'

Melody was excited to try these new experiences. 'Bring it all on. We both want to support you in any way we can.'

'That's amazing. Thank you both so much. I could do with the help.'

'And now you have it,' Patsy said, raising a hand for Lettie to give her a high five.

Melody saw the surprise on Lettie's face when she realised what Patsy was doing and laughed.

'I have a feeling having you both here is going to be a lot of fun.' Lettie smiled at them both. 'I'll show you around after we've eaten and tell you more then,' she said quietly.

'I'd like that,' Melody said, mouthing a thank you at Zac as he handed her a mug of steaming coffee.

Yes, she thought, she was going to enjoy staying here.

5

ZAC

When Lettie arrived for their meal, Zac listened to her talking to Patsy and Melody, explaining how she had only recently taken over the farm. He couldn't help thinking that even though she had decided to hold a wellness festival and had a smile on her face, she was worried. What else was she concerned about? he wondered. He decided to speak to her privately once they had finished eating.

'You seem a little distracted,' his mother said when there was a break in the conversation.

He wasn't surprised she'd said something – their mother didn't miss much and never shied away from facing things head on.

Lettie paused, her fork halfway to her mouth, and looked across the table at her mother. Zac watched as his sister seemed to consider something, then lowered her knife and fork and rested them on her plate. 'I wasn't going to mention anything because I didn't want you to worry while you were away.'

'What is it?' Gareth frowned. 'Is it one of the animals? They all seemed fine when I checked them earlier.'

Lettie shook her head. 'No, Dad. The animals are all fine. And anyway, I have Brodie minutes away if anything does happen while you're gone, don't forget.'

'Then what is it?' Lindy asked.

Lettie sat back in her chair and sighed. 'It's the barn roof.'

Zac sensed his sister's concern about sharing the insurer's decision with their father.

'The damage to the roof is covered, isn't it?' Gareth frowned.

'That's just it.' Lettie grimaced. 'Only partly.'

Their father went to stand, then thinking better of it sat again. 'What's that supposed to mean? I'm never late paying their premiums. Is it because the damage was caused by an act of God, or some other reason they've come up with? Is that it?'

Lettie shook her head. 'No. It turns out that our policy hadn't been pro-rata'd each year to keep in line with inflation.'

'What? But I paid what they quoted me. How can it be wrong?'

Lettie grimaced. 'I called them earlier and asked them the same question. Apparently, it's up to us to ensure the value of everything is covered correctly.'

He shook his head and Zac knew that he would have shown his frustration loudly if they didn't have guests. 'Go on. What else did they say?'

'Only that they're willing to cover seventy per cent of the total cost to sort out the roof.'

Zac looked from Lettie's concerned expression to his father's cheeks reddening in fury.

'But that means we must find a way to cover the rest.' He closed his eyes and Zac saw the muscle working in his father's jaw as he tried to remain calm. 'How much do we need to find to cover the rest of the repairs?'

'Five and a half thousand pounds, or thereabouts.' Lettie

gave Patsy and Melody an apologetic smile. 'Sorry. I hadn't meant to discuss this in front of you both.'

'Please don't worry about us,' Patsy said. 'We're here to help you all in whatever way we can.'

'Thank you,' Lindy said. 'We appreciate your offer.'

'Lindy,' Gareth said, putting his cutlery together, clearly having lost his appetite for his food. His father never left anything on the plate and Zac knew he must be very upset to have done so now. 'I'm not sure us going away tomorrow is the sensible thing to do.'

Zac caught Lettie's shock and knew he needed to say something. 'You're only away for a couple of weeks, Dad,' he said. 'I'm sure this can wait until you get back.'

'I agree,' Lettie said. 'Anyway, I've already discussed with Zac a way we might be able to raise funds quickly to cover the cost of the repairs.'

'You have?' Gareth looked askance at Lettie, then Zac. 'And what idea was that?'

'A festival,' she announced triumphantly.

'Melody and I will help in any way we can,' Patsy offered. 'Won't we, love?'

'We'd be happy to,' Melody assured her.

Zac saw his father scowl. 'If you're thinking of holding one of those noisy music festivals, you can think again. I'm not having my animals frightened by loud music,' Gareth said. Lindy coughed and he seemed to remember they had guests. 'But I think the idea of an event might be something to consider.'

'Actually, Dad,' Lettie said. 'I was thinking about holding a wellness festival?'

'I'm not sure we have many of those over here,' Lindy said thoughtfully. 'I used to go to Pilates and loved it but stopped after a while. I don't think I've ever been to a wellness festival though.'

'A what?' Zac saw the bemusement on his father's face and struggled to hide his own amusement.

Lindy shrugged and smiled at Gareth. 'Well, at least it wouldn't be noisy, Gareth.' Something occurred to her. 'Although I'm not sure any of us have much experience with wellness events. Can you explain what they are?'

Wanting to keep positive for his sister's sake, Zac thought quickly. 'You said you teach yoga, Melody,' he said recalling their earlier conversation. 'And know something about different therapies. Isn't that right?' He saw his father continuing to look bemused.

'That's right,' Melody said. 'I'd be more than happy to help come up with a programme for the event and Gran would help too, wouldn't you, Gran.'

'Happily.'

'You see, Dad,' Zac said, relieved. 'I think with Melody and Patsy's help, we should be OK.'

'That's a relief, because I wouldn't know where to start arranging something like this.'

Neither would he, Zac realised.

'I could round up my Book Club Girls and ask them to pop round tomorrow. I'm sure some of them will be able to help, or even suggest people they know who might want to be involved in something like this.'

'Thank you,' Lettie said. 'I was also thinking of bringing in local alternative therapists and suppliers of health foods, supplements, people who hold classes in things like sound baths, even meditations, that sort of thing.'

'Sounds good to me,' Zac said, noticing the relief on his

sister's face that they had the beginnings of some sort of plan to raise money for the roof damage to be fixed.

'It sounds amazing,' Lindy said. 'When were you thinking of holding it and for how long? A day, a week?'

'Not a week,' Gareth snapped. 'I don't think I could stand having loads of people wandering around the farm for that length of time.'

Zac struggled not to laugh. His father could be so unsociable sometimes.

'I was thinking over a couple of days. A weekend, probably.'

'And now we have Patsy and Melody's support there are enough of us to ensure people keep well away from the fields and the animals.'

'You see, Gareth? Lettie has everything under control. Or soon will have by the sounds of things.' She pursed her lips thoughtfully. 'Maybe some of The Book Club Girls could offer to keep an eye on attendees, or takings, or something?'

'I like that idea.' Lettie smiled. 'Those who can't contribute in any other way but wish to be a part of things could do some of the smaller jobs while we're busy elsewhere.'

Lindy rested an arm on Lettie's shoulder. 'Well done, Lettie. What a clever solution. Don't you think, Gareth?'

'I do,' he said, picking up his cutlery and continuing to eat his food.

'I'm pleased you all like it.' Lettie smiled at each of them. 'And grateful to the pair of you for offering to help so soon after arriving here.'

'I think it's the very least we can do after you've all kindly welcomed Melody and I into your beautiful home.'

'Gran's right,' Melody agreed. 'We're going to be there with you every step of the way.'

Zac half listened to the conversations around the table as

everyone continued eating their early supper. He noticed his father finish off the food on his plate. It was a relief. He hated to think of his parents' well-earned holiday being marred by worry about the barn roof. It seemed like Patsy and Melody had arrived at Hollyhock Farm just when they needed them most.

Once the table was cleared and his parents had gone upstairs to freshen up before leaving for the airport, Zac accompanied his sister as she showed Patsy and Melody around the farm.

'These are the two barns,' she said. 'If the weather's bad maybe we could hold the festival in the larger one. The smaller one has the damaged roof. It was hit by lightning during a storm earlier this year. We've been using it for as long as possible and covering the opening with tarpaulin. Some of the animals were housed in here until recently, but I don't want to risk them getting hurt, so I moved them out to the larger barn. Others who have shelters in the paddocks have spent their time outside.'

'Shall we have a look inside to see if we can use it for the event?' Zac suggested, leading the way.

Once inside, he could clearly see that this barn was out of action until the roof was professionally repaired. 'What a shame.' He felt sorry for his sister. Ever since she had taken over the farm she'd had to deal with so many issues. 'Never mind, Letts. I'm sure we can work this out.'

Lettie bent to pick up a tile. 'It's getting dangerous if the tiles are falling off,' she said, looking up briefly. 'Come along. We should get outside.'

She pointed to the unusable barn. 'We need to bring the animal feed and any tools and equipment stored in there that I'll need to use over the next couple of months,' she said sounding as forlorn as she looked.

'I'm happy to help you bring anything out and store it else-where,' Melody said.

'Me too.' Zac had a thought. 'We'll need hard hats, just in case any more tiles fall, but I can source a few of those from somewhere.'

'Thanks, both of you,' Lettie said, cheering slightly. 'I appreciate your help.'

'Just tell me what you need me to do,' Melody said. 'I'm here to help in any way I can.'

'So am I,' Patsy added. 'Although I don't think I'll be much use moving equipment.'

Zac was relieved to hear her say so. 'I'm sure my sister will find enough work to keep us all busy,' he teased.

Melody seemed cheerful but Zac had spotted a sadness in her eyes. Come to think of it, he mused as he waited for his sister to lead them back outside, there seemed a sense of mystery about the pretty girl with the pink-dyed hair. Zac wondered what could have happened to her to put that hint of sadness in her pale blue eyes. He wondered if he would get to know her well enough for her to trust him and open up about her life. He hoped so.

'Shall we take a walk around the fields now?' he asked, checking his watch. 'I've got about forty minutes before I need to take Mum and Dad to the airport and I'd love to be there when Lettie introduces you both to the animals we still have here. We can also show you the crops.'

'Good idea,' Lettie agreed. 'We can talk through some ideas for the wellness festival while we're at it. I've got a few ideas for utilising areas around the farm for some of the classes.'

'Such as?' Zac asked, intrigued.

'Well, I thought the yoga classes could be held in one of the

fields and maybe the sound bath and some of the other therapies in the lower meadow near the stream.'

'Sounds wonderful,' Patsy said, straightening the straw hat
on her head.

'It does,' Melody agreed, reaching down to pet Spud who
had joined them.

Lettie fanned her face. 'It's still very warm out here. Why
don't I show you around the farm and take you to meet some of
the animals. Afterwards we can go inside, pour ourselves some
drinks and brainstorm more ideas.'

'Now that is a good idea.' Zac laughed.

They were crossing the yard when a vehicle drew up and
parked.

'Callum?' Lettie said, looking at Zac. 'Maybe he could offer
some help,' she whispered to Zac. 'See what you can do.'

Zac felt a pang of jealousy when he noticed Melody's eyes
widen as Callum got out of his pristine Golf GTI. He wasn't
surprised. His friend had started modelling at a young age to
earn money to help pay his way through university, while most
of them, Zac included, earned a pittance working shifts in bars
or restaurants. Despite Callum seeming oblivious to his effect
on women, Zac was used to the way women in the village
reacted to this friendly, chisel-jawed man who looked as if he
had stepped out of a glossy commercial.

'Hi, everyone,' Callum said. 'I hope I'm not interrupting
anything.'

'Of course you're not,' Lettie said, introducing Melody and
Patsy. 'This is Zac's friend and these are Patsy and Melody.
They've come to help us on the farm for a few weeks.'

Zac saw Callum smile at Patsy before his gaze settled on
Melody. Zac waited to see if she blushed like girls usually
tended to when Callum turned his attention on them but she

didn't. He hid his relief. He might have only known Melody for a few hours but there was something about her he found magnetic. She was very pretty and obviously kind but it was something else. Maybe it was the sorrow he saw in her eyes that piqued his interest. Was it that he wanted to find out more about her and what had caused her to be sad so he could find a way to make her happier again? He had no idea, but whatever it was he knew he wanted to get to know her better.

'Hello there, Torels and guests,' Callum cheered.

Always so confident, Zac mused, unable to help smiling at his friend's exuberance. 'I hadn't expected to see you here this evening?' Zac said. 'We're about to show the ladies around the farm.'

'You're welcome to join us,' Lettie said. 'Although you've seen it all before many times.'

'Lead the way,' Callum said, falling into step next to Zac. 'I thought you were going to let me know if you could join the lads for a couple of drinks tonight.'

Zac realised he had forgotten. 'Sorry, must have slipped my mind.'

They followed behind the three women as Lettie led the way, explaining to Patsy and Melody about the different fields and what animals were kept where.

Callum stopped. 'Nothing's wrong, I hope.'

Zac explained about the issue with the insurance claim and Patsy's suggestion about the festival. 'I've no idea where to start but our guests seem confident they can come up with suggestions. We're going to have to hold it soonish though so that the work can be paid for before the weather turns.'

'I'm sorry you're all having to deal with this,' Callum said, continuing to walk once again. 'If there's anything I can do to help promote the festival on my radio show, you must let me know.'

'Thanks, mate.' Zac slapped his friend lightly on his back. 'I appreciate the offer.'

'No worries.' They caught up with the others.

They reached the alpacas and Lettie began introducing them to Patsy and Melody. 'This one is Gideon and this is Tinker Bell and Thumbelina.'

Patsy and Melody reached out to stroke the soft fur that had begun to grow a little since the alpacas had been shorn weeks before, and Zac spotted Melody glance across at Callum – probably doubly impressed by him now she had spent time with him.

He suppressed an envious groan. It would have been far easier if his friend wasn't such a decent man, but he was. They had grown up together, having fun and getting into all sorts of scrapes. Being friends with Callum had always been fun and, he reasoned, it was hardly Callum's fault he had been born with both good looks and character.

Callum smiled at Patsy and Melody. 'We're going to have to show you both how we entertain ourselves here on the island, aren't we, Zac?'

Lettie smiled at her guests. 'He means we can go to the pub and sample their menu over a couple of drinks.'

'Not necessarily,' he argued, laughing. 'Although that might be a good place to start.'

Zac heard his father bellow from the front door. He looked at his watch. 'Damn, I need to get Mum and Dad to the airport.' He smiled at them all. 'I'll catch you later, Callum. I'll see you ladies when I get back.'

'I should get going too,' Callum said. 'I'll walk back with you but maybe we could all go for that evening out sometime soon.'

6

MELODY

She watched Zac and Callum hurry back to the farm briefly before turning back to Lettie.

'Shall we introduce you both to the rest of Hollyhock Farm and its residents?' Lettie asked.

By the time Melody and her grandmother had strolled through various fields, been shown the produce they would soon be helping harvest in the vegetable areas and made friends with the goats, alpacas and retired Jerseys and various other waifs and strays Gareth Torel had been unable to resist homing, she was happy to follow Lettie through the meadow down to the stream.

Melody took off her shoes and sat next to her grandmother and Lettie, sighing with pleasure as she lowered her hot feet into the cool running water.

'Feels good, doesn't it?' Lettie asked, leaning back and resting her hands on the warm grass. 'I think this will be a perfect place to hold a sound bath and a few other events in the programme.'

'It's perfect,' Melody said honestly. 'This meadow is like

something out of a storybook or a film. It's like a piece of heaven.'

Lettie gave her a beaming smile and she was pleased she had made her hostess happy. 'I'm so glad you think so. It's taken me longer than it should to appreciate Hollyhock Farm and all that I've grown up with, but now I do I'm enormously proud of the place. It's become very important to me to make this place work and now we have the incentive to get on and make the event a success, I'm going to give everything I've got to make that happen.'

'And you have the pair of us here to support you every step of the way,' Melody said, happy to have a purpose to focus on once again.

Patsy leant forward and put her hands in the water, opening her fingers to let the water run through them. 'I'm smitten by the place.' She looked at Melody. 'And I can see by the smile on my granddaughter's face that she feels the same way. Don't you, love?'

Melody sighed. 'I do. I feel very lucky to be here right now.' She saw her gran give her a quick sideways glance and was glad Lettie didn't notice her doing it. She wasn't ready to share her situation with anyone yet, let alone her host who she hadn't known for long.

'I'm so pleased. We still have to iron out a lot of details,' Lettie said, 'but with your experience in wellness and mine in event planning – albeit arranging fashion shows – and Zac's in sound engineering, I'm sure we can make this festival idea work.' She groaned. 'We need to make it work.'

Melody hated seeing anyone anxious. She had felt that way herself far too many times before. 'We'll be fine,' she insisted. 'We still need to work out a programme and come up with a list of people we could ask to take part, but I'm sure we'll find a way to make that happen.'

'And don't forget that handsome friend of Zac's offered to interview you on his radio show,' Patsy said. 'So that's a good start.'

Melody thought of Callum and how generous he had been to invite them onto the show. 'That's true.' She moved her feet up and down in the shallow water, enjoying being able to cool down slightly. 'I think it all sounds very positive. I have enough experience to help you interview candidates for the rest of the programme if you'd like me to.'

'That would be brilliant.' Lettie smiled at her. 'I'm so relieved you're both here now. I think I would have found things far more overwhelming without your help.'

'We're happy to do whatever you need us to,' Patsy assured her.

Melody gave the event some thought. 'Do you know how many days you'd like the festival to last?'

'I'm not sure whether a weekend will be enough time if I'm to raise the funds I need.'

'Hmm,' Melody said, unsure how they would manage to run the event over more than two days when they still had the farm work to do. 'And when were you hoping to hold it?'

'I was thinking that with all the necessary planning we'll need to do for the festival, the earliest we could realistically hold it would be the end of September.'

Melody couldn't hide her confusion. 'But that's only six weeks away, isn't it? That doesn't give you much time to put everything in place.'

'I agree.' Lettie puffed out her cheeks. 'But any later in the year and the weather could be unreliable.'

Aware she wasn't helping by stating the obvious, Melody

decided she needed to backtrack. 'But that's fine. It'll give us even more incentive to work harder. I always find a deadline does that.' She had no idea why she'd said that, especially as she never had to work to deadlines teaching yoga. 'However, I do think that as you're already busy and only have a short time to prepare for the festival,' she said with a smile, 'and that it's your first time holding one, maybe you should start small and only hold it for two days.'

'I wasn't sure whether that would be enough time to raise the funds we need for the roof though?' She looked at Patsy, who gave an approving nod Melody was relieved to see.

'I've always found that people who have the most incentive to attend something want to be there at the beginning,' Patsy said thoughtfully. 'I think two days is about right, especially as you haven't taken something like this on before.'

'I suppose you're right. I am already overstretched and don't want to burn myself out by pushing myself too hard,' Lettie agreed. 'And I suppose it does make sense to keep things more manageable. Thanks, both of you.'

'We're here to help you in any way we can,' Melody reminded her, glad Lettie had agreed with her.

Lettie crossed her arms. 'I've been pushing myself a lot and have only recently finished a three-month trial to run the farm.'

'And you've done an excellent job, I'm sure,' Patsy said. 'It can't have been easy to take on all this as a novice.'

Lettie smiled. 'I had a lot of help but as much as I love working here now, I suspect I'm better suited to working in fashion.'

'I still find it exciting to think you had such a glamorous lifestyle before turning to farming. I'm not so sure I'd be able to give all that up to return home and rescue your family farm, especially as it's such hard work and long hours.' Melody hoped she wasn't overstepping by being so open with her opinion.

Lettie shrugged. 'Don't be too enamoured by what I'm doing. I was getting tired of the whole thing, if I'm honest, and was on my way to being made redundant. Even if I hadn't been, I would have returned and offered to take this place on.'

'That's still very loyal of you.' Melody gave her gran a grateful smile. Having someone loyal in your life was the most comforting thing and she couldn't ever imagine not having her grandmother around for her.

'My parents have always been there for me. And anyway, I love this place. Even living away since I went to university I still think of Hollyhock Farm as my home, and the thought of it being sold and possibly changed is heartbreaking.' She pursed her lips thoughtfully. 'I'm pretty sure you'd probably do the same thing anyway if this was your home at stake.'

'I suppose I would.' Melody decided to change the focus of their conversation. 'Your parents sound as if they've really got the travelling bug now.'

'They have, but they deserve to enjoy themselves. They've worked hard and given Zac and I wonderful childhoods and put us both through university. I believe it's the least we can do for them, as does Zac. He's taken months away from his work to help me get a hang of the work here. I couldn't have done it without his input and my uncle Leonard's. He's Dad's brother and his fields back onto ours.'

Melody pushed her fringe from her forehead, feeling hot but more relaxed than she had in months. 'I've only been here for a couple of hours and it's obvious how close you are as a family. And this place is beautiful, like something out of a picture book.'

'It is a special place,' Patsy agreed, giving Melody a knowing glance.

'I'm so glad you both like it here.' Lettie sighed happily. 'I'm feeling much more enthusiastic about putting on an event with you two helping me.'

Melody didn't know what she had done to deserve spending the rest of the summer at this blissful place but whatever it was, she was going to make the most of every minute. 'We're excited to get started with the planning, aren't we, Gran?'

'We are.'

Melody saw the tension in Lettie's tanned face fade slightly and noticed her shoulders lower and it dawned on her just how tense she must have been. Poor Lettie, she thought.

'Shall we go back to the farm and start making some notes?' Lettie suggested. 'We could have something cool to drink while we do a little brainstorming.'

'Good idea,' Melody said. An idea occurred to her. 'The most important thing we need to do first is get the word out about the festival. We can work on the details later, but we want to build people's interest in the event.'

'Where do you suggest we start?' Patsy asked.

Lettie nodded. 'We could set up a website?'

'I agree. And make the most of various free social media platforms.' Melody was glad she and Lettie were on the same page. 'Don't worry about how you'll fit in the marketing side of the festival. I'm very happy to do it all for you.' She saw the immediate relief in Lettie's face. 'You don't need a complicated website, just something basic,' she continued as they walked. 'With the dates of the event, asking people who might be interested in taking part to contact us, and I'll add an email address for them to do that rather than giving out your phone number and being inundated with calls. Emails are far easier to keep under control and at least everything is written down and in one place.'

'That sounds perfect,' Lettie said, giving her a grateful smile and making Melody feel much better about being invited to stay on the farm.

'I'll set up links to the different social media platforms to the site. I can draft a flyer to print off and pin to noticeboards around the village and nearby parishes, if you like.'

'I love that idea.'

Encouraged by Lettie's enthusiasm, Melody continued. 'Then I'll share a digital version of the flyer onto various local online groups, community notices, that sort of thing.'

Lettie beamed at her. 'That all sounds amazing, thank you. Feel free to get started as soon as you like.'

'I'll get on to it straight away,' Melody said, happy to see the relief on Lettie's face. 'Just lead the way to the nearest laptop,' she said, her mind whirring with ideas and possibilities. This would be the perfect way to keep her brain busy and away from troubling thoughts of Rhys and what he might do next.

7

ZAC

The following morning Zac stood behind his sister's and Melody's chairs in his father's study, watching as Melody talked them through the website she had set up for the wellness festival. His couple of drinks with Callum had ended up with them having a few more than he had expected and walking home from the pub. It was the first hangover he had endured for a long time and he wished he didn't have to stare at a bright screen this early, but he wanted to show his appreciation of her efforts so did his best to concentrate on what she was showing them.

'Where did you get that picture of me from?' he asked, grimacing. 'I look bemused by something.'

Lettie turned to scowl at him. 'We can always change the photo if you're that bothered by it.'

Melody laughed. 'We can. Anyway, don't blame me for it. Lettie found it and thought it was fine. And I have to agree with her. I think you look sweet,' she said, clenching her teeth together in embarrassment when she realised she had said the words out loud. 'That is...'

'Sweet? Is that what you think of me?' he asked, trying to keep his voice light but wishing she saw him as something far more exciting. 'Not mysterious, or...'

Lettie groaned. 'Zac, please stop going on about yourself. This is far too important and we have too much to do in far too little time. Be quiet and let Melody talk us through what she's done here.'

'I've kept it simple,' Melody said, glancing at Lettie. 'We only need a holding website to begin with. Later, when we know the dates the event is being held, what it'll entail and cost to attend, or more about requesting a stand, we can update it with that information. Then ask prospective businesses to contact us for further information.'

'Such as what if we don't have all the information yet?' Zac asked, wondering what else there might be to say.

Melody turned slightly in her chair and looked over her shoulder at him. 'People will hopefully contact us to let us know about their business and ask whether we feel it will fit into our plans for the two days.' She looked at Lettie. 'For example, we've discussed yoga and Pilates, but what about nutritionists, or people who sell products, or give talks on various complementary health aspects, like essential oils, crystal therapies, acupuncture and sound baths.'

Zac noticed a tab at the top of the website and pointed to it. 'What's that Market one for?'

'We don't have to keep it,' Melody said, 'but I thought it would be an added incentive to businesses if they thought we would share links to their websites, show their logo and contact details. It could simply be advertising for businesses unable to attend but encourage those considering the festival to take that step and sign up to join us in order to showcase the benefits of their business products direct to the public at the event.'

'Sounds good to me,' Lettie said. 'I like it.'

'Won't it be a lot of extra work for you to set each one up though?' Zac asked, concerned Melody might be taking on too much for herself.

She shook her head. 'No. Each one will only take a couple of minutes, if that, and it adds another layer to the site.'

Zac realised he hadn't been doing as much as his sister and Melody and wanted to rectify it. 'What can I do to help?'

Lettie thought for a moment. 'Maybe before you start work on the website, you could make a list of anyone, either business or person, we can think of who could be interested in signing up to take part, then contact them.'

It was a good idea.

'How about trying to find some sponsors?' Melody asked. 'It would help cover the merchandise we'll need to buy for the event.'

He hadn't thought of merchandise and by the expression on his sister's face neither had she. 'Like banners, stickers for them to take away, that sort of thing?' He tried to think of what else they might need.

'Yes,' Melody said. 'Also tote bags are good. They're light and easy to store somewhere and we can ask businesses who sign up to take part to send us their promotional products and add one of everything into each bag, ready for whoever is on the door taking admissions to hand out. All of this is good advertising for us for future events if we do decide to do this again, and also for businesses taking part.'

He noticed his sister looking thoughtful. 'What's the matter, Letts?'

She shrugged. 'I was just thinking how we had been planning to put on events anyway but not this soon.'

He wasn't sure what her point might be, but waited for her to continue.

'I had expected to have more time to consider what to do and then make all the preparations.' She smiled at Melody and then at Zac. 'I am grateful, especially to the pair of you and Patsy, but I'm worried that because we're having to rush this that we won't be making the most of the wellness theme and that it won't be as polished as the corporate events I'd hoped to hold.'

He understood his sister's concerns, but when she caught his eye, he inclined his head in Melody's direction, relieved she was too busy updating the wording on the website home page to take much notice of Lettie's fretting. It was all very well his sister worrying, but there was little time to change much now. Zac didn't want his sister's panic affecting everyone else's confidence in their plans especially with all the effort Melody had already put in to help them set up the event.

Lettie widened her eyes and grimaced. He saw her swallow then turn to look at Melody. 'I don't mean to downplay everything everyone has been doing,' she said. 'Especially you, Melody. You've been amazing and I know we could never pull this off at all without all the help you've given us.'

Melody smiled and looked back at Zac. She stared at him for a couple of seconds, then turned back to face the screen. 'It's perfectly natural to worry when you're trying to do something for the first time. I'm sure that everything will work out.' She smiled at Lettie. 'We're here to support you and do our best to see that it does.'

Lettie gave her a grateful smile. 'I think I'm panicking about not succeeding in raising enough to cover the shortfall on the insurance.'

'It will be fine, Lettie,' Melody assured her. 'I know it will.'

She looked away from Lettie for a moment and Zac watched as she bit her lower lip thoughtfully, wondering what was going through her mind.

'What is it?' he asked, unable to stand the tension a moment longer.

'Only that we want to entice as many people here as we can.' She thought for a few more seconds. 'It occurred to me that you have a wonderfully close community here and maybe we should mention the reason behind putting this event on this quickly to them?'

Zac thought of people setting up crowdfunding pages online. 'I agree. If people we know understand why we're doing this it's bound to encourage them to come along and support us in any way they can.'

Lettie pulled a face. 'You don't think it's taking advantage of people's kindness though?'

Melody turned to look up at Zac. 'I don't think that, but what do you think, Zac?'

He considered her question and came to the conclusion that there was nothing dishonest about doing it. 'I suppose it will answer anyone's question about us pulling this together in such a short time. Add to the transparency of the thing too.'

'Yes, it would, wouldn't it?' his sister said, seeming happier at that point of view. 'Go on then, Melody. Add something about our reasoning behind this. Maybe put in a paragraph letting people know we're also looking for sponsors, or suggestions for sponsors.'

'Yes,' Zac said, liking the idea the more they spoke. He recalled something from his night out. 'I forgot to mention Callum has offered to interview one or two of us about the festival on his radio show.'

'That's kind of him,' Lettie said.

Melody nodded. 'It is.'

Relieved to have remembered to share this snippet of information, Zac peered over Melody's shoulder at the website again. 'The logo.'

'Sorry?' Melody turned her head to one side and looked at Lettie. 'He's right. We don't have one yet. Damn. We're going to need one quickly if we're to order promotional merchandise. Well done, Zac.'

'I could give it a go – coming up with one?' he said, wanting to be helpful.

Lettie shook her head and grinned at him. 'No, it's fine. I think I know just the person who will enjoy doing this for us.'

'Who?' he and Melody asked in unison.

'Brodie's sister, Maddie. She's an interior designer and loves anything creative. I'll ask her. Then if she doesn't think she can do it the three of us can put our heads together and come up with something. Or—' she smiled at him '—you could do it for us.'

Zac thought of the doodles he had always done on notepads and on the front of his schoolbooks when he was growing up. His teachers were always telling him off about drawing on things but none of it was very artistic. 'I'm not the one to do that,' he admitted.

'The first thing we should do though is come up with a name for the festival,' Lettie said thoughtfully.

'Now that I can do,' Zac said proudly. 'How about Hollyhock Farm Wellness Festival.'

Melody laughed.

Trying not to be offended by her amusement at his suggestion, he shrugged. 'What's so funny?'

'Sorry,' she said, resting her hand on his arm and making

his skin tingle from her touch. 'It's such a simple but perfect name for it, I think. Don't you, Lettie?'

Lettie nodded. 'I do. It's to the point and at least people will automatically know where the event is being held too.'

He hadn't thought of that. He glanced at Melody's hand on his arm just as she removed it, his skin cooling immediately when her hand moved away. He really needed to rein his emotions in. She was only here for a short while and he had no intention of getting his heart broken again. Although he suspected she had the power to do that to him, even if unintentionally.

8

MELODY

By the following week, Melody felt as if she had lived at Hollyhock Farm for months rather than days. The Torel siblings were funny, friendly and made her feel as if she was one of their close relations rather than someone who had only recently started working for them. She liked them very much and wanted to do her best to be helpful wherever she could.

She was sitting in Gareth's office having just ordered tote bags, T-shirts for the volunteers they hoped to find to help run the event, several banners, stickers and biros, all with the cute logo of the outline of a hollyhock flower with the word *Wellness* underneath, which Brodie's sister had designed for them.

She felt satisfied that their efforts were finally coming to fruition. It was a relief. When she had made her initial suggestion for the festival it hadn't occurred to her exactly what it would entail. This was an important fundraising event for the Torel family and she wanted to make sure nothing she did took away from any success the event might bring.

Today she was excited that they were meeting with a group

called The Book Club Girls that Lindy had apparently contacted.

She looked at the list she had printed earlier that morning with the different businesses they had signed up so far. There weren't many, which was a worry, but they still had six weeks before the event and although Melody would rather they were further along in the planning, it couldn't be helped. She intended to make the best of what they did have. Positivity was key, she decided.

Hearing footsteps, Melody closed her file, ready to go and meet their visitors. She looked up as Lettie entered the study. 'Ready?'

'As I'll ever be,' Lettie said, sounding nervous.

Melody presumed her new friend was anxious because this was her first event at the farm. 'You've got this,' she said, hoping to reassure her. 'After all, you've arranged events at the fashion house so it's not as if you don't have experience.'

Lettie sat on the edge of the desk. 'Those were with people who knew what they were doing, and only for a few hours. I've never arranged anything like this that's going to last two days.' She groaned. 'To be honest, I think I should have started with just one and taken it from there.'

'Rubbish,' Melody said. 'You were only being ambitious and two days is manageable, especially as you now have me and Gran on board to help with everything.'

'I've been thinking about that too,' Lettie said thoughtfully. 'You were only going to come and stay here to help work on the farm initially. Now, you're doing all this work for the event, setting up websites, doing marketing for the festival, and heaven only knows what else. It's unfair of me to expect you and Patsy to do this without any payment.'

Melody raised her hand. 'Stop right there. We've offered to

do this because we want to help you. Being here has been a wonderful experience for us both and I know Gran would agree with me when I say that neither of us expect or want any payment.' Lettie went to argue. 'No, I mean it. I needed to get away for a bit and I'm loving every moment being here. I don't want any more payment than to stay here and be involved in everything that's going on.'

Lettie didn't seem convinced. 'But that doesn't feel right, or fair.'

'Seriously, Lettie. I don't want paying for what I'm doing.' She smiled. 'Now, let's focus on the festival. Right now, my most important concern is you being stressed about everything. I know it's vital you make money from this event, and that the worry is getting to you.'

'You're right. I get in a state and then panic. I think it's because I was comfortable in my job in London after doing it for a few years and these past few months have pushed me to learn so many new things. Maybe I'm a little tired. I'm not sure.'

Melody suspected she knew what might help her friend. 'I was thinking when I was on my mat in my room this morning, that I should really give you and Zac some yoga classes. It's very good for relaxation and will also show you how I work for when I host a couple of classes during the festival.'

'I'd love that,' Lettie said. 'I suppose Patsy does yoga too. She seems very fit and strong.'

'She's always loved it, as does my mum.'

Hearing a couple of cars, Melody presumed Lindy's friends had begun to arrive. She stood and picked up her file. 'I'll wait for our prospective programmes to finish printing, then go and find Gran. We'll join the rest of you in the kitchen...'

'Sure. Let's hope they're ready to offer their help. We could do with as much as possible.'

* * *

Melody watched Lettie leave and as soon as the last sheet had slid from the printer, picked up the small stack, grabbed a few notebooks and pens and went to join them in the kitchen.

'What can I do to help?'

Lettie indicated the pantry with her head. 'I picked up a couple of cakes from the bakery yesterday. You'll find them in of the cake tins.' She lowered her voice. 'The group are used to coming here. Mum always hosts them because she has the largest space, or that's what they tell her. I suspect it's because they like her baking. She always treats them to cakes and scones.'

Just as Lettie had expected, Melody found two cake tins in the neat pantry. She lifted them out and set them down on the table.

'Aw, how typical of Lindy to think of us even though she isn't here,' one of the women said, beaming at the tins.

Melody counted eight women in total. As she fetched plates and cake forks, she wondered if Zac might be joining them. She hoped so. She hadn't seen him since the previous day and was surprised to find she missed his company.

Melody placed the notepads and pens on the table and, not wanting to hold up the gathering, quickly took a seat.

'Thank you all for coming. Mum said she had asked you to meet here because you might be able to help us with the wellness festival we're putting on very soon.'

'We're more than happy to help where we can,' said the grey-haired lady who seemed to be the head of the group. 'I'm not sure how yet, but I'm sure we'll all figure something out.'

'Well, it's very kind of you.' Lettie sat at the head of the table. 'Maybe we should begin with introductions.'

Melody grinned at her gran's friend. Kathleen had been kind introducing the pair of them to the Torels and Melody was very grateful. She hadn't met Kathleen's daughter Phyllis before though and neither, it seemed, had Patsy. The two women who worked at Brodie's practice, Tina – a friend of Lettie's – and Bethan, the practice nurse, introduced themselves and Melody listened as the others gave their names. She couldn't help thinking what a lovely sense of community there was in the village.

Lettie indicated Melody. 'This is Melody, she's staying here for a couple of months with her grandmother, Patsy.'

'Hello, everyone,' Melody said. 'It's good to meet you, and lovely to see you again, Kathleen, and finally meet your daughter I've heard so much about over the years.'

'Likewise,' Patsy agreed, exchanging smiles with the other women.

'Welcome, Melody,' they all said in unison.

She looked at the smiling, friendly faces, each of them happy to be there. 'Thank you,' Melody said. 'I look forward to getting to know each of you.'

'These lovely ladies have kindly agreed to bring their expertise in wellness to help the festival,' Lettie explained. 'They've been a wonderful help already.' Lettie took two large plates and lifted the cakes from the tins. She picked up a knife ready to start cutting slices. 'I really appreciate your offers to help but want you to only do whatever you're happy with. Some of you will probably have more experience in wellness than I do.' She grimaced. 'Which won't be very difficult. Melody, would you like to start sharing the ideas we've already been working on?'

Melody flicked back the cover of her notepad, opened her file and handed out copies of the plan to each of the women. As she pushed the pieces of paper towards each of them, she got ready to speak but then heard footsteps coming down the tiled hallway.

Everyone looked up to see who was coming and Melody did the same, the words she was about to say lost as Zac stepped into the room.

'Hello, everyone,' he said in his usual cheery way.

She felt the atmosphere in the room lighten and she relaxed slightly. She had been unaware of just how tense she was.

'I hope these ladies haven't been giving you a hard time,' he said, bending to kiss Kathleen and then Phyllis on their cheeks.

Kathleen slapped his arm, frowning, but Melody couldn't miss the amusement in her eyes. 'Behave yourself, you cheeky devil.'

'Stop winding everyone up,' Lettie said, shaking her head. 'Make yourself something to drink and come and join us.'

'Have I missed much?' he asked, as he passed Melody. He clicked the kettle on and took a cup from the cupboard.

'We've just started,' Lettie said.

Melody sensed him looking at her but daren't catch his eye. She had only just met these women and needed to get along with them, so didn't want their first impression of her to be acting silly with Zac. He clearly knew everyone well and there was obvious affection for him by their reactions.

She wasn't exactly sure what being a sound engineer entailed, but presumed his work involved some lifting and shifting of equipment. His T-shirt did little to hide his impressive biceps and she had to force her eyes from them back to his face, horrified to realise he had noticed her reaction.

He sat down and Melody was relieved there were two people between them. She had already made a bit of a fool of herself and looking across the table she caught Kathleen's eye and saw the lady's amusement as she raised a grey eyebrow and gave Melody a kind smile.

'I was expecting you to be here earlier,' Lettie said, rolling her eyes. 'Where've you been all morning?'

'Places to go, people to see,' he said mysteriously.

'He's always been a cheeky boy, this one,' Phyllis said to her mother.

'He has,' Lettie agreed. 'He's been allowed to get away with too much, being the baby of the family.'

'Baby?' Zac raised his eyebrows and gave Phyllis a questioning look.

Melody giggled. She loved this friendly banter between the siblings.

'I think it's more to do with the dear boy needing time to himself,' Kathleen said sombrely.

Melody saw the change in the woman's expression. There was no less affection in her tone, but she seemed to be referring to something only the others were privy to.

Lettie's expression was serious. 'Maybe.'

Melody looked from one to the other of them, her focus resting on Zac. He was scowling and didn't catch her eye. She sensed he wasn't doing so on purpose and wondered what might have happened to him to cause this reaction from the women.

'Er, I am in the room, you know,' he said quietly. 'And secondly, I'm fine. I promise you. All of you.' His amused expression returned and he shook his head at Melody. 'Don't believe a word they say about me.'

'I won't,' she said. She realised she liked him very much but couldn't help wondering what had happened to him. Whatever it was the others cared very deeply for him, and that only happened when someone was considered lovable. She knew it was silly of her, but Melody couldn't help wondering if Zac might ever have any feelings for her. Not that she was at a stage in her life when she was looking for a new partner. Heaven forbid. She studied Zac's handsome face as he spoke. She had experienced enough heartbreak to keep well away from men. Especially handsome men with this much confidence.

9

ZAC

He sat at the table and picked up one of the draft programmes, not wanting to dwell on his past errors. Or one in particular, he mused. He had spent far too much time running away from responsibility in his personal life, and that blip in his life had been the incentive he needed to take a break from work and spend several months in Jersey when his sister needed him most.

He pushed the unsettling memory away, not ready to think about it and wishing it hadn't been such public knowledge. Determined not to slide back down to the mortification he had only recently recovered from, he focused his attention on the sheet of paper in his hand. His sister and Melody had already done a lot.

He was intrigued to get to know Melody better. She mesmerised him for some reason. It wasn't her looks, although she was beautiful in a quirky way, or her quiet strength that appealed to him. He couldn't put his finger on it. There was something else. An underlying sadness maybe. He had picked up on how Melody's grandmother watched out for her in an understated way that made him think Patsy was trying to hide what she was doing from Melody. As if letting her feel independent while being watched over and he wondered what might have happened to cause Patsy to fear for her granddaughter.

'Don't you think so, Zac?' Lettie asked, interrupting his musings.

'Sorry, what was that?' He looked at the faces around the table and saw that each of them was watching him, some amused by his lack of focus and others, like Phyllis and Bethan, unimpressed. He supposed he would be too if he had taken time out from work to come here. 'I was thinking about what microphones or music you might need,' he said quickly.

He saw Phyllis give Kathleen a gentle nudge only to be rewarded with a scowl.

'We were saying how useful your knowledge of sound is, Zac,' Kathleen explained.

'That's right,' Lettie added. 'But as you were already thinking about sound arrangements for the event, I think you've already answered my question.'

He was relieved. 'Good. We can talk in more detail later if you like, but I'm fairly certain I know what you'll need and will soon set everything up.'

He caught Melody's eye and, forgetting the others' gazes were focused on him, smiled.

'Hello, everyone.'

Zac heard Brodie's voice. 'Good to see you here.'

Brodie laughed as he stood behind Lettie and bent to kiss the top of her head. 'You seem a bit outnumbered here.'

'You could say that,' Zac replied, glad to see his sister's friendly boyfriend had joined them. 'Are you here for the animals, to see my sister or to volunteer your help for the festival?'

Lettie took Brodie's hand in hers. 'He's already volunteered, if you must know, and when we've finished here we're taking Spud and Derek for a walk at Les Landes.'

Melody lowered her biro. 'I think we've probably gone through everything we need to at this point.' She narrowed her eyes briefly. 'Although, while you're all here, I was thinking...'

'Go on,' Zac said, intrigued. He leant slightly forward, waiting for her to share her thoughts.

Melody looked at Lettie who nodded. 'Go ahead.'

'Well, it's just that I thought it might be a good idea to hold a yoga class for any of you wishing to join me down at the beach one evening this week.'

'I love that idea,' Kathleen said instantly. 'Although I'm not sure about exercising in all that sand.'

Zac pressed his lips together worried he was about to laugh. 'I'm sure we can take towels and yoga mats.'

Melody gave him a surprised look and he wasn't sure if it was because he knew what a yoga mat was.

Maybe she was waiting for him to show interest so the others would follow. 'Count me in,' he said.

Melody gave him a beaming smile, just as the others immediately began chattering about it.

'I'm not sure it's my sort of thing,' Kathleen said. 'But I'll come and watch you all if I'm free.'

Tina, Bethan, Phyllis and Lettie all expressed their interest.

'How about you, Brodie?' Zac asked, hoping not to be the only chap doing it.

Brodie gave a lazy shrug. 'Fine by me. Although, if the surf is good I might duck out at the last minute and make the most of the waves.'

'Good plan,' Lettie agreed.

They went back to discussing the festival and when his

sister said they didn't need him for anything else, Zac left the noisy kitchen. They didn't need him to add to the chatter; Lettie and Melody knew what they were doing better than he did, especially as his expertise was the sound, rather than who did what and when. He would wait for them to let him know the finalised programme when it was ready and would then work out whether they needed him to set up microphones for people like Melody who would be holding classes at the event, or pull together playlists for background music.

He had discussed ideas enough to know where some of the events would be held and decided to go and check out the barns and outbuildings to try and get an idea of what might be needed of him and his electrical equipment.

Standing in the largest barn, he studied the sheet of paper in his hand. It looked as if Lettie was suggesting having a few stalls across one of the walls at the back of the room, with the rest of the room cleared to give space for yoga displays and classes. He had no experience of an event like this, having mostly been a sound engineer in recording studios and at music festivals. He would have rather this be for music, too.

Zac looked at the plan again and the notes Lettie had printed on one side, trying to imagine how it would work. It seemed that various aspects of a healthy lifestyle would be brought together covering mental health, physical fitness, as well as emotional and spiritual wellbeing.

Some of the place settings had been reserved for the experts taking part. Zac wondered if he might have a chat with the personal trainer. He also liked the look of the aromatherapy. Anything that was calming was good as far as he was concerned.

The barns were going to need a lot of work, he decided. They might be clean but they were not ready to invite in people wanting to do exercises, even if the attendees were using floor mats. He leant against one of the stall doors. This event meant a lot to his sister. To him, too.

He thought of Melody and how much of a support she was being to Lettie and knowing she was there for her was bound to be reassuring to their mother. Melody. She was so different to most of the people he came across and he felt that her entry into their lives had happened for a reason. He wasn't sure if that was purely to help his family over the next few months, or something else. He knew that he liked her though and not only because she was attractive, but also because she was calm, kind and enthusiastic, and wanted to help his family.

An hour or so later, he heard voices coming out of the house and realised the meeting must be over and the friendly group about to leave.

Not wishing to spend ages chatting to them all again, he decided to nip out of the barn and go up to the field and check on the animals. They were all outside for the day and although he knew Lettie would have sorted out their feed and checked their water, it was a good excuse for him to take a walk and go and check that everything was fine while getting a bit of exercise.

10

MELODY

Melody helped Lettie harvest plums and tomatoes to wash, weigh and pack up into brown paper bags for the honesty box. She loved that here in Jersey people could still leave produce on a stall by the side of the road and know that most of those taking bags would leave the correct money in the money tin. Several staff had come to help the previous day for deliveries to local restaurants and a few of the smaller parish stores. Her grandmother was sourcing yoga mats for the festival. She had offered to help with the harvesting but neither Melody nor Lettie had thought it a good idea, especially in the heat. And Melody suspected her grandmother had only offered her assistance because she had thought it was expected of her.

It had been another beautiful, cloudless day and Melody wondered if she should take a walk over the fields to see where she ended up. She liked the idea of going for a walk but wasn't sure where. She was in the kitchen washing her hands, trying to think of places she had heard the Torels mentioning, when Zac came in humming to himself.

'There you are,' he said, smiling.

'I've been helping Lettie around the farm.' She wasn't sure why she was stating the obvious because what else would she have been doing? 'Have you had a good day?'

She listened as he told her about starting work clearing the store area at the back of one of the barns and how he thought both barns needed a thorough deep clean before the festival.

'I agree,' she said, thinking about rolling out the yoga mats they would be using on a floor that wasn't spotless. 'We should make fairly short work of it with several of us doing it though.' She took the hand towel from the hook it was hanging from and dried her hands, unsure if she had missed something when he didn't reply. 'You weren't thinking of starting the cleaning this evening, were you?'

He shook his head and seemed to relax slightly. 'No. I was hoping you might accompany me for a walk instead.'

She hadn't expected him to say that. 'I'd love to go,' she said, then a thought occurred to her.

'Is something the matter?'

She didn't feel comfortable admitting she had been about to ask him what Kathleen had meant when she had referred to his past the other day, deciding straight after she'd had the urge that she didn't know him well enough to broach something obviously personal. Her next thought had been about how she was keeping her own past a secret from him, so really wasn't in a position to ask anyway.

'I was thinking of Gran,' she fibbed, certain he would believe her. 'Lettie and Brodie have gone out somewhere for the evening and I don't like to leave her here alone.' She wasn't sure if her grandmother might in fact enjoy a bit of time by herself. 'Although...'

'Why don't you go and ask her if she wants to join us? I'll wait here for you to ask her, then we can head off.'

'I won't be long,' she said, hurrying past him and running up the stairs to find her grandmother. She reached her bedroom door and knocked lightly, not wishing to wake her in case she was dozing.

'Come in, Melody.'

Melody pushed the door open. 'Er, how did you know it was me?' she asked as she walked into the room to find Patsy reading.

Patsy raised an eyebrow at the question.

Her grandmother lowered her book to rest it on her chest. Melody noticed she had pulled across one of the curtains to block the sun from shining on her face but left the other drawn back. Both were swaying lightly in the wind.

'Did you want me for something?' Patsy asked.

Aware she had probably interrupted an interesting part in her grandmother's book, Melody said, 'Zac has invited us both out for a walk and I've come to check if you want to join us.' She smiled. 'You seem rather comfortable where you are, but the offer is there.'

Patsy gave her a knowing look.

'What?'

'I have a feeling three would be a crowd if I did join the pair of you.'

Surprised, Melody shook her head. 'I've no idea what you mean.'

Patsy put her hand up to her chin and tapped the side of her jaw. 'No?' She laughed. 'I'm only teasing. Although it is obvious that there's chemistry between you two.'

Melody pointed to the novel with the brightly coloured cover in her grandmother's hand. 'I think you've been reading too many romances lately.' She laughed. 'Although I can't say I blame you. We all need cheering up these days.'

'I am enjoying this, very much. Anyway, it's been a long day and I'm happy lying here relaxing. You go and enjoy yourself and I'll see you later.'

'You're sure?'

'I am. I've been looking forward to putting my feet up and reading more of this book all day. It's the perfect way for me to stop thinking about the one I'm working on.'

Melody walked over and kissed her grandmother's cheek. 'Fine. I'll come and check up on you when I get back.'

'I'll look forward to hearing how it went.'

Melody shook her head at her grandmother's wry grin and left the room, closing the door quietly behind her. Not wishing to keep Zac waiting too long, she ran downstairs and when she couldn't find him in the kitchen went outside and saw him leaning against Lindy's car.

'Was I very long?'

'Not at all.' He looked past her. 'Patsy not coming then?'

Melody shook her head and walked over to join him. 'She's happily reading in her room. She said for us to enjoy ourselves.'

They got into the car and strapped themselves in. Zac looked up at the attic windows. 'I'm glad Patsy's happy here. That you both are,' he said, turning on the ignition.

He turned left out of the farm driveway, and she was excited to be shown a different part of the island to what she had already seen. Zac had driven her past a couple of the beaches on their way from the harbour to the farm. He had pointed out the beautiful areas where the pale sand met the turquoise sea. When Melody had remarked on the glorious colour, Zac had been quick to let her know that it changed according to the weather and she looked forward to seeing the sea on different days.

Zac had given snippets about the area and their names,

which Melody couldn't remember, probably because they sounded as if they were in French.

She was happy she hadn't allowed herself to think too deeply before agreeing to come to the island, even though her mother had recently given her one of her kindly lectures about taking time to consider her choices more carefully. This was a visit to a place a few hundred miles away though, Melody reminded herself, not embarking on a marriage that might only last a few years. She pushed away the memories of her disastrous, short-lived life with Rhys and vowed never to allow herself to be swept up by a man again and to follow her instincts instead.

A few minutes later they pulled into a parking area and got out of the car. As she walked gingerly down the long, cobbled slipway, she tried to be careful not to slip on the seaweed that had probably been washed up on the last high tide, but the sole of her trainer must have caught a piece and skidded out in front of her. It was only Zac's quick reaction, grabbing her arm, that stopped her from falling.

'That was a close one.' She laughed, embarrassed.

'Here, take my hand.'

He reached his hand out to her. She stared at it for a second, feeling awkward about taking it. Holding his hand felt so intimate for some reason.

Not wishing to seem silly or wanting to slip again, she did as he suggested. Focusing on keeping her footing, she tried to recall the last time she had held hands with any man apart from Rhys. She was relieved when they reached the sand, but felt the coolness on her skin when his hand let go of hers. They began walking and she listened as Zac told her about the tower that rose from the islet in the sea. He really was good-looking in a tousle-haired, outdoorsy kind of way.

It had only been a couple of months since that last disastrous encounter with Rhys and although Melody knew for
certain that any love she'd had for him was gone, his controlling behaviour still made her anxious. As much as she told
herself he had no idea where she was, she still struggled to
remember that he wouldn't be watching and seeing something
suspicious in an innocent gesture.

Zac turned to her, and she realised with embarrassment
that she hadn't been following what he was telling her.

'You all right?'

She saw the concern on his face and tried to come up with
something plausible without admitting that she hadn't been
listening. 'Yes, sorry. I was, um, breathing in the delicious sea
air.'

He smiled, seeming happy with her reply. 'It is special here,
isn't it? I can't get enough of the beach. Whenever I'm away
working, however exciting the job is, it only takes a few days
before I long to get back to this place.'

He frowned and listened for something. He then turned to
look at a rocky area where the receding tide lay in rock pools.
'Over there.' He pointed at some birds congregating noisily on
the rocks.

'What are they?' she asked, studying them. They were quite
a bit smaller than seagulls with black heads and bodies, and
white chests with long, thin, orange beaks. Bobbing on the sea,
they peep-peeped among themselves.

'Oystercatchers. You get a lot of them down here. I'm sure
they're increasing by the year.'

She wondered if he was trying to change the subject and
happily went along with him. 'I don't think I've ever seen birds
like those before.'

A couple of seagulls flew near to them and the entire flock

swooped up, then flew in a large circle before landing again and congregating further along the water.

'It's lovely here,' she said almost to herself.

'It is, isn't it? I'm aware how lucky I am to have this place to return to whenever I want.'

'Which is why you and Lettie have been so determined to try and keep Hollyhock Farm in your family, I imagine.'

'Exactly. Of course we could rent flats in town, or maybe somewhere in the country parishes, but it wouldn't be the same as living at the farm.'

'I can understand why, although from what I've seen of the island there seems to still be a lot of character here. Has it changed much over the decades?' It was one of the things she loved about growing up in Edinburgh, especially the older part of the city – that it had seen little change in the architecture for hundreds of years.

He sighed. 'Well, it is changing. In fact, it's changed a lot but when I was moaning about it to one of my friends from the UK they said that the island seems to be changing far slower than most of England, and for that I'm extremely grateful.'

'That's good to hear.'

'How about you? Do I hear the hint of a Scottish accent?'

Melody laughed. 'More than a hint, I imagine. I'm from Edinburgh. My family moved around a lot, but that's where I call home.'

'I've only been once,' he said. 'But it was years ago. I thought it a very atmospheric place. I loved it.'

She liked that he did, although she rarely came across anyone who didn't. 'I agree. It's very special there.'

He turned to her. 'So why leave and come here? Were you and Patsy hoping for a break from the place or just a summer trip away?'

'A bit of both,' she admitted.

'But you like what you've seen of the island so far?'

She laughed. 'How could I not? The weather is glorious and everywhere I've seen so far is beautiful. Hollyhock Farm is especially pretty. The farmhouse is gorgeous in that pink-tinged stone.'

'It's our local granite. Guernsey's granite is blue. You'll see many more homes and walls built with this stone as you visit more of the island.'

His phone buzzed. Taking it out of his pocket, Zac sighed as he read the text that had appeared. 'Everything all right?' she asked, concerned.

He pushed the phone back into his pocket and looked out at the rocky area again. 'A message from Callum.'

Suspecting Callum was inviting Zac out for a drink somewhere, Melody decided to broach the subject. 'I know you invited me out for a walk, but please don't feel like you have to put your friend off for me. We can do this another time.'

He stilled briefly. 'No, it's fine,' he said. 'I can see Callum any time.'

She liked Zac but hadn't picked up any vibes that he was attracted to her despite what her grandmother had said. Callum seemed nice enough but she wasn't ready for anything romantic. 'I don't want to keep you from your plans though,' she said, feeling guilty that he was putting himself out for her. 'Maybe the three of us could go out for a drink at the village pub together sometime,' she said eventually.

They continued walking and seeing a beautifully marked shell, Melody bent to pick it up. She brushed the sand off it and studied the browns and creams. She slipped it into her back pocket. Then, noticing a discarded crisp packet, picked it up to take to the bin when they left the beach.

Zac nodded. He took his phone back out of his pocket, typed in a reply to Callum and sent it.

'There,' he said. He bent to pick up a similar shell a few strides along the beach. 'Here's one. It's a limpet shell.'

She took the pointed shell and decided it would look perfect on her windowsill. 'Thank you, I like it.'

'It's not very beautiful, but it has a sort of rough and ready charm about it, I think.'

She didn't like to say that he did too.

'Did I say something?' He smiled.

She realised she had shown her amusement on her face and immediately shook her head. 'No, not at all.' She thought quickly, not wanting to show him how attracted she was to him. 'I was just wondering how many I'll manage to collect in the brief time I'm on the island. Quite a few, I should imagine.'

He laughed. 'I wouldn't blame you. I'm always collecting them. Always have done. We used to find them in our back garden a lot of the time when I was a kid.'

Intrigued, she asked, 'Did you live next to the beach then?'

'I grew up living at Hollyhock Farm It might be up the hill from a beach and far enough for a decent walk to get there, but it's also close enough to hear the sound of the waves when I'm lying in bed. The shells were brought to our garden at some point though because we kept chickens.'

She wasn't sure how that made sense. 'I'm sorry, I don't understand why having chickens means you'd have seashells.'

He thought for a moment, then said, 'It's to do with the calcium in them. It helps them produce healthier shells on the eggs they lay.'

Melody had never heard such a thing.

Zac laughed. 'I know, it sounds odd but I recall Mum telling me that having seashells for chickens to peck at helps them lay healthier eggs. It's like them being given a supplement, I guess.'

'I never knew that.' She sighed and gazed out to sea. 'I've only been here a short time and I'm already learning so many things.'

'I'm glad you're enjoying yourself.'

'I am.'

Zac looked at his watch. 'We should probably turn back here,' he said. 'We should be thinking about supper and I don't want to be a lousy host and not make sure Patsy has something to eat.'

'I suppose so,' she said, feeling guilty towards her grandmother that she would rather stay on the beach with Zac. 'I was enjoying myself.'

'So was I.' He smiled at her. 'Maybe next time we can plan our outing a bit better and give ourselves more time. Maybe stop off somewhere for a coffee or snack? What do you think?'

She loved the idea. 'That sounds good to me.'

'Great. Maybe once the festival is over, we can take off to one of the smaller islands for a day.'

'Like Herm or Sark?' she asked. Melody smiled at him. Why hadn't she thought to come and visit this place and its friendly locals before now? She had been missing out on so much. If only she had thought to come here before meeting Rhys and having to face all the nastiness that her marriage with him had brought about.

She had relaxed so much already since her arrival on the island but knew she had a long way to go before feeling more like her old self again. She looked around at the wild landscape and listened to the birds and sea, and she knew she had made the right decision agreeing to join her grandmother and come here.

11

ZAC

The following day Zac met up with Callum for a late breakfast down at the beachside café in Ouaisne Bay. He had tried to suppress his disappointment that his best friend had taken a liking to the woman he was attracted to but so far wasn't doing a very good job, if the scrutiny of his friend's gaze was anything to go by.

He and Callum rarely went for the same women, which was a relief as far as Zac was concerned. He took another bite of his sausage and egg burrito. Ordinarily Zac loved coming here and eating this delicious food, but today he was struggling to find his appetite. Not wishing to let Callum know how badly his message had affected him, Zac focused on his food. It was too good to waste.

Callum set his cutlery down on his plate, turning his attention from his tortilla. 'What is it?'

Pretending not to understand, Zac shook his head. 'I don't know what you mean.'

When Callum didn't say anything Zac looked at him. They had been best friends for too long for Zac to be able to fob

Callum off that easily. He placed his burrito into the bowl. Callum was a good bloke and Zac knew almost certainly that all he would need to do to deflect his friend's interest in Melody was to let him know how he felt. And he had considered doing that. Many times over the past few hours. But his conscience wouldn't allow him to be that selfish. What if Melody wanted to spend time with Callum? What if she preferred Callum to him? What right did he have to get between two people who had feelings for each other? None, that's what.

'Zac,' Callum snapped. 'I can tell something's bothering you. Is it something I've done?'

Zac shook his head. 'Of course it isn't.'

'Why don't I believe you?' Callum squinted in the bright morning sunlight before shading his eyes with his hands. 'Lend me your cap or your sunnies, will you?' Zac took off his cap and handed it to his friend to put on. 'That's better. I can see properly now. So, come on, out with it. What's bothering you?'

Zac groaned inwardly. Callum rarely let anything go before he was ready to. Zac didn't want to ruin any potential relationship between Callum and Melody, so he needed to think quickly to assuage his friend's concerns. When Zac hesitated, Callum pointed at him.

'I know. You're finding it harder being back on the island full-time than you expected, aren't you?'

Relieved to be given a reason he could use, Zac shrugged. 'A bit, maybe.'

Callum leant forward. 'Listen, mate. I know this is all very new for you, but we've had this discussion before.'

Zac knew where this conversation was going and, aware he was about to get one of Callum's friendly lectures, picked up his burrito and took a bite. He needed food if he was to listen and not react.

'Look, I know you never expected your folks to ever want to leave the farm, but you have to admit ever since you and Jazz ended things after she lost the baby, you've found ways to distance yourself from the island as much as possible.'

Not just from the island, Zac mused, aware he had also not allowed himself to become too emotionally involved with any other woman he'd dated since the devastation of his and Jazz's relationship ending so painfully.

'I've been travelling for work,' Zac argued, aware there was some truth in what Callum was saying.

'I know that, but you've also spent as little time here as possible,' Callum argued. 'Speaking as someone who also travels for jobs, I don't mean to criticise you, Zac. But even though this farm business is unexpected for both you and Lettie, I think that in your case it's probably the best thing that could have happened.'

Zac swallowed his food. 'What's that supposed to mean?' he asked, irritated. 'Look, I admit I felt more comfortable being away knowing I had little chance of bumping into Jazz, but you know that's all in the past now.' He thought back to seeing her and the chap she had married when they returned to the island on their honeymoon the previous year. 'We chatted and put all our issues to rest.'

'So you've said, which is why I don't understand your reluctance to spend more time with her after that, Zac.'

He had a point. 'I can see why you'd be confused.'

Callum scowled. 'You must admit you've been hard to pin down since your split though and that you've avoided most opportunities to come back to Jersey.'

Callum was right. He knew he was. 'It's true.'

He had thought himself in love with Jazz and although he had been shocked about the pregnancy, Zac had quickly believed himself ready to marry her. He closed his eyes, hating to have to think about that period of his life. It had put him off becoming deeply involved with another woman.

He thought of Melody. He had known her for barely a couple of weeks but already his feelings were stronger for her than they had ever been for Jazz. Was it his fear of being hurt again that was stopping him from being honest about his feelings for her?

He realised Callum was still speaking. 'Sorry, I missed that.'

Callum sighed heavily. 'I was saying that it's time you set down roots here.'

'Here?'

'Or somewhere. Don't you think?'

Zac ate the last mouthful of his food to give himself time to think. Callum was right. He could be based here and still go on tour with artists when the need arose. 'I suppose you're right. My sister does need my support now our parents have stepped back from the farm business.'

'I'm pleased.'

Zac was at a loss as to why it meant so much to his friend. 'Why does it bother you so much?'

Callum stared at him for a moment. 'Because it was painful to see you shut down your emotions when Jazz lost the baby and the pair of you drifted apart shortly afterwards. Each time I've met up with you I've wondered how much it still affected you.'

He had no idea Callum had been so concerned about him. 'Really? It bothered you that much?'

Callum looked hurt by his disbelief.

'Sorry, I didn't mean that to come out how it did,' Zac said, not wanting to offend him. 'You never said anything though.'

'Of course I didn't. Hurt like that can be difficult to come to terms with, especially when it happens to someone young.' He ate a mouthful of food and swallowed. 'I mean, you were what? Eighteen?'

'Nineteen,' Zac said.

'I hoped you knew I was there for you if you needed to talk to me, but you never did so I presumed you were dealing with it in your own way.'

Zac thought about his decisions since then and realised Callum was right. He had distanced himself from his family and friends, choosing to spend ninety per cent of his life working and most of that on tour with various artists. He had told himself it was the buzz he got from the work, but really he had been doing just as Callum had said. He had been running away from the loss of his and Jazz's baby.

He stared at Callum. 'Do you know something?'

'What?'

'You're far more clever than you look.'

Callum pretended to be offended for a moment, frowning before throwing his head back and laughing. 'Some things never change,' he said eventually.

'Like what?' Zac laughed.

'Like you being a plonker.'

They roared with laughter.

Eventually Zac shook his head. 'I suppose I am.'

'Not about the Jazz thing,' Callum said quickly. 'Just with your terrible insults.'

Zac folded his arms and leant on the table. 'You're right though. I have been running away from relationships and it is a good thing that Lettie needs me to help her here.' He thought of the farm and how much he had enjoyed helping out. 'It's not been nearly as bad as I expected either.'

'Good. That's what I like to hear.' Callum finished his coffee.

'Now, are you going to give me Melody's number, or not?' he asked, smiling.

Zac had to force himself to keep looking cheerful. He might be almost ready for a relationship again, but had sworn off long-distance relationships after being on tour when Jazz had needed him most. He couldn't help feeling anxious in case he became close to Melody and then found he couldn't commit to her. Anyway, she would be returning to Edinburgh with Patsy at the end of the summer, so it wouldn't be wise to risk falling for her only for her to leave.

He took his phone from his jeans pocket and was about to read out her number to Callum when it dawned on him that he should check first that she was happy for him to do so.

'Is something wrong?'

Zac shook his head. He reassured himself he knew Callum well and that his friend was trustworthy. 'She's a lovely girl, so no messing her about or you'll have me to answer to.' Satisfied, Zac gave Callum her number.

Zac watched Callum tap Melody's contact details into his phone and save them. He hoped he hadn't just made a very silly mistake.

'Don't worry,' Callum said, wiping his mouth and standing. 'I wouldn't dream of being anything less than a gentleman to her.'

12

MELODY

Melody's phone pinged. She picked it up from the window ledge in her bedroom and saw an unknown number. Tensing in case it was from Rhys, she hesitated. How could he have discovered her new number? She had been careful to dump her mobile back in Scotland, determined he wouldn't have a way to contact her. Surely her mother hadn't given it to him? She might not have told her all the details that led to her leaving Edinburgh, but she had asked her mother to keep the number to herself, insisting she needed distance from Rhys while she got her head straight and decided what to do next.

Leaving her phone for a few minutes, she kept glancing at it. Forcing herself to think rationally, Melody considered who she had given her number to. Her mum, Gran, Lettie and Zac had it and possibly Lindy. If they had passed it on then it wouldn't have been to Rhys because none of them knew him.

Feeling silly for her knee-jerk reaction, she picked up her phone again and unlocked it, opening the text to read it.

> Hi Melody, this is Callum, Zac's friend. He
> kindly gave me your number so I could ask you
> out for a drink one evening if you were
> interested in joining me at the village pub.
> Looking forward to hearing from you.

Surprised that Zac hadn't asked first whether she minded him passing on her number, Melody then realised him doing so showed his lack of interest in her. She stared out of the window miserably. A cow mooed in the distance somewhere, distracting her from her disappointment.

What was she thinking? It shouldn't matter whether or not Zac fancied her. Hadn't she sworn off men forever? Her horrible experiences with Rhys should be enough to remind her that single life was far better than spending time in a bad relationship. She had never felt so alone as during those last months with Rhys. She now knew that being lonely and being alone were two completely different things.

Her thoughts returned to Zac and she pictured his adorable face, always ready with a quirky smile. He wasn't often serious, but he was kind and made her and her gran feel welcome. Being upset that he didn't feel the same attraction for her made her realise she must like him more than she had expected.

She looked at her text from Callum again and pictured the tall, handsome model and smiled to herself. Who did she think she was – feeling underwhelmed that a perfectly charming man, a model no less, had asked her out for a drink? She needed to get a grip. She hadn't even met a model before coming to this place. She supposed she should reply but wasn't sure what to say.

Should she mention Rhys to the Torels and Callum? Was it necessary? She tried to think what her grandmother would say and knew without a doubt that she would insist it was no one else's business but her own.

She should be making the most of being on the island and getting to know new people though, and Callum had only asked her out for a drink. She didn't need to make a big deal about someone being friendly. Anyway, she reasoned, if she didn't enjoy his company for any reason the village was close enough to the farm for her to walk home.

Deciding to reply before giving herself too much time to think about it and no doubt end up changing her mind again, she replied.

> Hi Callum, thanks for the invitation. I'd like to meet up for a drink sometime. Melody

She went to push her phone into her back pocket when it pinged. She turned it over to look at the screen and saw Callum had already replied.

> Are you free tonight? C

She gasped. What the hell? Melody took a calming breath. She hadn't expected to hear from him immediately.

'What's the matter?'

Melody shrieked, not realising someone else was in the room. She looked up and saw her grandmother standing near the doorway.

Patsy hurried towards her, resting her hand on Melody's arm. 'It's not you-know-who, I hope?'

Hating that she had just given her grandmother a fright, Melody quickly shook her head. 'No, Gran. Sorry. I was surprised when you spoke, that's all. I was deep in thought.'

Patsy tapped on Melody's phone screen. 'If it's not your ex, then who's put you in this strange mood?'

Melody explained what had happened. 'I'm not sure I should have agreed to go now.'

'Why ever not?' Patsy shrugged, clearly unsure why she was being so worried about the whole thing.

'You know my situation. Is it wrong to act as if I don't have a care in the world? As if I'm single?' She felt her grandmother's hands take hers and waited to hear what she had to say. 'Go on.'

Patsy smiled. 'I was just thinking that you should make the most of this time here, being free of all the nastiness you've had going on back home. It's all harmless and there's nothing wrong with going out for a drink with a handsome young chap.'

Melody thought of Zac and wished again that he had been the one to suggest a drink. She wouldn't be feeling anxious or conflicted with Zac. She just liked his company. She shook her head. 'You're right. You think I should reply to him now then?'

Patsy let go of her hands. 'Unless you're waiting for another invitation.'

Melody knew her grandmother had picked up on her feelings for Zac. 'No, Gran. I'm not,' she said, aware Patsy wouldn't be that easily dissuaded.

'Come along. Let's go down to the kitchen.'

Anyway, she mused, how could she expect to kid her grandmother when she knew she was only kidding herself?

'Well?' Patsy said, pointing at the screen once they reached the kitchen. 'Are you going to reply to him?'

Not wishing to commit to going out with Callum just yet, Melody shook her head. 'Not yet. I think I'd like a cup of tea and some toast first.'

Patsy arched an eyebrow. 'Haven't you eaten breakfast yet?'

Melody opened her mouth to answer when Zac walked into

the kitchen, a troubled look on his face. He exchanged glances with Melody, then looked at Patsy.

'Sorry, I didn't mean to interrupt anything.'

Unsure why he was acting oddly, Melody shook her head. 'You're not. Gran was just about to tell me off for not eating anything yet.'

She expected him to smile or at least relax a little, but his expression didn't alter. What was wrong with him?

'Um, I've just realised I've forgotten something in my bedroom,' Patsy said.

'Let me fetch it for you, Gran,' Melody said, taking a step forward, stopping when her grandmother raised her hand.

'No, I'll do it.' She looked pointedly from Melody to Zac, and Melody took a moment to realise she was trying to be discreet.

'OK.' Melody wasn't sure if she was missing something. When Zac didn't move or say anything, she turned to the kettle and lifted it to check there was enough water in it for several cups of tea. After topping it up under the tap, she then plugged it in and pressed the lever down. Clearly she was going to have to get the conversation with him started.

She turned to him and opened her mouth to speak, but before she had a chance to do so, he said, 'I'm so sorry, Melody. I did worry that I hadn't asked your permission first.'

Confused, she shook her head. 'I don't know what you're talking about.'

He pointed to her mobile phone lying in front of her on the kitchen table. 'I gave your number to Callum.'

'Oh.' So that's what was bothering him. She realised she should have been displeased with him, but he seemed so worried and as it hadn't occurred to her to be anything other than disappointed up until this point, she smiled. 'It's fine. I've already heard from him so this isn't news to me.'

'I see.' He moved his weight from one foot to the other. 'Did he ask you out then?'

'He did.'

'And you don't mind?' He laughed. It wasn't a happy laugh, she noted, rather it held a tone of sadness for some reason. 'Why would you mind?' He shook his head. 'Sorry.'

Determined to change the mood of the conversation, Melody indicated the kettle. 'I'm not sure what's going on, Zac, but I have a feeling you might need to chat.' When he didn't react, she added, 'Or might a coffee be more in order?'

'Coffee would be great, thanks.' He pulled out one of the chairs and sat at the table. 'So you said yes, then.'

She noticed it wasn't a question, more of a statement. He was acting oddly but didn't seem to be fazed by Callum asking her out. Hurt that he hadn't thought to ask her himself, she nodded. 'I did.'

'Right.'

The kettle finished boiling and Melody quickly made Zac a cup of coffee and herself a green tea. Setting the cups down in front of their places, she sat down.

'Are you going to tell me what's the matter or shall I try to guess?'

13

ZAC

Why was he acting like a love-sick teenager, Zac thought, irritated with himself for the mess he was in.

'Zac?'

He stared into Melody's light blue eyes and desperately tried to come up with something plausible that wouldn't result in him ending up looking like a complete fool. Why had he given Callum her number when he wanted to take her out himself? Because he assumed she would be more interested in his handsome friend, that's why, he reminded himself.

'Is something the matter?' Patsy said, entering the room carrying a book. She looked at the table. 'And my tea?'

'Oh, sorry, Gran. I forgot. I'll make it now.'

Patsy waved for Melody to remain seated. 'No, it's fine. I was only joking.' She took a mug down from the shelf and Zac noticed her turn to look at him. 'I sense an atmosphere in here,' she said as she dropped a teabag into her mug and poured water over it. 'You two haven't fallen out about something, I hope?'

'No!' They answered in unison and Zac caught Melody's eye again.

Patsy sighed heavily. 'Give me a couple of seconds to finish making this drink, then I'll leave you to sort out whatever it is that's going on here.'

He watched as Patsy finished making her drink. Then, picking it up, she grabbed her book and turned to them. 'I've no idea what's going on, but I do know that there's too much to do here for you two to fall out.'

'We haven't, Gran, I promise,' Melody said.

'Really, it's nothing,' Zac assured her, wishing he hadn't been such a prat and caused this tension in the first place.

He waited for Patsy to leave. 'Look, I'm sorry. I'm acting weird – I know I am.'

'Why, though?' She tilted her head to one side and studied his face.

Because I don't want you to go out with my friend, he wanted to shout.

Her phone pinged and they both looked at it. He took a mouthful of coffee, wincing as he realised too late how hot it still was, and waited for her to pick up her phone and read it.

'It's Callum,' she said, reading the text.

Zac tried to push away his instant jealousy to think of his best friend with Melody.

'He must think me rude.'

'Why?'

'Because I didn't get round to replying to his last text.'

Not wishing for her to feel guilty, Zac said, 'Callum is a chilled guy. He probably doesn't mind.'

'I hope you're right.' She stared at her screen.

'He's sent you another text, so he's obviously not fazed, or anything.'

'Good point.' She smiled, looking relieved. 'He's suggested we go out to the pub tonight.' She stared at him thoughtfully for a few seconds. 'He's asking if I'd like him to pick me up or if I'd rather meet him there,' she said, looking as if she was trying to work out what she would prefer.

He watched her put the phone back onto the table. 'Do what makes you more comfortable.'

She flushed slightly. 'I'm not sure I should be going out with him, if I'm honest.'

Unsure why she would say such a thing, Zac asked her.

She went to say something, then seemed to stop herself. A cloud appeared to cross her face and he wondered what could be bothering her. A boyfriend maybe?

'Do you have someone in Edinburgh?' he asked, expecting her to say no. When she didn't reply, but just looked at him, he suspected he had hit a nerve. Maybe she had fallen out with her partner and that was the reason for her coming to the island with Patsy?

She didn't deny that there was someone, but her face lit up and she bit her lower lip for a second. 'Why don't you join us this evening?'

'Me?'

She laughed. 'You do know us both and I barely know Callum. I wouldn't have to walk into a new pub by myself if you were with me.'

He didn't like to remind her that Callum had offered to pick her up. 'If you want me to, then of course I'll come with you.'

'Great.' She picked up the phone and tapped in a reply. Her phone pinged again almost immediately. She laughed. 'Callum. He says he'll meet us there.'

Zac knew he should feel happier to be accompanying Melody on her date with Callum, but instead he felt ridiculous.

If he didn't like the thought of his friend being with Melody, how was it going to feel if she and Callum kissed? He closed his eyes. Why hadn't he just let the pair of them get on with their evening out and stayed out of things? The last thing he wanted from Melody was for her to feel sorry for him.

He finished the rest of his coffee, careful to drink more slowly and blow on the hot liquid before taking a mouthful of it. Then it dawned on him that all he had to do to rectify the matter was walk in with her, have one drink and then make an excuse and leave them to it.

Melody stared at him for a moment and, wanting to fill the silence, Zac decided to change the subject to something more neutral and bring up arrangements for the festival.

'I'll be glad when we have everything organised for this event.'

'Me, too. I feel responsible for bringing as much of my expertise as possible to help make it the success Lettie hopes it to be,' she said. She was looking up at him with an expectant expression on her face.

Zac couldn't work out why, then wondered if he could make a suggestion that might show her he still enjoyed her company despite passing on her contact details to his friend. He didn't want to be obvious about his feelings for her, especially now he knew she was happy to go out with Callum, but didn't want to ruin the friendship they had made by being distant.

'I know what you mean. I feel the same way about making sure all the sound is up to scratch. Maybe we could go out for coffee together and chat about—' Zac stopped, realising that was exactly what they were currently doing.

'Yes.' She looked down. 'I mean, I'd like that.'

Thrown by her enthusiasm, Zac was happy to think she still wanted to spend time with him. 'Um, OK. We could run some ideas between us and think of ways we can help Lettie. I want this to be as much of a success as possible.' He thought of the amount of money they needed to raise. 'It's not going to be easy though. We haven't had time to build up any momentum with advertising.'

'We'll do the best we can,' she insisted.

'We will.' He shrugged as a thought occurred to him. 'I'll do all I can to help towards the cost of the repairs.'

Her smile vanished. 'We'll all try to think of ways to help do that,' she said. 'For now though, I think we need to focus on making this festival as slick as we can.'

'Yes.' He held up his hand for her to return his high five.

Melody laughed and slapped her hand against his.

14

MELODY

Melody heard voices and turned to look out of the window. She watched as Lettie kissed Brodie in the yard before waving him off. 'Lettie's back,' she said, getting to her feet. She had enjoyed spending time with Zac and wasn't ready to leave him but she was staying at the farm to help out and didn't want to be caught chatting when there was so much to do on the farm and for the festival.

'You off then?' Zac asked, standing and taking their mugs to the sink.

'I should be helping your sister with all she has going on.'

'And I should be answering some of the emails from work that have been sitting in my inbox for far too long.'

She watched him leave the room then went outside to join Lettie.

'Hello there,' Lettie said, giving her a beaming smile.

Melody really liked her new host, although she seemed more of a friend already than someone she worked for in exchange for room and board. 'You're looking...' She tried to come up with the right word to fit what she wanted to convey.

'As if I'm on a mission?' Lettie laughed.

That was it. 'Yes, exactly. Has something happened?'

She followed Lettie into the barn, listening as she explained that she had bumped into Kathleen who had called her friends together to come up with ways they could help at the festival.

'That's good of them,' Melody said, remembering how Kathleen had been the one to contact Lettie's mum, Lindy, about her and Patsy coming to stay and help out at Hollyhock Farm. 'She's such a kind lady.'

'Very pro-active too,' Lettie said. 'I think we can safely say we'll have enough helpers greeting people at the gate and taking money, which is an enormous relief because I'm going to need to be free to go where I'm needed during the festival.'

Melody agreed. 'Yes, and I'll be there as backup for you when I'm not giving a class.'

Lettie grinned. 'I'm feeling a little more confident about the whole thing.' She laughed. 'Not much, but a little.' She frowned. 'I thought that as well as you pinning flyers at various places like the noticeboard in the supermarket, pub and even Brodie's practice, that maybe we could also place an advert in the local paper.'

'Good idea,' Melody agreed. 'I've also set up a Facebook page about the festival that's starting to gain some traction and lots of followers who have been sharing my post, so that's another audience discovering what we're planning.'

Melody thought of her and Zac going to meet Callum in the pub later and told Lettie about it. She saw Lettie's eyebrows rise in surprise. 'It's not a date, or anything.'

'With which one?' Lettie smiled.

Aware her friend was teasing her, Melody relaxed. 'Either one of them.' She wasn't sure but she thought she had seen a look of disappointment momentarily cross Lettie's face. Melody wondered which part might have given her cause to react in that way.

'I, er, am not long out of a relationship,' she explained, hoping it was enough to deter Lettie from getting any ideas about setting her up with someone.

Lettie raised both hands. 'Not my business. You're my friend and helping me both here on the farm and with the festival, and I'm just grateful to have you here.'

It was a relief to hear her say so. Melody remembered her reasoning behind telling Lettie about meeting Callum at the pub. 'I was thinking about when Callum offered to have us on his radio show,' she explained. 'I thought Zac and I could speak to him about it tonight and hopefully arrange for us to go on air as soon as possible.'

Lettie beamed at her. 'What a brilliant idea. Callum is a lovely bloke and if he said he'd help promote the event, then he'll do it. Let's hope he can have you on his show soon.'

'I'll bribe him with lagers later, if necessary,' she said and laughed.

She was feeling much better about agreeing to meet up with him now that she could justify doing so. Her friend's event needed publicity and hopefully Callum would be able to give them the biggest amount via his show.

15

ZAC

Zac was surprised by how much he was enjoying helping out on the farm. Most years he would be inundated with work during the summer months with music festivals and events, but this year he had found a replacement for several of his bookings in order to help his sister prepare and run her wellness festival. He thought it was the least he could do to help her keep their childhood home.

He pressed send on his final email and sat back in his father's office chair with relief. He checked his watch and realised he had been working for three hours. He promised himself he wouldn't leave his admin for so long next time. Strangely enough working on the farm had seemed like being on holiday, despite the strenuous physical work. Maybe it was because it was so different to being in a recording studio or touring with a band, but the simplicity of the fresh air and doing what his sister told him to was like taking a proper break, which he supposed it was.

He thought of Melody wanting him to take her to meet up with Callum later. He didn't intend staying for long and end up playing gooseberry for the evening. The most he intended doing was staying for one friendly pint and then leaving.

He closed his laptop and went to find Lettie and Melody. Seeing Lettie in the top field with the alpacas, he whistled for Spud to follow him and went to join them.

'Can I help with anything?' he asked, stroking the soft fur of Gideon.

'Where have you been all this time?' Lettie grumbled, a hammer in one hand and several nails in the other.

Zac leant to one side to peer around his sister. 'Something broken?'

'Not any more, it isn't,' Melody said, coming up behind him.

'Where did you come from?' he asked, surprised to see her there suddenly.

Lettie handed the nails to Melody. 'I noticed a couple of the rails were getting old and a bit unstable, so Melody has been helping me replace them.'

Feeling guilty for not helping out, Zac grimaced. 'You should have let me know. I could have done it for you.'

Lettie pulled a face. 'With all due respect, Zac, I don't think you'd have been any better at this than we were.'

Not wishing Melody to think badly of him, he gave her an apologetic smile. 'Can I help fix them now?'

'Nope,' Melody said, holding up the hammer. 'I only need to put in one extra nail to a rail back there and we're done.'

He patted the alpaca once more and joined his sister, following Melody to where she still had to fix the last rail. He watched her working and seeing how proficient she was said, 'You're right, I wouldn't have been any better than either of you at this.'

'Maybe you need some practice,' Lettie joked.

'Hey, I'm happy to give anything a go here, so just point me in the right direction and tell me what you need doing.'

He gave Melody a satisfied smile and could see she was amused. Wanting to change the subject, he told them about one of his emails.

'I've been offered a job going on tour with one of the bands I've been employed by a few times.' He was surprised to see Melody's smile vanish.

'When?' Lettie asked. 'I hope you're not thinking of leaving before the festival is over, Zac. I need you here to help with everything.'

Wishing he had been clearer about his next booking, he pulled an apologetic face. 'Sorry, I was going to say that I'd be leaving soon after the festival but you interrupted me.' He hated the thought of Melody thinking he was being selfish. 'I'll do all I can to help clear up in the time I have, but don't forget I'm a sound engineer and these jobs pay decent money.' Hoping to soften the blow, he added. 'I'm hoping that with what I'll make I should be able to contribute more to the cost of the barn repairs.'

'Really?'

His sister seemed surprised and, concerned that her expectations might be unrealistically high, Zac decided to explain further. 'Don't get me wrong, I wouldn't be able to cover a large amount, but I should be able to let you have a couple of thousand.'

'Pounds?' Lettie asked.

He frowned. 'Of course pounds. What else would they be?'

'That's wonderful, Zac,' Melody said.

Lettie gave him a hug. 'It is. Thank you.' Her arms dropped away from him and she stepped back. 'We forgot to mention that Melody has had an idea about tonight.'

Unsure where the conversation was going, Zac looked at Melody. 'Tonight?' Had she forgotten they were going to meet Callum at the pub? If she had, was that a good thing?

He listened while they explained about Melody's idea for locking in a time for them to appear on Callum's radio show.

'So,' Lettie said. 'What do you think he'll say?'

Zac shrugged. 'Well, yes, of course. He's already said he'd happily give you, or us, a spot on there and he will have meant it.'

'Brilliant,' Lettie said. 'Then don't either of you forget to ask him. We need all the publicity for this event that we can get.'

That evening as Zac accompanied Melody up to the pub's front door, he greeted a few people he knew then stopped by the door to hold it open for her when he realised she was a short distance away. Melody seemed nervous about something and he watched silently as she looked around her. It was almost as if she was expecting to see someone there.

She noticed him and hurried over, thanking him as she passed him and walked into the pub.

'Everything OK?' he asked quietly, not wishing to draw attention to any concerns she might have.

She gave him a look that made him think he had imagined what he had seen. 'Yes, of course. Why?'

Confused, Zac shook his head. 'Nothing. Take no notice of me.' He thought he saw a shadow of shame cross her face and knew she was hiding something from him. But what? Who could she have expected to appear outside? It couldn't be Callum because he had said he would meet them inside the bar. Callum had just spotted them and was waving them over.

And anyway, Zac reasoned as he walked with her to the other end of the bar, she had no reason to be bothered by Callum.

Strange, he thought, deciding to keep alert in case he spotted her doing it again. If he did, he would definitely have to press her to tell him what was wrong. He hated to think that Melody might not feel completely safe here in their village.

'Good to see you, Melody,' Callum said before frowning. 'And you, Zac,' he said, putting his arm around Zac's shoulder and laughing to show he was only teasing.

'I'll only stay for one drink,' Zac said. Even though he was sure Callum didn't mind him being there too much, he didn't want to interrupt their date. Well, he did, but had more pride than to do so. 'Melody and I have something we'd like to ask you, so I thought I'd make the most of enjoying a cool pint of lager before I leave you both to your evening.'

'I'm intrigued,' Callum said, motioning for them to quickly grab the table next to them as a couple stood to leave. 'I'll get us some drinks.'

'No, I'll get them,' Zac insisted. 'I've come to ask a favour of you and you can consider it your payment.'

As soon as they were seated with their drinks, Zac brought up their being featured on Callum's radio show. 'I'm a bit nervous but we need all the publicity we can get and you did say we only had to ask.'

Callum smiled at him and then at Melody. 'And I meant it.' He narrowed his eyes and thought for a moment. 'We really need to get on and do this soon. How about in two days' time? I can give you twenty minutes at, say, three fifteen. Would that suit you? If you're busy...'

Zac was relieved and by the look on Melody's face, she was delighted. 'We'll be there.'

'You won't need me to talk too, I shouldn't think,' Melody said, before taking a sip of her lemonade.

'Er, you're the one who knows all about this wellness stuff,' Zac argued. His idea of any entertainment involved him being very much behind the scenes. 'You're going to need to explain what it's all about.'

Melody pulled a face. 'I suppose you're right. But I'm not doing it by myself. You'll have to be in the studio with me.'

'Fine then,' he agreed.

Callum laughed. 'Honestly, you two are like an old married couple the way you bicker.' He smiled when Zac glared at him. 'And you, Zac. I know you well enough that once you get going there'll be no shutting you up. You'll be fine. Chatting on the radio isn't scary at all.'

'Hah,' Zac scoffed. 'Says the radio DJ. Of course it isn't for you. For us it is though.'

'Yes, it is,' Melody agreed.

Zac felt her elbow in his side as she nudged him, and he looked questioningly at her. 'What is it?'

'We're going to have to sit down before we go on and make some notes. I don't want us to mess this opportunity up by not mentioning something important about the event.'

Happy to have a reason to spend more one-to-one time with her, he agreed. 'Absolutely. We still haven't gone out for that coffee yet, have we?'

'No, we haven't.' Melody smiled thoughtfully. 'And I presume you're suggesting that would be the perfect time to discuss our promotional strategies?'

'That's exactly what I had in mind.'

'Sounds good to me.'

16

MELODY

Melody woke after a restless night's sleep. She wasn't sure why she felt troubled by having a drink with Callum the previous evening, although maybe it was because she liked him. She liked Zac too, rather more than she wanted to admit. She thought of the strange feeling she had experienced as she and Zac arrived at the pub and shivered. She could have sworn someone was watching her. The only person who would spy on her would be Rhys, and she was sure he had no idea where she was.

She couldn't shift her feeling of guilt despite knowing she was being silly. The only reason she and Zac had been going to meet Callum was to ask him to help with the promotion of the festival, she reasoned. At least that was a reason for Zac coming with her. That and him dropping her off for her drink with his friend. Surely not even Rhys could find fault with that. She closed her eyes. Of course he could. Rhys could find something to be jealous about when she spent time with her parents without him, so why wouldn't he be apoplectic about her having a drink with two men he didn't know?

Not that she knew Callum well, or Zac really, for that matter. At least Callum had agreed for her and Zac to go on his radio show together. Lettie would be pleased, and she was relieved to be helping get the word out to the locals about the event. Callum had been more fun than she had expected, entertaining her with anecdotes about modelling shoots and how much he preferred being a radio host and not being in front of the camera. She had been sorry when Zac had left early. Melody recalled how Callum had walked her back to the farm and gone to kiss her, having wished her goodnight. Why had she stepped back as if he was about to do something wrong? She pulled the covers over her head and groaned, mortified to think that she would have to face him soon. What must he think of her?

Hearing Zac's voice outside calling for Spud to follow him, Melody threw back the covers and got out of bed. She pushed her window open wider. It was another hot, sunny day and she breathed in the sweet air and stretched her arms above her head.

'Hey, sleepyhead.'

She tensed, hoping he wasn't talking to her. She pushed her hands quickly through her messy bed hair, relieved she had thought to sleep in a T-shirt for once rather than going to bed naked. Why hadn't it occurred to her that he would notice her?

'Yes,' Zac said, amusement in his voice. 'I'm talking to you in the attic.'

'I presume you don't mean me,' Melody heard her grandmother say, laughing at her own joke.

'Morning, Patsy.' Zac pointed to Melody's window. 'I saw Melody was awake and was going to ask her to join me and Spud for a walk down at the beach. I thought we could talk through our ideas for what we want to include in our interview with Callum on the radio tomorrow. You're welcome to join us.' He put his hand up to his eyes to shield them from the sun that Melody realised was reflected off her window. 'Will you be coming?'

Melody rested her elbows on the windowsill, wishing he hadn't reminded her about seeing Callum again so soon. She hoped there wouldn't be an awkward atmosphere between them when she saw him the following afternoon.

'Give me a couple of minutes to take a quick shower, then I'll be down.'

'Patsy, how about you?' he asked.

'No, thanks, Zac,' Melody heard her grandmother reply. 'I need a coffee before venturing out anywhere in the morning. Maybe another time.'

As Melody showered, she thought of Zac and how much she liked the friendly farmer's son. He always seemed cheerful, and she wondered if he actually was, or if it was a front he put on to hide past hurts. She wondered if she was letting her imagination get ahead of her or if she simply recognised a hidden sadness in him because that's the way she faced the world too. Whatever his story was, she appreciated the way he seemed to make everything exciting and fun, at least for her. And he was dedicated to his family. In fact, the Torel family as a whole seemed dedicated to caring for each other. It was what families were all about or should be.

Her thoughts turned to her father, who made a point of not getting involved with anything outside his work, and her mother who, as much as she knew loved her, never seemed able to see Rhys as anything other than a gentleman. Her mother had known Rhys since Melody and he were in school together and was best friends with his mother, who thought him the perfect son. Then again, Melody thought as she stepped out of the shower, she had kept most of her issues with Rhys to herself. She wondered why she had always felt like she was to blame for the way he treated her and supposed it was because he had coerced her into believing she was at fault. She now knew better thanks to her grandmother's patience and many hours of sitting and listening to her.

Not wishing to keep Zac waiting, she quickly towel-dried her hair, then her body and pulled on a pair of shorts and a clean T-shirt. After running a brush through her hair, she grabbed her trainers and a pair of socks, and headed downstairs.

She took a moment to see where he was and spotted him to the right of her with Spud, staring at the flowers.

'Sorry you had to wait,' she said, her stomach doing a flip when he smiled that bright, blue-eyed smile of his. As usual his chestnut hair was messy and it was all she could do to stop gazing at him. Remembering she still had bare feet, Melody leant against the front-door frame and pulled on her socks before pushing her feet into her trainers.

'Take your time,' he said calmly. 'There's no rush. Spud and I have been having fun watching the bumblebees humming around the hollyhocks.'

She sensed he liked her and wouldn't mind there being something between them romantically, or was that just wishful thinking on her part? Anyway, she reasoned as she pushed her foot into her second trainer, she had too much baggage to allow herself to give in to any feelings she might have for Zac. He was far too nice to deserve becoming involved in hers and Rhys's battles.

Plus, she thought, stepping into the garden to join him and Spud, Zac had mentioned being offered a job touring soon, so it wasn't as if either of them would be near the other one to have any kind of romance.

'You look lovely,' he said, almost to himself. 'Um, that is...' He patted Spud's head, clearly deciding not to finish that thought. 'Shall we get going then? The tide is on the way in and if we still want to have any sand to walk on we'd better not leave it too long to get down to St Ouen.'

She wasn't sure whether to thank him for his comment, or why he had said it as it had clearly made him uncomfortable.

Maybe he had said what he did because he liked her and now felt awkward. She cringed inwardly, dismissing that thought, and got into the passenger's seat of his mother's old Golf and closed her eyes briefly. She wasn't sure what could have happened to her to make her fall for him so quickly. Especially as she had decided not to open her heart to any man since her previous relationship had ended so horribly. She pushed away the thought of Rhys and his increasingly violent behaviour that led to her leaving him. That was part of her problem with Zac now though and why they couldn't have any future as far as she was concerned. She had walked away from Rhys. If he had been the one to end their relationship, the one in control, then maybe she would be free to move on from him with Zac. But he hadn't done, and she knew he wouldn't let go of her easily. She felt sick at the thought of what he might be capable of and hated to think of Zac becoming involved in her dramas in any way.

She was an emotional mess and was beginning to suspect Zac might have noticed. She hoped not. She would hate it if he was only being kind to her because he felt sorry for her.

17

ZAC

Zac wasn't sure why Melody was quiet during the short drive to St Ouen's Bay but supposed it was because she hadn't been awake all that long. He had heard her come home the previous evening and looked out of his window to tell her that the front door was unlocked, only to see Callum leaning forward to kiss her. He'd immediately stepped back, not wishing to seem as if he was watching a private moment.

Zac had never been a jealous person, but the pang of envy seeing his best friend and the woman he was falling in love with about to kiss one another stung. Damn it. Why hadn't he told her how he felt about her? If he had, then maybe she wouldn't be kissing his best friend on his front doorstep.

That morning he had been about to take Spud for a walk on the beach when he spotted two ducks flying over the roof and happened to notice Melody watching them from her bedroom window. Deciding to mention the ducks to her when they next met up he was pleased with himself for his quick thinking. At least now he had something to talk about to get past what he had seen the night before. The last thing he wanted was for her to know he had seen them about to kiss and not act rationally in front of her. They were friends after all and if she was attracted to his mate, then he would simply have to get over his disappointment that he wasn't the one Melody felt romantically towards.

Maybe her quietness had nothing to do with how early it was, or her date with Callum, and rather it was down to her regretting agreeing to be interviewed on the radio. 'I've been thinking,' he said as he parked the car and got out. 'If you'd rather not do the interview tomorrow, I completely understand. I know speaking on the radio isn't everyone's cup of tea.'

She seemed surprised by his comment. 'Sorry, I've been a bit quiet, haven't I? I'm just not really awake yet,' she said, waiting for him to let Spud out of the car. 'I don't have a problem chatting on air.'

She seemed very confident. 'Have you done it before then?'

She shook her head and laughed. 'No, not on the radio, but Gran has a monthly podcast.'

'Patsy has a podcast?' Why wasn't he too surprised? 'What does she talk about on it?'

'Oh, this and that, but mostly about wellness, living your life to the full. She chats with people who give courses either online, or in the local area and shares ideas about how to keep active both mentally and physically.'

'Good for her.' He smiled, thinking of the sprightly lady and her enthusiasm for life. 'Hey, maybe she could do an episode to promote the festival? What do you think?'

'I can ask her. Gran is a great one for making the most of opportunities that come her way. She's always encouraging me to do the same thing.' Melody grinned. 'I've had to go on that a few times when she needed someone to step in. As Gran constantly reminds me, technology isn't only for the young.'

Seeing a horse and rider about to make their way down the cobbled slipway, Zac decided to take another route there. 'I think we'll go this way,' he said, walking towards the long grass above the high beach wall towards a round Martello tower with a Second World War bunker next to it. 'Please don't let Patsy know I was surprised to discover she has her own podcast.'

Melody laughed. 'I won't but you should understand Gran well enough by now to know she loves nothing better than shocking people. She says it helps her feel less invisible.'

Zac couldn't understand why anyone would feel that way. 'Invisible? What a strange thing to say.'

'Not really,' Melody said, slowing to look at the deco house she had just spotted ahead. 'Gran says that the older she gets the less she feels noticed by people.'

Zac turned to her, surprised. 'I can't imagine anyone not noticing your grandmother. It's as if she has some sort of magnetic field shining from her. She's great fun.'

'I'm glad you think so.' She pointed to the property overlooking the sea built in the shape of a boat. 'What is that? A house?'

'It is,' he said. 'It's one of my favourite places here. It's called Barge Aground but the name embossed on the building is Seagull. It was built sometime in the nineteen thirties and was one of several Art Deco follies dotted along this coastline. People rent it out for holiday stays from Jersey Heritage.'

'Can we go closer to get a better look?'

'Of course.' He led the way and soon they were standing right in front of it at the short path. 'Isn't it beautiful?'

'I'd love to stay in there sometime,' she said wistfully.

He watched her gazing at the place he had loved his whole life and decided that if possible he would try to arrange for her to see inside the boat-shaped house overlooking the expanse of the bay. 'I'll see what I can do.'

She turned to him, a look of surprise on her face. 'Really? You'd do that?'

He wasn't sure why she was taken aback by what he had said, but nodded. 'I'll do my best.'

Spud barked, distracting them. Zac called out to him to wait, but Spud was too focused on another dog down by the water's edge and immediately ran towards the granite steps leading down to the beach. 'Spud, I said wait,' he bellowed.

Ignoring him, Spud hurtled down the stairs, his black and white tail wagging.

'I'd better get after him.'

'He's quick, isn't he?' Melody called as she raced after Zac.

'Especially when he's doing something he shouldn't.'

* * *

The following afternoon, as he and Melody were at the radio station waiting in reception to be taken up to the studio for their interview, Zac hoped he would remember everything he needed to know.

'Are you nervous?' Melody asked, resting her hand on his.

Not wanting her to remove her hand, but aware he didn't dare forget all they needed to bring up with Callum, he said, 'I know we need to mention our website, so people can find out more about the event.'

'Yes, and that they can contact us that way and book a stand for their business, or to sponsor us.'

'That's right. We can also mention the programme and that you'll be giving a yoga class among other things we have planned.'

She gave his hand a squeeze. He turned so that he could take her hand in his and his heart raced when she smiled at him. Reminding himself she was only trying to comfort him and calm any nerves he might have, he focused on their impending interview.

'We've got this,' she said. 'Anyway, Callum knows why we're here today and I'm sure he'll mention anything he can think of that we might forget.'

She was right. 'I think I'm aware how last minute this festival is,' he admitted. 'I'd hate for us to come across as being shoddy.'

Melody frowned. 'I think we can safely say that won't happen. We've all done a lot of work to make this festival the best we can and all of us, especially Lettie, have worked tirelessly to bring things together. It'll be fine. Don't worry.'

The door next to the reception desk opened before he had a chance to respond and a young woman smiled at them. 'Hi, I'm Kiera one of the producers here at the station. They're ready for you now,' she said, holding the door open.

Zac's nerves increased as he followed Melody and the producer upstairs to a side room filled with sound equipment above a desk where a pair of headphones now lay. There was a large window on one side. Through it he could see Callum, looking every part the professional radio host. He listened as he introduced the next record before waving for them to go and join him in the studio.

'Great to see you both,' he said, motioning for them to take a seat at one of three high stools. 'Kiera will be setting you both up. How are you feeling?'

They waited while Kiera arranged microphones in front of each of them and then, after checking they were fine, left them to it.

'I'm good,' Zac said, having to force his cheerfulness and try to dispel the image of his best friend homing in to kiss Melody two nights before.

'Yes, me too.' Melody cleared her throat.

Callum smiled at her. 'You'll both be great,' he said. 'Right, when the record ends, I'll introduce you and then ask a few questions. Lettie kindly forwarded some information about your festival earlier today, so we shouldn't forget anything. How does that sound?'

'Great,' Zac said, certain he couldn't recall the first thing he was there to talk about now he was seated opposite Callum.

'Sure.' Melody patted his leg and gave him a reassuring smile. 'This is going to be fun.'

He hoped that once he started speaking he would somehow relax enough so that his voice didn't quaver. The record ended all too soon and Zac clenched his fists and rested his hands on his legs. He tried to calm himself, aware that he was breathing too fast and that it would come across over the microphone. Then, taking a long slow breath, he exhaled just as Callum introduced them.

'That was one of my favourite records and I hope you enjoyed hearing it. I mentioned earlier that my guests today were Zac Torel and Melody from Hollyhock Farm here on the island. Welcome, both of you.'

Zac opened his mouth to speak, but found it was completely dry. What the hell was wrong with him? He shot a terrified look in Melody's direction.

'Thank you for inviting us,' Melody said.

Zac saw Callum give him a confused look when he didn't speak. 'They've joined me this afternoon to talk about the well-ness festival being held there in a couple of weeks. I know I try my best to look after myself but sometimes am overwhelmed by all the information that's out there. Zac, Melody, I'm interested in attending this festival and was wondering what you can tell us about the event and who it might be for.'

Melody gave him a reassuring smile and he realised she was checking to see if he wanted her to reply to Callum's question. Zac could see her smile was slightly forced but was relieved when she began talking.

'That's right, Callum,' she said, her voice clear and confident. 'I've been to wellness events in the past and they've always been interesting, but the setting for this one is exceptional. Hollyhock Farm is a beautiful place, surrounded by rolling fields and views out across the bay.'

'Sounds incredible,' Callum said, grinning and tilting his head briefly on one side. 'I've noticed that the forecast is suggesting bad weather coming our way from the south. We could have showers, but they will be a bit hit and miss thankfully. What are the plans in case that happens? Can you explain about that, Zac?'

This was something Zac didn't want to think about. Realising his concern about the bad weather had dispelled his anxiety about speaking, Zac went to respond. 'We have two barns at the farm, a larger and smaller one, so will utilise those for the event.'

'Sounds good.' Callum smiled at him. 'And what can those of us attending the festival expect to find there?'

Feeling more confident, Zac continued, 'You can find out much more on our website, which you'll find at HollyhockFestival.org, but essentially we will be showcasing various businesses, each of which will have their own stall. There's an area where Melody, who is a trained yoga teacher, will be giving classes and answering any questions about yoga. We also have other complementary therapies that attendees can try out, like sound baths, ice baths, talks by experts in crystal therapy, aromatherapy and experts in herbal remedies to mention just a few.'

'Yes,' Melody said. 'We still have a couple of stands available, so any businesses wishing to hire one for the two-day event can find our contact details on our website. And if anyone wishes to sponsor the event, there's still time for us to add their information to our website, where you'll also find a market directory for each of the businesses taking part that will link directly to their own website.'

'It sounds incredible,' Callum said, and by the look on his face Zac saw that he meant it. 'I'm definitely coming along,' he said. 'So any of my listeners wanting to say hi to me will be able to find me there at some point too.'

Zac noticed lights flashing in the corner of his eye and saw the producer's workstation was busy and Kiera was indicating the phone and giving Callum the thumbs up.

Callum seemed impressed. 'I was wondering if this will this be a one-off festival, or are you planning another next year?'

'We're going to see how things go,' Zac replied. 'My sister Lettie runs the farm now. We're an organic farm with various rescue animals living there too. We had intended taking longer to decided what to do for the best, but necessity has caused us to bring this event forward by quite a few months due to repairs being needed on our larger barn roof after it was hit by lightning a couple of months ago and caught fire.'

'That sounds daunting,' Callum said and Zac could hear the sympathy in his friend's voice. 'Hopefully you'll raise enough money for the repairs.'

'Yes, that would be a great result. And to answer your question, I imagine that if enough people attend and we can see that there is a call for this sort of thing, then we will most probably do this again next year.'

Callum asked them a few more questions. The time seemed to fly by and soon their interview was over and Callum was thanking them. 'Well, Zac and Melody from Hollyhock Farm, thank you for coming in today to explain about the upcoming wellness festival. I'm sure it'll be an enormous success and look forward to seeing you both there.'

'Thanks, Callum,' they said in unison.

He realised Callum had finished with them and was speaking to his audience.

Melody smiled at Zac. He returned her smile, eager for Callum to announce the next record so they could leave the studio and get back outside.

Hearing the record start playing, Callum removed his headphones and smiled at them.

'Thank you both for coming in today. It was fun chatting to you both.'

'Thanks, mate,' Zac said.

Callum walked around the huge console in front of him and gave Melody a hug before kissing her on the cheek. He moved to Zac and patted him on the back. 'You both did well there,' he said. 'You sounded like you've done this before, Melody.'

Zac waited while she told him about Patsy's podcast and could see Callum was visibly impressed.

'Any time you or your grandmother want to come and chat again, you only have to ask,' he said.

As Zac drove back them back to the farm, they reflected on everything they had said in the studio.

'It was exciting being at a real radio station and seeing a professional studio for the first time,' Melody said. 'Gran has a decent set-up, to be fair. Although hers is in her spare bedroom, so not nearly as impressive.' She grinned at him. 'I loved it, didn't you?'

He thought about it as he drove up Beaumont Hill. 'I did actually. Once my nerves vanished.'

'I thought you'd be far more relaxed about it,' she said thoughtfully. 'Especially with your experience in the music industry.'

He had thought he would too, but didn't say as much. 'I'm not sure what happened. I'm relieved I did finally manage to speak. I know Lettie will have been listening to the show and I'd hate to let her down.'

'You definitely didn't do that.'

'Neither did you.'

'I'm glad you think so.' She sighed. 'Gran was going to listen too. I'd be mortified if I had said something silly.'

'You certainly didn't do that. I thought you were amazing,' he said, hearing his voice soften and wishing he could hide his emotions even more than he already did.

'Did you really?'

They stopped behind a row of cars at the top of the hill, waiting to go through the filter in turn. He looked at her, trying to gauge the tone in her voice and realised that if he didn't know better, he might be persuaded to think that Melody also had feelings for him. Someone hooted behind him and Zac saw the car in front had driven forward. He raised his hand by way of an apology.

Realising he hadn't answered Melody, he decided to be honest. 'Yes, I really did.'

18

MELODY

She wondered what Zac really meant when he called her amazing. She watched him discreetly as he drove, willing him to say more, disappointed when he just made small talk about jobs they still needed to do for the event.

They arrived back at the farm minutes later to be greeted by Lettie and Patsy who gave them a round of applause when she and Zac got out of the car.

Zac took a bow and for the first time Melody sensed he hid a lot of his feelings from everyone. It was a shock to discover that the man she had assumed to be an open book, always cheerful and wanting to make everyone around him as happy as him, might not be what she had at first assumed. It was a revelation.

'You were both brilliant,' Patsy said, hurrying over to wrap Melody in a tight hug. 'I'm very proud of you, darling girl.'

'Thanks, Gran. I'm sure it was all your training.'

Patsy laughed. 'Forcing you to chat to me about crystals and other alternative treatments when my planned interviewee chickened out, you mean?'

'Yes, exactly that.'

Lettie hugged her as soon as Patsy stepped back. 'It stood you in good stead,' she said. 'You sounded perfect.'

'Hey, what about me?' Zac asked, giving Melody a wink and putting his arm around her shoulder, making her tingle with delight at his closeness.

'You were a perfect double act,' Patsy said.

Melody knew her grandmother was up to her usual tricks. 'Never mind that, I'm sure we still have a lot of work to do today.'

'We do,' Lettie agreed. 'Brodie has a quiet day at the surgery so he's kindly offered to come along and help us.'

* * *

By the time Brodie arrived, the four of them had begun sorting through most of the equipment in the smaller of the two barns. It wasn't too bad at all, Melody mused, impressed at how efficiently the farm was run and how neatly everything was stored. With Brodie's help they soon finished all they needed to do.

'This is looking so much better,' Lettie said, arms folded. 'I finally feel as if we're getting somewhere.'

Melody thought of the work they had done in the larger barn a few days before and how all that now needed was to have the floors thoroughly washed just before the festival to allow tables and stands to be set up. 'It is. I told you we could do it.'

'I know, but I thought I was busy before looking after all the animals and keeping an eye on the produce we grow here, but having the extra help—' she pointed to Patsy and then Melody, then blew a kiss to Brodie '—you lot, that is, has been amazing.'

'Er, what about me?' Zac asked, sweeping the last pile of dust into a dustpan that Melody was holding for him.

'You've been helpful too, but it is your family farm as well as mine, don't forget, so you have an added incentive.'

Melody enjoyed the siblings and their banter. She thought of the exchange between Lettie and her lovely boyfriend and couldn't help wishing for gentle romance for herself. She pushed the thought away. She was getting ahead of herself. Anyway, she was very fortunate she and her grandmother had ended up being invited to stay at this beautiful place. She loved the work and it helped keep her mind off her personal troubles.

If only it wasn't temporary, she mused, reminding herself that she would have to return home to Scotland at some point. Right now though she was going to make the most of being on this pretty island and enjoy every moment with these kind people.

Lindy appeared at the barn door. 'There you all are.'

Lettie gasped. 'You're back.' She ran over to Lindy and hugged her.

'Why didn't you call and let us know?' Zac asked, joining them and stepping into his mother's arms as soon as they were free. 'I'd have come to fetch you both from the airport.'

'We did tell you when we would be back.' Lindy sighed. 'I suppose the pair of you have been too busy to think about much apart from this place and the festival you've been planning.'

'Something like that,' Zac said. 'You should have called for one of us to fetch you from the airport though.'

Lindy frowned. 'We did try to call a few times, but couldn't get through to anyone,' she said. Zac went to say something, but she held her hand up to his mouth. 'In the end we thought it was quicker to take a taxi.'

'We?' Zac said. 'So you didn't leave Dad behind on some Mediterranean coastline somewhere then?'

Lindy glanced over her shoulder. 'Don't think I wasn't tempted on several occasions.' She laughed. 'But no, he's here. In fact, I'd be grateful if one of you could go and help him carry the luggage up to our bedroom, if you don't mind.'

'I'll help him,' Brodie said, going to leave the barn.

'Thanks, Brodie,' Lindy called after him. When Zac went to follow she raised her hand to stop him. 'Right, I'm going to freshen up and then if one of you would like to come and help me set up for dinner that would be wonderful.'

'I'm happy to make us all something,' Patsy offered before she handed her broom to Melody, who noticed for the first time that her grandmother looked flushed and realised she was probably desperate for a break and a cup of tea.

'You're very kind. Thank you, Patsy.' Lindy pointed to Zac. 'Could you go and help your father set up the barbecue? He won't be long upstairs because he always leaves the unpacking to me and you know how much of a mess he makes with the coal and everything.'

'Happy to, Mum.'

Once the three of them had gone, Melody waited for Lettie to tell her what she needed doing next.

'We can finish up here by putting the cleaning utensils away in the back room,' Lettie suggested, leading the way to a small room to the rear of the barn. 'I think we've done well today.'

'I think so, too,' Melody agreed, looking forward to taking a shower and washing her hair.

'Brodie and I are going to fetch Spud and take him and Derek for a walk on the beach.' She thought for a moment. 'You're welcome to come with us, if you'd like.'

Aware how busy Lettie and Brodie were most days, rarely

getting time alone, Melody knew her friend was only being polite inviting her to join them, so quickly tried to think of a reason not to. 'Thanks for the offer but I'm going to take a shower then thought I'd take my sketch pad and sit in the meadow down by the stream and draw for a while.'

Melody knew she had been right to decline when Brodie returned to the barn and took Lettie's hand, giving it a gentle squeeze. 'Ready to go?' he asked, kissing her.

'See you later,' Melody said, noticing the subtle movement between the pair. 'I'll finish tidying up in here. Enjoy your walk.'

She watched them go hand in hand looking very much in love. From what she had gathered they had only been seeing each other for a couple of months and it didn't seem fair to interrupt their time together.

Once she had finished, Melody left the small room at the back of the barn and closed the door, bolting it behind her.

She hadn't intended going to spend time by the stream but it had been a hot, tiring day and now she thought about it there was little she would rather do than go and sit with her sketch book and draw with her bare feet in cool running water.

Twenty minutes later, as she lay back on the warm grass enjoying the sensation as the running water cooled her feet, she closed her eyes, covering them with her forearm against the bright sunlight. 'This is the life.' She sighed deeply.

'It certainly is.'

She gasped, not expecting to hear Zac's voice, and sat up.

'Sorry.' He laughed, sounding apologetic for surprising her. 'I thought you could hear me coming. I didn't mean to give you a fright.'

She slapped his arm. 'Well, you did.' She wasn't really annoyed, just surprised and extremely happy that he had found her there and was about to join her. 'Are you here for the same thing?'

'Er, and what might that be?' he asked, sitting on the grass next to her. He took off his trainers and socks, slung them to one side and slid his feet into the water. 'Ah, this is bliss.' He lay down and closed his eyes.

'Taking a moment to relax and cool down.' Melody studied his dark brown lashes as they rested on his tanned cheeks. He really was adorable to look at.

'Are you staring at me?' he asked, opening one eye and peering at her before she had the chance to deny it.

'No,' she lied, laughing because it was such a silly thing to say. Wanting to change the subject, she said, 'Your family are going to have a battle on their hands to get me to leave at this rate.'

'Is that because this pretty island has won you over, or...' He made a point of pretending to think. 'Maybe you've fallen in love with Hollyhock Farm like the rest of us.' He closed his eyes again and smiled. She could tell he was amused at something. 'Could it be that I'm the appeal for you here?'

Melody laughed, realising how that must have come across when his smile disappeared. 'I didn't mean that was funny,' she said hurriedly.

'It's fine,' he said, opening both eyes. 'Lie down and rest. You deserve the break and I have interrupted your peace.' She did as he suggested then saw him turn on his side and rest his elbow on the grass and his head against his palm. 'I was teasing you, by the way.'

Enjoying their banter and wanting to keep it going, Melody said, 'What, about falling in love with the farm or about you being the main attraction?'

He fell backwards laughing loudly. 'I never said that about myself.'

Melody couldn't help giggling. 'You did say something like that though.'

'I noticed a sketch pad next to you when I got here,' Zac said, turning to face her again. 'I didn't realise you were an artist.'

'I'm not really. I've only ever sketched as a hobby, for relaxation mostly. That was until Gran needed someone to illustrate her books.' She felt her cheeks heat slightly, embarrassed in case he thought she might be showing off. 'Gran insisted my work was professional enough and kindly employs me to sketch then paint specimens for her books.'

'Specimens?' he asked. 'Hang on, did you say your gran's books? How many has she written?'

She could tell he was intrigued, and she realised she liked telling him something new about herself. 'She's had three published so far. Gran's a botanist and it's been a dream of hers to have books published and two years ago she realised that dream.'

'That's impressive.'

Melody liked to hear him say so. 'I think so too.' She thought of her grandfather dying several years before Gran achieved her dream.

'You look sad.'

She shrugged. 'My grandad died five years ago and had always insisted Gran would find someone to publish her books, but she didn't ever think it would happen.'

'He didn't live to see the books then?'

She shook her head, sad at the reminder.

'I don't think I've ever knowingly met a botanist before,' Zac said after a brief hesitation. 'I thought she was some sort of therapist though. Crystals, that sort of thing.'

Melody liked that he was interested. She had come across many people who knew very little about alternative therapy and thought that the best way to show their ignorance was to be insulting about it.

'She does that too. Gran is a creative lady and needs outlets for that creativity.'

'Like her podcast, you mean.'

'Yes.' She smiled.

'Have you always painted?'

'I've tried to do it since I could hold a pencil or get my hands on paints at school,' she admitted, thinking back to how surprised her parents had been when her art teacher insisted she had artistic talent.

'I'm impressed.'

'I think most people are good at what they love doing, don't you?' she asked, interested to know what he thought.

He shook his head. 'Not necessarily. I believe we can all improve with practice but if you don't have a natural talent with something I can't see how someone might have that extra...' He struggled to find the word.

'Sparkle?' she suggested.

He smiled. 'I'm not certain that's the word I was searching for, but it will do.' He stared at her.

Melody's neck was getting tired, so she turned to lie on her side, mirroring him. 'What is it?' she asked, wanting to know what he was thinking.

'Have you drawn me?'

She smiled and shook her head. 'No. Why, do you want me to?'

'Maybe.' His mouth drew back into a cheeky smile. 'I'd like to see some of your work first.'

'What? You're scared I might make you look like one of the flower fairies, or something?'

Zac fell back laughing again. This time he didn't stop and soon his infectious laughter caused tears to run down her cheeks.

Melody wiped them away with the back of her hand as she slowly gathered herself and noticed he was staring at her. 'What?'

'I want to kiss you,' he said, becoming serious.

She hadn't expected that answer. Unsure what to say, it dawned on her that if she didn't speak soon her chance to kiss him might disappear, never to return. 'Go on then.'

19

ZAC

She had said he could kiss her. Scared she would change her mind, Zac leant over her, letting his mouth find hers. His lips touched Melody's and she immediately responded, slipping her arms around his back, pulling him down to her and kissing him back.

She groaned quietly as they kissed and Zac didn't think he had ever felt so strongly for someone simply from a first kiss. He felt her hands travel under his T-shirt, sliding up the warm skin on his back and taking it as encouragement he kissed her more urgently, his hand moving down to her waist.

He felt Melody still and before he could wonder why, heard Spud barking.

'What is it?' she whispered as Zac sat back.

'Someone is coming. Spud never comes this way unless he's with someone.'

'Melody?'

Hearing Lettie's voice, both of them sat up and began straightening their clothes. He saw Melody run her fingers through her hair and take a calming breath.

Sitting next to her, Zac returned her gaze. 'That was...?' He couldn't find the right word to describe how much his senses were racing.

'Unexpected?' she offered, one eyebrow raised.

Zac smiled, happy that the intensity of a few moments before had been calmed. 'Yes, you could say that.'

He didn't hear Lettie's footsteps until she had almost reached them and Spud was pushing his wet nose into Zac's right ear.

'Eugh, get off, Spud.' Zac laughed, catching Melody's eye and seeing the amusement there.

'This is where you've both been hiding.' Zac saw his sister look from him to Melody and back again. 'Um, I hope I haven't come at an awkward time.'

'Not at all,' Melody said quickly, leaning to pick up her sketch pad and pencil.

'Why would you ask that?' Zac said, hoping to distract his sister.

Lettie wasn't that easily distracted though and pressed her lips together thoughtfully as if she was trying to stop herself from saying anything else.

He picked up his trainers and got to his feet. Then as soon as Spud moved away from him he reached out to take Melody's hand to help her up once she had put her trainers back on.

'I presume the food must be ready with all this urgency,' he said, starting to feel irritated that his moment with Melody had been interrupted.

'You know what Mum's like about mealtimes. She's probably been looking forward to this barbecue for days, so we can't disappoint her.'

He and Melody exchanged glances, but it wasn't obvious to him how she was feeling. Was she as frustrated as him that their kisses had been interrupted? His sister was talking about the steaks their father had been sent out to buy but all Zac could think of was that they could have eaten at any time if their parents had still been away. He pushed his annoyance away. He was being selfish. His mother was happy to be home again and her way of showing her love was to feed people. He should be grateful for that.

As they entered the yard, he spotted Callum's car parked to one side. 'Callum's here?' he asked, guilt flooding through him when he thought about what he and Melody had been doing minutes earlier. He looked at her just as she looked from Callum's car to stare into his eyes, immediately looking downcast.

Zac felt Melody's hand brush his wrist. He took her hand in his and was about to give her a reassuring smile when Callum and Brodie strode out of the front door.

'There you are,' Brodie said. 'We thought you two might have got lost somewhere.'

He was joking and Zac knew what he was saying was spoken in all innocence, but he spotted Callum's cheerful expression vanish and his eyes look down at Zac's hand holding Melody's. They immediately let go of each other, but he didn't miss the look of hurt on Callum's face.

It seemed as if nobody spoke for ages, but Zac supposed it was only a few seconds. Brodie had slipped his arm around Lettie's shoulders and was walking with her into the house. Callum was standing with one hand on Spud's head but clearly didn't know what to say and Zac knew he needed to take charge somehow.

'Shall we go in then? We don't want Mum panicking about food being spoiled. You know what she can be like, Callum.'

'What? Oh, yeah.' Callum didn't move but said, 'It's good to see you again, Melody.' His face softened. 'I see you've got your sketch pad. Been drawing plants, or this reprobate?'

'I was intending to draw some plants I'd seen earlier in the meadow, but was interrupted by this one,' she said, giving a gentle laugh. 'Shall we go and join the others.'

Zac led the way to the farmhouse, down the hallway and out the back door to the terrace where the smell of cooked food wafted towards them as they stepped outside.

'Smells delicious,' he said.

* * *

Brodie and Lettie were serving themselves and Lindy waved for Callum and Melody to do the same.

'When you're all sitting down, Gareth and I can tell you all about our trip.'

Zac didn't dare look at his sister, certain she would rather give their parents an update about the festival preparations and all they had managed to achieve since they had gone on their trip.

Zac sat next to Brodie and his mother motioned for Melody to take the seat next to him, putting Callum on the other side of the table. He could feel the heat from her skin her knee was so close to his.

'Sorry it's a bit of a squash,' Gareth said. 'I went to bring out the other table and chairs but couldn't find them.'

'Sorry, Dad,' Lettie said. 'We've been sorting out the store-room at the back of the smaller barn where you kept the extra table.'

'I saw it was very neat in there,' he said after finishing a mouthful. 'Which is good, I'm not complaining. However, maybe next time you decide to rearrange my things, let me know where I can find them.'

Zac knew his dad wasn't too bothered but liked to remind them all that this was still his farm even if he wasn't actually running it full-time any more.

'Yes, Dad.' Lettie walked over to him and kissed his cheek.

Lindy extolled the virtues of cruising around from place to place on the ship. 'It's incredible. If you've never tried it you really should,' Zac heard her say. He had heard this before several times, when they had been deciding where to visit, when his mother was packing and other times when he probably had just not been paying attention. 'You unpack your case only once and wake up in a new, beautiful location most days. There are sea days, of course, when there's more distance between two places, but I love those.'

'She spends her days lying on a sun lounger reading,' Gareth said, rolling his eyes. 'Don't you, love.'

Lindy sniffed. 'Yes, well, I'd much rather do that than sit in one of the pubs waffling to another holidaymaker for hours.' She addressed the rest of them. 'I want to go away to relax, not spend my time talking to people I don't know.'

Gareth took a drink from his glass of wine. 'You would know them if you bothered to talk to them though, wouldn't you?'

Zac looked at his sister who rolled her eyes. They were used to their parents squabbling, but it was never anything serious and there was always a form of teasing and amusement in their bickering.

'I thought they said they enjoyed their trip,' Melody whispered, leaning her head closer to him.

Zac saw the concern in her face. 'They did. This is them sharing that with us.'

Callum laughed. 'You'll get used to them.'

Zac had forgotten his friend was sitting next to them for a moment. He agreed with him and searched Callum's face for any disappointment. There didn't seem to be any, but he knew Callum was used to hiding his emotions. If Callum had any reservations about Zac and Melody becoming closer, Zac knew he would confront him about it at some point. He also knew his friend probably wouldn't let on how he felt until he was ready to say something. The anticipation was worse than being confronted, of which Callum would be well aware.

Melody went to reach for the pepper just as Zac reached for the salt. The skin on the back of her hand grazed his and she jerked it back.

Anxious that Callum would pick up on her reaction, Zac picked up the pepper and placed it in front of her. 'Sorry. There you go.'

'Thank you.' Her voice was tight and Zac wished the pair of them could relax. Clearly Melody was feeling at odds about what had happened between them, too. Deciding to direct the conversation to something neutral, he asked her about her sketches.

'You mentioned that you sketch plants for Patsy's books. That must be interesting.'

'Yes,' Callum added. 'You were going to show me some of your work, if you remember.'

'I was.' She took a sip of her wine and set her glass back down on the table. Zac wasn't sure if she was feeling calmer but hoped she was.

'Yes, I'll show you some of them after we've eaten, if you like?'

Callum had only just taken a mouthful of food from his fork

and gave her a thumbs up as he chewed. He swallowed. 'I'd like that.'

Melody looked at Zac and again he felt his stomach tumble under her gaze. 'It is interesting. It's also fun, except when Gran decides to add a couple of paintings to the book and only gives me a short time to get them right. We do work well together most of the time though, and I love what I do.'

'Do you have much work to prepare while you're here?' Lettie asked from the next table.

Zac realised that everyone's attention had moved to Melody.

'You draw?' Lindy asked. 'I've always thought myself a little artistic, but nothing on a professional level.'

'She's very talented,' Patsy said, giving Melody a proud look.

'Thanks, Gran. Yes,' she said, continuing. 'I do need to refine some sketches and add more to what I've already done while we're here. That's part of why Gran suggested we come here, for the different fauna and flora found here on the island.'

'And why you were in the meadow, I imagine?' Callum said without a hint of sarcasm, Zac noticed.

'That's right,' she said. 'I wanted to study some of the flowers I'd spotted there a couple of days ago, so that I could paint them later.' She looked around and pointed towards the wooded area to her right. 'I want to spend time in that area after I've finished in the meadow. I'm sure I'll find all sorts of things.'

'It's a shame you weren't here a bit earlier in the year,' Lindy said. 'We have rare orchids in a couple of wet meadows that you can arrange to see.'

Patsy nodded. 'I had read about them. Maybe we can arrange to come over next year and see them?'

'You'll both always be welcome to stay here at the farm,' Lettie said.

'Thank you,' Melody said.

Zac was enjoying the conversation and getting to know more about Melody and her interests. 'Is it only rare plants that interest you?'

'Not at all,' she said, standing and walking over to the side of the lawn where she picked a buttercup before returning to her seat. 'Most people would look at this little flower and do one of two things.'

Zac studied the shiny yellow petals.

'I suppose the first one would be to think how pretty buttercups are,' Lettie suggested.

'And the second?'

Recalling when he was a child and Lettie had held a buttercup under his chin, Zac said, 'I suppose they would hold it under someone's chin and say something like, let's see if you like butter.'

Melody smiled. 'Exactly. I've done that myself in the past. Now though, I would take out my magnifying glass that I always carry.' She pulled a small magnifying glass out of her shorts pocket to prove the point. 'And study every angle of it before taking it to my room and painting it, spending time getting the exact shade of each part of the flower and stem correct.' She held the delicate flower in front of him and handed him the magnifying glass.

Zac studied it for a few seconds, surprised how different a change in perspective could make something seem. 'I've never looked at a flower in that much detail before,' he said.

'Neither had I until Gran asked me to start sketching for her books. Now I've fallen in love with doing it.'

'You've always drawn though?' Brodie asked.

'I have. I don't think of anything else when I'm focused on a drawing.'

Zac noticed a haunted look in her aquamarine eyes.

She closed her eyes as if she sensed him peering into their depths, then looked at Patsy. Zac saw Melody's grandmother give her a subtle nod and wondered why Melody seemed to be waiting for her agreement.

He waited silently with the rest of them while Melody took a few seconds to think. 'I had a bitter break-up at the beginning of the year,' she said simply. Zac waited for her to continue but it seemed that was all Melody wanted to tell them.

He saw a flash of pain cross her face and sensed the break-up entailed far more than she was willing to divulge.

'I sense there's more,' Lindy said, leaning back in her chair, her arms folded across her chest as if she was waiting to hear a detailed account.

'Mum, maybe Melody doesn't want to share more right now.' Lettie looked around at the rest of them.

Melody sighed heavily. 'Unfortunately, my mother is very fond of Rhys. We'd known each other most of our lives, dated when we were both seventeen and then met up again two years ago. She was over the moon that we were together and I'm not sure if she's partly to blame for him still believing I might forgive him for what happened between us.'

'And you won't,' Callum said gently.

It was a statement rather than a question, Zac noticed.

He saw Melody nod. 'No. I know everyone has their own views on situations like these and that each relationship break-up is different and, to be honest, I haven't confided in my mother about all the details, so she doesn't have the whole picture.'

Zac wondered how bad the relationship had become to make her leave him, but it wasn't his business to ask. He hoped his mother would keep quiet and resist asking more too.

He saw his mother watch Melody thoughtfully before

opening her mouth to speak but before she could, Lettie got to her feet. 'That was delicious, Dad, Mum. Thank you.' Zac joined the others, adding his thanks. 'I spotted some tasty puddings in the fridge earlier.'

'Puddings?' Brodie asked and Zac suspected he was trying to keep Lindy's conversation from returning to questioning Melody.

'Yes, there's an apple pie.'

Zac felt Melody's little finger touch his. Before she could move it away from him, he wrapped his little finger around hers gently but didn't look in her direction. Her finger tightened around his.

Zac felt his heart race to know she felt comfortable with him and picked up his bottle of lager to take a drink. As he looked up he saw Callum watching Melody, then look at him. He tried to read his friend's expression but couldn't tell what he might be thinking. Feeling Melody's finger moving from his, Zac assumed she had seen the exchange and was feeling as uncomfortable about Callum as him.

'Can I take your plate?' Brodie asked, interrupting their silence.

Zac looked up at his sister's boyfriend, aware that it should be him helping and not Brodie. He stood, happy to do something to take his mind off things. 'You're a guest,' Zac said. 'You should be relaxing not helping. Let me get these.'

'It's fine,' Brodie said. 'I don't mind.'

'Then I'll help you,' Zac said, taking Melody's plate and placing it on top of his.

20

MELODY

Two weeks later

Melody couldn't believe they were already in September. The weather was still warm, but the forecast was for a cold front to pass over the island and Brittany over the following few days. The festival was in a week's time and everyone was concerned that the inclement weather would hamper their preparations, or worse, cause disruption to the festival itself. She really hoped it wouldn't happen, especially after all the hard work everyone had done to make it a success.

'The worst thing,' Lettie said to her and Patsy as they sat eating a cooked breakfast on the terrace overlooking the garden, 'will be if people need to camp but are unable to due to heavy winds or rain.'

Melody hoped the bad weather would pass the island by somehow. She hadn't been in Jersey long but was aware that the island was small enough to miss odd showers that passed by. She desperately wanted to help Lettie resolve her concerns.

'I think that camping outside will be fine but maybe we

could set up an area with tables and chairs in the barn where people can eat in the evenings, or sit and chat to each other.'

Lettie finished her mouthful and gave Melody's comment some thought. 'We could keep aside some space for that. I will need to be able to house some of the animals if the weather's bad though.'

Determined to help find a solution, Melody tried to come up with another alternative.

Melody saw Patsy's expression change. Then her grand-mother drank some of her tea and after placing her cup down on the saucer turned her attention to them. 'I think giving over space for attendees to relax each night when the festival ends is a great idea. We can tidy the furniture away in the morning before that day's programme begins, if necessary.'

'Hmm,' Lettie said, clasping her hands together and narrowing her eyes thoughtfully. 'We've hired portaloos for the site, and as the event is over two days we'll need to offer shower facilities too.'

'Yes, that's what I was thinking,' Melody agreed. 'Maybe keep one of the smaller storerooms for people's personal belongings.'

'I don't foresee too many people wanting to camp here,' Lettie said. 'It's only a small island and I'm sure most people will want to go home at the end of the day.'

By the time they finished breakfast, Melody knew that Lettie was feeling much calmer about the weather forecast. Melody was beginning to look forward to the entire thing being over with and getting back to her sketches and helping Lettie with harvesting produce and looking after the animals. That was more than enough work as far as she was concerned.

'Where will you find camp beds though?' Zac asked, coming

out to join them. She saw him look at the food on their plates. 'Hey, where's mine?'

'You know where the kitchen is,' Lettie said. 'If you'd have got out of your bed as early as we did, then I'm sure Patsy would have cooked some for you.' He grumbled something and went back into the house.

'Going back to what you were saying,' Lettie said, chewing her lower lip. 'I'll give some thought about who hires out camping gear on the island.'

'It is still a busy time of year, so we really should enquire about it soon,' Melody suggested. 'Zac seems to know most people here,' she said. 'Maybe he could give someone a call,' she added, realising that might be the better option.

She hadn't seen much of Callum since the barbecue a few days before because he had been away on a modelling shoot somewhere. Zac had seemed quieter since that evening too and somehow kept himself busy with jobs for the upcoming festival. If he wasn't delivering leaflets, he was putting up posters. He had met with a couple of late sponsors and there always seemed to be emails to respond to and calls to take.

Melody wasn't sure if him being constantly busy was due to his discomfort about the two of them kissing. She suspected it might be, especially as he and Callum were good friends. Maybe though, Zac's distancing himself had something to do with him discovering she had only recently gone through a difficult break-up, and he wanted to give her space to come to terms with that? Whatever it was, she missed having him around as much as he had been before.

'Yes, please. That would be perfect.' Lettie gave her a thumbs up.

Melody tried to retrace her train of thought to understand

what Lettie was talking about. Remembering her suggestion, she said, 'I'll ask Zac to make some calls.'

Melody watched Lettie lean back in her chair. She sighed happily. 'This is finally all coming together. Although I'm beginning to wonder why I ever thought this might be a good idea. I suspect this is going to end up costing more in time and effort than we'll ever see back in revenue.'

When Zac joined Melody and Lettie up at the top field later that day, Melody explained to him about the camp bed idea. 'We were wondering if you had any thoughts about how to source some? We only need them for the two days of the festival.'

Lettie walked on ahead, continuing to harvest the beetroot crop they had been busy working through.

He thought for a moment. 'I might be able to come up with something. We have a few hire shops over here but apart from a carpet cleaner I hired once, I've no idea what else they might stock.'

'Carpet cleaner?' She grinned, unable to help herself picturing him with his sleeves rolled up and an apron around his waist.

'Er, I can see by the expression on your face that you're having unnecessary thoughts about me.'

'Unnecessary?' Melody laughed. She wasn't sure what he meant but by the cheeky expression on his face could take a good guess. It was a relief to have Zac back to how he usually was around her. 'I am not.'

'No? Then what were you thinking, because it wasn't about the carpet cleaner – I'm certain about that.'

She giggled, enjoying their fun flirtation. 'I was imagining you with a pinny around your waist.'

His eyes widened. 'I hope I was wearing something underneath.'

Melody threw her head back in laughter. 'Of course you were. Honestly, what do you take me for?' Although now he had asked the question, her thoughts raced back to him lying on top of her kissing her in a way she had only ever imagined being kissed before. The thought of his toned arms as he lowered himself onto her and how his muscular back would feel under her fingers made her mouth go dry.

He raised an eyebrow and she realised he was watching her, a smile on his face. Could he sense what she was thinking? 'Fine. I am thinking that,' she fibbed, 'but I wasn't until you said something about not wearing any clothes.'

'Nosedive?' Patsy asked, a glint in her pale blue eyes as she walked up behind Melody.

Melody closed her eyes, mortified to have the attention on them. There was nothing wrong with her grandmother's hearing; that much was obvious. She racked her brains to come up with a believable answer but couldn't think of anything.

Patsy noticed Lettie. 'I'm not sure why the pair of you are standing here messing about when poor Lettie is doing all the work.' She picked up a basket by Melody's feet and handed it to her. 'Come along then. It's not as if any of us have time to stand around chatting.'

Zac went to pick up one of the sacks Lettie had left on the ground waiting to be filled while Melody followed her grandmother. He was soon walking next to her again and Melody felt her hand brush his before taking hold of it.

'I'm sorry I've been distant,' he said, holding her back slightly to give some distance between them and Patsy.

'It's fine,' she said, enjoying having his hand holding hers.

She had rarely held hands with Rhys and loved the feel of Zac's skin against hers. His hands weren't soft like her ex's who spent his time working at a computer. She liked the firmness of Zac's grip. Of every part of him that she had come across so far. Not that she had come across much, apart from his arms and back, but she had also felt his hard stomach when she had pulled him against her in the meadow and they had kissed. His lips. Now they were probably the best part of him, she decided. His lips against hers. Forgetting she was supposed to be looking where she was going, she felt his hand pull on hers, only just managing to stop her slamming into the back of her grandmother.

'What are you doing?' Patsy asked, spinning round to face her.

Zac let go of her hand. 'Sorry, Gran,' she said. 'I was thinking about something else.'

She saw Zac smile from the corner of her eye and wondered if he had been thinking similar thoughts to hers.

She wasn't sure how long she and Zac would have this connection, or if they had any future at all, especially as she was supposed to be returning to Scotland in a month when her time at Hollyhock Farm came to an end, but she had no intention of thinking about that too deeply today. Today she was happy and wanted to keep that joy in her heart for as long as possible.

21

ZAC

Zac was conflicted. On the one hand he couldn't wait for the festival to be over and get back to some sense of normality. On the other hand, he knew that when it was over Melody would probably be heading back to Scotland with her grandmother and he would be setting off on tour for a few months. The thought saddened him. He wasn't ready to part ways with her. He wondered if he would ever be ready.

He and Melody had been given the job of adding the final businesses to the marketing page on their website and finalising the programme, and so far it had taken them hours. Six long hours. As much as he resented being inside and having to sit still for so long and stare at a screen on such a beautiful day, at least he was spending the time with Melody.

He was relieved their friendship, if that's what it was, appeared to be back on track and the awkwardness they had felt after their kiss and Callum's arrival at the farm that same night had gone. He enjoyed her company the more he got to know her, but she still hadn't confided in him any further about her ex and their relationship. Maybe it was a good thing he didn't know how serious her past relationship had been. He liked her and thankfully she seemed to like him. Melody was a free spirit like her gran and the pair of them had certainly brought a fun atmosphere to Hollyhock Farm.

Right now Lettie was with Patsy delivering posters to be put up at the library, cafés and bookshops. He and Melody had produced them and he had been impressed with her idea to add a QR code to promotional material for people to scan and see the latest version of the programme and buy their tickets.

'I have a feeling you, me, Patsy and Lettie are probably going to need to treat ourselves to some of the treatments on offer at this festival.'

'Especially your sister,' Melody said, leaning forward and peering at the screen. She clicked the mouse a couple of times. 'There. I think that's it. At least I hope it is.' She sat back and closed her eyes, pressing the heels of her palms against them.

He heard Lettie's voice chatting to Patsy seconds before they entered the study.

'Oh dear, that bad, is it?' Patsy asked, walking in and leaning on the desk.

Melody lowered her hands and stretched. 'We've been in here the entire time you two have been out.'

'How are you getting on?' Lettie asked, walking around their father's desk to have a look over Zac's shoulder at the programme on the screen. 'You're coming along well.'

'So we should be,' Zac groaned. 'We've taken long enough to get this far.'

Melody gave Zac a gentle nudge in his ribs. 'Take no notice of him – he's fed up because I'm a perfectionist.' Zac heard the amusement in her tone but knew there was some truth in what she was saying. 'We've also updated the spreadsheet with all the new additions, like the rubber flooring we've had to hire for the class areas in the barns and any costings that have come in over the past few days.'

Lettie groaned. 'Urgh, I hate to think how much this is costing us when we initially planned on doing it to make money.'

'I'm sure you'll make some money,' Patsy said. 'We just need enough people to come along and pay their entrance fee.'

'The festival will pay dividends,' Melody assured Lettie. 'We just need to make sure enough attendees come along on both days so that those with stands do well.'

'I'm sure they will,' Zac said.

He felt Lettie give his shoulder a slight squeeze. 'Maybe you can contact Callum and ask him to give the festival another shout-out on his show, to remind people about it.'

He knew it made sense. 'I will but I'm not sure whether he's back on the island yet.'

'Give him a call and find out then,' Lettie said, walking back around the desk and pulling a face at him. 'Honestly, is there something going on between you and Callum?'

'No.' Zac sensed he had answered a little too quickly by the way his sister's eyes narrowed thoughtfully. 'Why would you think that?' He hoped she couldn't tell he was bluffing.

Lettie shrugged. 'I thought he'd given up doing all that modelling.'

So had Zac. 'Maybe they made him an offer he couldn't refuse,' he suggested. 'I don't know.'

Lettie sighed wearily. 'Would you prefer it if I called him?'

Feeling silly for making a big deal about speaking to his best friend, Zac shook his head. 'No, of course not. I'll call him in a bit.'

Melody stood and, pressing her hands to her sides, stretched backwards. 'I've been sitting for far too long.'

Seeing an opportunity to call Callum in private, Zac held his hands out to the three women. 'Why don't the three of you go and take it easy for a bit? I'll finish up in here, then make that call to Callum and I'll catch up with you later.'

He watched them go and sat back in his chair, trying to think what to say when his friend answered his call.

22

MELODY

Melody was relieved to know that Zac and Callum would be speaking. She hated to think that her presence had caused a rift between the two close friends. It wasn't as if she was completely free of Rhys yet, or that anything much had happened between her and Zac. Which was a good thing, she decided, not liking to think of Rhys discovering she was attracted to anyone else. Not until she knew he understood that their relationship was well and truly over.

An hour later she heard a van coming down the drive followed by Lettie's excited voice a couple of minutes later. 'Girls, come and look at what's just arrived.'

Patsy nudged Melody as they walked along the hallway to the kitchen. 'I love how she includes me when she calls for the girls to join her.'

'When you have more energy and enthusiasm than the rest of us, I think I can understand why she would class you as a girl.'

They walked into the kitchen and Melody noticed two

boxes. The first one had the flaps open already and Lettie was busily cutting the tape on the other with a knife.

'What is it?'

'Have a look,' Lettie said, giving a satisfied sigh as she released the tape on the other box and opened it.

Melody delved into it, pulling out rolls of rubber. 'Are these mats?'

'Yes, yoga mats and hand towels for people to use. In here —' Lettie lifted a corner of the second box for Melody and Patsy to peep in '—are exit signs, first-aid signs and coffee and tea station signs.'

Patsy looked bemused. 'Exit signs?'

'Yes,' Melody explained. 'The first thing we'll need to do after welcoming everyone and opening the event is to do some housekeeping and let attendees know where the exits are.'

'Why, won't they realise they can leave out of the barn doors they've just entered through?' Patsy asked.

Melody understood her confusion. 'I know it sounds a little odd, but we need to let people know. The insurers I contacted about the event insisted we did.'

'We never needed to jump through all these hoops in my day,' Patsy grumbled, shaking her head. 'It's all very odd, if you ask me.'

'I dread to think of the lack of health and safety arrange-ments at events in your day.' Melody laughed. She decided to change the subject. 'Lettie, do we know yet when the chairs and trestle tables we've ordered will be arriving?'

'I phoned earlier this morning and they promised me they'll be here first thing tomorrow, in good time for us to set every-thing up. We also have the tea and coffee urns and deliveries of pastries being brought in by a vegan baker Mum discovered recently.'

Lettie's phone pinged and Melody watched as she peered at the screen. 'This is amazing,' Lettie said, holding up her phone and showing somebody sitting in what looked like half a barrel of ice. 'We've had confirmation that one of the women from the book club has a sister wanting to do ice baths for our attendees. I think the smaller barn will be better for those. We still have a little space to the right-hand side to set them up.'

'That's brilliant. This really is coming along well,' Melody said. As well as that, she had checked the long-distance weather forecast earlier and relaxed when she saw that the mention of inclement weather seemed to have been wrong and that when the event was being held in a few days constant sunshine with only a gentle breeze was expected. At least the animals could be left out and it was one thing less to worry about. The temperatures were comfortable, so that was another thing she was relieved to know.

As she helped clean the barn for the final time before they began setting up, Melody couldn't help wishing she could have some time away from the preparations to continue with her sketches. The deadline for the next book was looming ever closer and she had no intention of letting her grandmother down.

'You OK there, Melody?' Zac asked, bringing in another couple of boxes that must have been delivered at some point.

'Fine, thanks,' she said, wondering how his call with Callum had panned out. 'Do you need a hand bringing anything else in here?'

He cocked his head over his shoulder. 'Dad and Lettie are bringing stuff in behind me.' He shot a look to the door and lowered his voice. 'I don't know about you, but I can't wait for this thing to be over and done with. I'm desperate to get back to normal. We had enough to do without all this extra stuff.'

'Stop moaning, Zac,' Lettie said coming up behind him. 'Anyway, did you manage to get hold of Callum?'

'I did.' He gave a satisfied nod. 'He's giving the festival another shout-out on his show today and tomorrow.'

'That's kind of him,' Lettie said. 'But then he's a lovely bloke and always willing to help others.'

Melody decided that she probably should have a chat with Callum too. He hadn't asked her out again after that initial drink at the pub, but she presumed he must have picked up some chemistry between her and Zac. She decided she needed to do the right thing and catch him on his own and check that he really was fine about any misunderstandings between them.

Feeling a little better, Melody realised she hadn't asked Lettie whether she needed her to help. She leant the mop handle against a stall door and went over to her. 'Here, let me take those from you.'

'These aren't heavy but they're awkward,' Lettie said. 'If you take the top one that'll be great.' Melody lifted the box. 'Follow Zac through there,' Lettie said.

Melody followed the siblings and Gareth through to the back storeroom.

'We're storing everything in there until tomorrow when I know this place is spotless,' Lettie explained. 'You're doing a brilliant job by the way, Melody. You and Patsy have been amazing through all of this.'

'Thanks, we're only too happy to help out.' Melody wondered what was in these boxes.

'There seems to be a lot of stuff,' Gareth said.

Melody placed the box on one of the trestle tables Zac had set up. 'Is there much more to come?'

'Only fresh stuff, like food and milk,' Lettie said, motioning for her father to place what he was carrying on the table next to hers and Zac's. 'The stallholders will be bringing in their products and any banners tomorrow afternoon. I said they could arrange everything and let them know we would padlock the barn doors closed at six-thirty. I thought that way they would be able to arrive fresh for the first day of the event and at least they would feel confident that all their wares were safely behind locked doors.'

It was a good idea. Melody hoped that Lettie's confidence was building. She was far better at arranging these things than she probably thought she was and if this was a success then there was no limit to what she could do to make money in the future.

'I could do with some fresh air,' Melody said. 'I'll finish washing the floor after I help you with the animal feed.'

'OK, thanks.' Lettie led the way as the three of them left Zac to carry on checking everything while they went outside.

'When were you thinking of starting to put your ecotourism plan into place?' Gareth asked.

Lettie held out a hand in Melody and Patsy's direction. 'We're already doing it, Dad. Melody and Patsy are staying here as guests but also getting a flavour of what living on an organic farm entails by helping out with the work.'

Gareth nodded thoughtfully. 'I hadn't thought of that. Yes, I suppose that is what these hardworking ladies are doing. But what I really meant to ask was when you're going to try and make a going concern out of it?'

'I hadn't got that far,' Lettie answered. 'Once this festival is over with I'll put more thought into how to go about it and what to charge.'

'So you're still thinking of doing it in the future then?' He seemed impressed with the notion.

'I think so.'

Melody saw her grandmother's expression change. She knew that look. 'What were you thinking, Gran?' she asked, intrigued to hear what she had to say.

'Only that I have quite a few contacts,' Patsy replied. 'Well, friends, mostly younger than me who I'm sure would be interested in trying something like this. I would be very happy to mention it to them when I go home. Spread the word for you, if that's what you'd like me to do.'

'You're both thinking of leaving soon then?' Gareth asked, looking surprised.

Pasty seemed surprised by the question. 'Don't get me wrong, I'm sure we'd both much rather stay here than return home.' She sighed. 'In fact, I know Melody would probably move here in a heartbeat if she was free to do so.'

Melody saw Zac give her a quizzical gaze.

'Then what's stopping you both?' Gareth asked. 'I'm sure Lettie and Zac could do with the extra help.'

Gareth's eyes focused on Melody, making her wish her grandmother hadn't said anything about her being unable to stay. 'I don't understand. What's stopping you from staying here if you wanted to?' he asked.

Melody cringed. She wasn't ready to divulge more about Rhys. Thinking quickly and aware that the family knew that she had been in a relationship that had ended badly, she said, 'It's just that Gran and I have this next book to finish working on, and I need to sort everything out with my ex. Finalise things completely.'

Gareth didn't look as if he understood but was clearly too polite to say as much. 'I see. Well, you're both always welcome here.'

'That's very kind of you, thank you,' Melody said, grateful

for his kindness even though Lindy had already made the same offer to them.

Or maybe she was simply overthinking things after having to be on high alert with Rhys for all those months. She shook the thought away, deciding to focus instead on the Torel family. She went to find Lettie.

'I was thinking that maybe I could finally give you all a yoga lesson on the beach this evening?'

'Yoga?' Lindy asked, walking into the kitchen to join them. 'Tonight?'

Melody smiled. 'Only if you want to. It occurred to me how busy we've all been and I thought it might help calm us all before the event to have a go if you'd like to.'

'On the beach?' Lindy asked, looking unsure.

Lettie clasped her hands together and beamed at each of them. 'I think it's a great idea. We could make an evening of it and take a picnic down with us. I'm sure the tide is on the way out by now and it would be exciting to try something like that.'

Lindy pursed her lips. 'I think I'll keep an eye on the food and watch you do it,' she said, making Melody and Lettie laugh.

'Fine, Mum. You do that.'

'You don't mind, do you?' Lindy asked, resting one arm on Melody's.

'Of course not.' She shrugged. 'If we're going to do this, I'd better go and let Gran and Zac know.'

'And I'll tell Dad and Brodie,' Lettie said.

23

ZAC

Zac sat on the towel waiting for Melody to roll up her yoga mat and join him.

'So,' she said, grinning at him. 'What did you think? Was it your first time?'

He laughed. 'Couldn't you tell?'

'I could,' she teased.

He rested back on his elbows next to Melody, watching the sky morph into deeper golds as the sun slowly slid below the sea on the horizon. He had watched sunsets many times from this beach but never with someone he liked as much as Melody. He had enjoyed the beach yoga more than he had expected. Maybe he should take it up regularly, he thought. He certainly had a great teacher to hand to show him how to do it.

He looked at her, his heart rate increasing. She really was special. He would have preferred to be sitting here by themselves, rather than with his family.

'It's a long time since I've sat and watched a sunset,' Lindy said dreamily.

'Rubbish, you watched at least two from the ship,' Gareth

argued. 'Although both were during the sail-away parties, so you probably weren't paying all that much attention to them.'

Zac thought how lucky he was that he had both his parents around to share special experiences like this one. So many of his friends growing up had fathers who worked away a lot of the time and mothers who were frazzled trying to keep everything going.

'This is so beautiful,' Melody said quietly, her voice filled with awe. 'I've queued to watch the sunset in Santorini in the past but what they don't show you when you look at the travel websites are the hundreds of people around you each vying for a photo. This is perfect. There's hardly anyone else here but us and there's nothing else to distract from the view.'

He was glad Melody was impressed. 'It is special, isn't it? Keep looking and you might see the green flash just before the sun disappears completely.'

She turned to him but he pointed at the sunset. 'Don't look away.'

'I've never heard of a green flash before,' she said, amusement in her voice. 'Are you sure you're not having me on?'

'He's not,' Lindy said. 'I've watched the sunset many times and I've only ever seen it twice.'

'I've seen it once,' Zac said, hoping that he might be lucky and see it again tonight.

'Wow.'

'It's a mirage,' Gareth said. 'Where the sunlight disperses through the atmosphere like a prism.'

Zac wondered why he hadn't ever thought to look up the phenomenon. 'Is it?' he asked, without taking his eyes from the view.

'It's something like that anyway,' his father said. 'Keep watching. If we're going to see it, we need to try not to blink.'

Zac stared but the sun finally disappeared and there was nothing at all apart from the sea to look at. 'Ah well,' he said, trying not to show the depths of his disappointment. He had wanted to give Melody something special to remember their evening. Maybe next time, he thought, hoping there would be one. 'We tried.'

Melody looked down at him and pouted. 'That's such a shame,' she said, lying back on her elbows next to him. 'Mind you, it's so beautiful down here that it's not as if we're not already spoilt with the scenery around us.'

He supposed she was right. He stared into her eyes, deciding to bring her back down here another evening, just the two of them. 'Would you like to come here again with me sometime?' he asked, before losing the confidence to say what he was feeling.

'Just the two of us?' she asked as if she had read his mind.

He smiled. 'Yes. We can bring something to eat and watch the sunset again.'

'I'd like that,' she said, smiling. 'Very much.'

Zac didn't think he had ever felt happier. He wished again that they were alone so he could kiss her, instead he moved his hand so that it rested on hers. 'Then that's what we'll do.'

'Let's eat this food Lindy's put together for us,' Gareth insisted.

The words were barely out of his mouth when everyone moved. Zac pulled a face at Melody, reaching out his hand to help her to her feet. 'We'd better get ours before it all goes. This lot seems hungry.'

He stood next to her watching their mother and father help serve food on to everyone's plates. After an immediate move to the table, Brodie, Zac and Melody were waiting with Lettie for Patsy to get her food first.

'This looks delicious,' Patsy exclaimed, holding out her plate while Lindy offered her various bits of meat.

'Gareth will serve you any salad,' Lindy said. She pointed to the second trestle table. 'You'll find the condiments, cutlery and napkins there. Please help yourself.'

Zac motioned for Melody to follow her grandmother and select what food she felt like eating. Once seated again on the picnic rug, he sat eating and enjoying being among friends and family. Even with his disappointment not to have time alone with Melody, he knew he was lucky to have such a close family. It dawned on him that he hadn't felt this settled and contented since, well, since forever, he mused. If only Melody could stay on the island and they could give themselves a chance to have a real future together. He looked at her for a few seconds before continuing to eat. If only they had met before now. Been together for more than a few weeks. Maybe then he would have the confidence to broach the subject of her staying for a bit longer. It didn't help that she travelled with Patsy. He loved that the women had such a close bond and knew Melody must treasure her connection with her gran, but he couldn't see why she would ever choose to stay with him rather than return to Scotland.

'Something wrong?'

He hadn't realised Melody was watching him and didn't want her to think he wasn't enjoying her company. 'No, I was just thinking about how much I've enjoyed spending time with you here.'

She looked doubtful. 'You didn't look very happy about it though. Are you sure there's nothing the matter?'

He appreciated that she kept her voice low. The last thing he needed was his mother to overhear and try to help by saying something that would end up embarrassing him. He looked into Melody's beautiful eyes and saw concern.

Not wanting her to get the wrong idea, he gave her a reassuring smile. 'Fine, I admit it. I was feeling a little sad.'

She rested a hand on his arm. 'Why? What's wrong?'

'I was thinking about us,' he said, wanting to be open with her and see if he could pick up anything in her reaction that might give him some hope that he meant as much to her as she did to him.

'What about us?' she asked, her expression not giving her feelings away.

Unsure what to say next, Zac hesitated.

'Zac? What were you thinking that you didn't want to share with me?'

He struggled to think how to reply. Glancing to his right past Melody, he saw Lettie and Brodie chatting. One of them said something and they both laughed. He could hear his mother's voice a little way behind him chatting with Patsy and his father. Satisfied that no one was listening, he decided to be honest. What was the worst that could happen? Melody could rebuff him, he decided. Then again, what else could he do but tell the truth? To come up with something random might only end up confusing things between them and he didn't want to do anything that might put her off him.

He sighed. 'I was thinking what a shame it was that you're not on the island for all that long.'

Her eyes lit up and he immediately knew he had done the right thing confiding in her. 'I was thinking the same earlier today,' she admitted. 'Just when we're getting to know each other, I'm also getting ready to leave.' She turned from him and stared at the horizon for a moment before addressing him again.

He understood why she would worry – hadn't he just done the same thing? He took her empty plate from her hands and lowered it with his onto the blanket behind them before putting his arm around her shoulders, happy when she snuggled closer to him.

'That's exactly what I hoped to hear you say, yet didn't expect you to.'

He kissed her cheek, and she immediately turned her face to him and kissed him properly. Zac lost himself in her kiss, wrapping his arms around her and forgetting they were with other people until someone pointedly cleared their throat behind them.

Melody looked over Zac's shoulder. 'Oh, sorry, Gran.'

'Maybe keep that sort of thing until you're alone later,' her grandmother suggested, leaning forward in her chair to address them. 'Although I can see why the romance of this place might affect a couple.'

'Pudding, Patsy?' Lindy asked. Zac could tell by his mother's voice that she was smiling.

Zac loved that his mother was trying to distract Patsy from telling them off. And he grinned at Melody who grimaced back.

'Oops,' she whispered. 'Gran is very open about most things but I think she worries that I'm only recently out of my last relationship.' She stared out to sea. 'She worries about me.'

Zac shrugged. 'I think apart from my mum she was the only other person to notice.' He cocked his head to his right. 'That lot are too busy chatting to notice.'

'Good. That's a relief.' Melody sighed. 'I won't feel quite so embarrassed now.'

'Don't, it's fine.' Despite what he said, he wanted to kiss her again. Desperately. The beach went on for a few miles though, and unless they went up one of the slipways or stairs there wasn't really anywhere for them to be alone without people seeing. Deciding that just being a bit of a distance away was probably good enough, he nudged her with his shoulder. 'Shall we take that walk now?' Hearing his mother calling the others for pudding, he added, 'Unless you'd rather wait until we've eaten some of the sweet things Mum bought with her?'

Melody shook her head and smiled. 'I can eat sweet things anytime I choose.' She grinned. 'Your mother always seems to have an abundance of delicious treats in her cupboards. Right now though I want to take a walk with you and, hopefully when we're far enough away from my gran, kiss you again.'

Zac laughed. 'You really are a woman after my own heart.' He stood and held out a hand to take hers.

She took his hand and stood. Then, keeping hold of it, began to lead him away. 'We're only going for a bit of a stroll, Gran.'

'Wait a sec and we'll join you,' Lettie answered.

Zac tensed, not wishing for his time alone with Melody to be interrupted by his sister and her boyfriend.

'No, lovey,' Lindy said quickly. 'Why don't you help me serve the tasty puddings we've brought with us. I don't want to have to take them all home again with me. Come along.'

Zac caught his mother's eye and gave her a grateful smile. She waved for him to make the most of the distraction and go.

His mum really was the best, he decided as he gave Melody's hand a gentle squeeze and they began walking towards the La Pulente end of the beach.

24

MELODY

Melody strolled away from the small group excited to have some time alone with Zac. She didn't want to seem ungrateful though and Lindy, Gareth and Lettie had gone to a lot of trouble to make their evening on the beach a perfect one. Noticing a chocolate cake that she supposed was one of Lindy's specialities and a bowl of what looked like tiramisu next to it, she decided to have some later, if there was any left.

'I've been thinking,' Zac said as they walked barefoot in the soft creamy gold sand. 'When the festival is over maybe the two of us can go and visit the other Channel Islands, or at least one or two of them. Would that be something you'd like to do?'

Excitement coursed through her. 'I'd love to. I'd have to check with Lettie that she can do without me for a few days, but I can't think of anything I'd rather do. I've been desperate to visit Sark ever since reading *Appointment With Venus*. Could we make sure one of those islands is Sark?'

He laughed. 'Of course. We'll do whatever you want.' He frowned thoughtfully. 'I don't think I've heard of that book before.'

'It was made into a film in the early 1950s and starred David Niven, Kenneth More and Glynis Johns. It's one of Gran's favourites and when it was on television a few years ago she persuaded me to watch it with her. I've read the book many times.'

Zac raised a finger. 'Did you know Kenneth More lived in Jersey for a while?'

'No, did he?'

'He did,' he confirmed proudly. 'His father worked on the railway we used to have here until the occupation. He went to Victoria College.'

She clutched his forearm with her free hand. 'That's so exciting. I never knew that. Oh, I can't wait to see Sark for myself.'

'I can't wait to visit again.' A tennis ball flew towards them, a wet spaniel racing after it.

Then Melody noticed a dog owner holding one of those long plastic arm-like things she had presumably used to fling the ball for the dog to chase.

'Sorry,' the lady shouted. 'Got my aim a bit off.'

'It's fine,' Zac said, bending down to pick up the ball and throwing it away from them. Immediately the dog changed course and followed it.

'That was close.' She laughed. 'I thought we were going to get wet and sandy from that dog for a moment there.'

'So did I.'

Wanting to return to their interrupted conversation, Melody said, 'You were saying about visiting some of the other islands.'

'Yes, I'd love to show them to you.'

'I'd love to go with you.'

'I tell you what, you speak to Lettie and find out some dates when she'll be happy for you to take time off and then plan around that. Sound good?'

'Sounds great.' It really did, she thought. To be able to visit one of the places she had dreamed of ever since she had read the old copy of the book she had discovered in her aunt's bookcase one summer when she was staying at her home, was a dream come true. She thought of the stories she had read about the Dame of Sark during the Second World War and La Coupée, a narrow isthmus of land connecting Great Sark with Little Sark. She could barely wait to go there and travel over that high narrow strip herself after so many years imagining what it must be like to do so.

She thought of Patsy and how much she would also enjoy the islands and felt guilty.

'What is it?' Zac asked. 'Something troubling you?'

'It's Gran. I couldn't possibly leave her behind when I visit the islands. She's the reason I came here in the first place and the least I can do is include her when I'm visiting places I know she would want to see.'

He pulled her to him. She felt the warmth of his strong arms around her and calmed immediately. She looked up at him, wanting him to kiss her, and when he lowered his head so his lips met hers, she closed her eyes and lost herself in the moment. He was an incredible kisser, this charming, cheeky man she was falling for. Melody wondered where this would all lead, but not daring to wait for the alternatives of what their future might be to come to her, pushed the thoughts away and focused on the moment and the pleasure of being in Zac's arms.

After a while, he led her towards the lowering tide and they made their way back to the others, walking the entire way with their feet in a couple of inches of water. She glanced down at her toes with their crimson nail varnish and gave his hand a slight squeeze.

'Enjoying yourself?'

'Very much,' she said. 'This summer has been exactly what I needed. I'm so glad I let Gran persuade me to come here.' She looked up at him and saw he was staring at her thoughtfully. 'What?'

'You're very mysterious,' he said quietly.

She shook her head. 'I'm not really.' Not wanting to see the questioning look in his eyes and feel like she had to open up more about her situation with Rhys, she looked ahead again.

'It's fine. I won't push you to tell me anything you don't want to, but I sense there's a lot more to Patsy's reasons for wanting to bring you here.'

Believing he deserved some response, she shrugged. 'And you wouldn't be wrong.' She looked at him again and gave his hand a gentle tug when she stopped walking. 'One day I'll probably tell you more,' she said, hoping that she would have the courage to do so. 'Right now though, I just want to enjoy being here, with you and your lovely family, and Gran of course, and make the most of every second of happiness that this place brings me.'

He gazed at her with a look of such sadness that she couldn't bear it. Wrapping her arms around his back, she pulled him to her and rested her head on his chest. 'This has been an amazing summer, Zac, and most of that is down to you and how lovely you are.'

She felt him kiss the top of her head. 'If there's anything you ever need, Melody, I want you to let me know.' When she didn't answer his finger went under her chin and lifted it slightly so that her face was turned up to his. 'You will do that, I hope?'

She stared at him and sighed. He really was amazing. 'Yes, I will.'

By the time they joined the others, the temperature had dropped and Gareth suggested they pack up and make their way back to the farm.

'You're all welcome for a nightcap, if you wish, and for you, Brodie, having to drive home, I'm sure I can make you a cup of coffee.'

Once everything was packed into the back of Gareth's car, everyone started getting into vehicles for the short drive back.

'We're being spoilt tonight.' Melody got into Zac's mother's Golf, happy to have a few more minutes alone with him again.

'We are,' he said as he turned on the ignition. 'I noticed my mother insisting Patsy went with her and Dad when Brodie offered her a lift with him and Lettie back to the farm.'

'Where are we going?' she asked when Zac turned right as the others went left out of the car park.

'I'm taking you for a short drive towards L'Étacq and up towards the racecourse. As far as I'm concerned the view from the top of the hill is the best on the island. You can see the entire expanse of St Ouen's Bay from there.'

She sat back happily and gazed out of her lowered window. The moon seemed enormous for some reason and its light on the sea was like a painting from one of her childhood books that she had loved reading time and again. They barely spoke and she wondered if he was just making the most of being alone with her. She hoped so.

They arrived at the farm about ten minutes after the others must have done.

'I wonder who that is?' Zac asked.

Melody peered through the windscreen, noticing Brodie

and Lettie chatting to someone standing next to a car with an H on the numberplate to the side of the registration number. She now knew these were hire cars, so presumed the person must be a holidaymaker who had got lost. It was a man and she noticed there was something familiar about his stance, but she dismissed her initial thought as ridiculous and pushed it away.

Zac parked his car in the shadow of the larger barn and, having waited for her to step out of the passenger side, slipped his arm around her shoulder as they walked towards the front door of the farmhouse.

'Ah, there she is,' Lettie said. 'I told you she wouldn't be too long, didn't I?'

She? Melody tensed. No one off the island knew she was here, apart from her mother, and she doubted she would have come this far. She and Zac stopped and turned.

'I was wondering where you had got to,' said a voice that made her light-headed and the blood in her veins turn to ice.

Melody stared at the outwardly charming man who was smiling at her, unsure whether she was about to pass out or throw up.

'Melody?' Zac whispered. 'Is everything all right?'

She couldn't move. Finally managing to swallow, Melody took a step away from Zac, his arm slipping from her shoulders. 'What are you doing here, Rhys?'

She sensed Zac still behind her as she stared at the man she had hoped never to see again.

Rhys stepped forward, his hand outstretched as he looked past her and went to shake Zac's hand. 'Didn't she mention me to you?' Rhys laughed, shifting his gaze and looking into her eyes. 'I'm surprised you didn't tell your friends that you were married, Mel, sweetheart.'

'Um, I think we should go and take the last of the stuff

inside and join Patsy, Mum and Dad,' Lettie said, lifting a cool bag from the boot of the car that Brodie immediately took from her.

'He's your husband?' Zac asked quietly, standing next to her.

She heard the unmistakable hurt and shock in Zac's voice.

Mortified to be at the centre of this horrible scene, Melody wished the ground would open up and swallow her whole. 'Unfortunately, he is,' she said, hoping that Zac would understand that their marriage really was a thing of the past.

She saw Zac look from her to Rhys then back at her again. 'You two clearly have things to discuss,' he said matter-of-factly. 'Would you like me to leave you to it, or would you rather I stay?'

Melody was relieved to hear him offer to stay with her. On the one hand she would much rather Zac be there with her. The thought of spending time alone with Rhys wasn't one she relished, but would it be fair to Zac? She studied his face, her feelings for him increasing as she saw his concern and that he wanted to support her. Then turning to Rhys and the smug expression on his face, she knew he thought once again that he was in control of the situation. He was about to start dictating what she should do next, of that she was certain.

'If you wouldn't mind staying, Zac,' she said, giving him a grateful smile. 'I'd prefer you to do so.'

Rhys stepped forward again, all smugness vanished and fury on his tight-lipped face. 'Now, Melody, you know we have private matters to discuss that others shouldn't be party to.'

'I think Melody has decided what she would prefer,' Zac said, his voice calm. 'And that's enough for me.'

'This is nothing to do with you,' Rhys said, scowling first at Zac and then at her.

Melody's stomach ached and she felt sick, instantly taken back to the many other times he had bullied her into submission. Well, not this time. She had finally managed to get away from him and although she had no idea where she would go after her time at Hollyhock Farm came to an end, she was determined that it would be somewhere far away from this vile man.

Zac glanced at her and when she didn't speak, he said, 'I think your opinion isn't relevant.'

Hearing Zac's firm voice, she managed to find the courage to speak again. 'You came here uninvited, Rhys. I don't have to speak to you if I don't want to. And I don't, so you may as well leave.'

She heard footsteps and saw Brodie and Lettie coming back outside.

'What's going on?' Brodie asked. 'Is this man bothering you, Melody?'

'I'm her damn husband,' Rhys spat. 'And I'm here to speak to my wife.'

'What?'

Melody heard the shock in Lettie's voice and guilt rushed through her that she hadn't yet confided in her friend.

'I left you, Rhys. I think we can safely assume that I have endured enough of your behaviour,' Melody snapped, sounding far stronger than she felt. 'And I've already told you I don't wish to speak to you.'

Zac folded his arms and Lettie and Brodie walked over to stand on Melody's other side.

'I think you've been asked to leave,' Lettie said. 'Now I believe you should do so.'

He glared at each of them in turn. Melody's heart raced as his gaze stopped on her for a few seconds and it took everything in her power to stop from withering under his scrutiny. *Hang in there*, she told herself. *Keep strong.*

His eyes moved to rest on Zac. 'And who is this, Mel? My replacement?'

Melody cringed. 'Just leave, Rhys.' She began to tremble, then felt Zac's arm go around her shoulders and calmed slightly.

'I think it's obvious from what Melody has told us that you are separated, so what I am to Melody really isn't any of your business,' Zac said. 'Now are you going to leave this farm or would you rather I accompany you off it?'

Rhys's eyes snapped to Melody. 'Whatever your boyfriend seems to think, we're still legally married and don't you forget it.' He laughed. 'This isn't the last you'll see of me either. I have things to say to you and you will listen to them.'

She knew he wasn't bluffing but didn't give him the satisfaction of showing how frightened she was to hear his threat.

'What on earth is he doing here?' Patsy shrieked, hurrying to Melody and slipping her arm around her granddaughter's waist. 'Get the hell out of here now, Rhys. You have no right to be here.'

Hating to hear Patsy upset, Zac stepped forward and Rhys raised his hands. 'It's fine. I'm going but this isn't the last of it. Not by a long shot.'

They watched as he got into his hire car and sped down the driveway, the tyres kicking up clouds of dust.

'Are you OK?' Zac asked gently.

She nodded, seeing the unmistakable confusion in his face. 'Our relationship is not how he made it sound,' she said, desperate to explain, aware that it was too little. As long as she hadn't left it too late that was what mattered most, she reasoned.

He stared at her briefly. 'But you are married to him, though, aren't you?'

Melody nodded, hoping desperately that Zac's discovery about her marriage wouldn't ruin any trust he had in her. She couldn't bear to think that their fledgling relationship might be brought to an end thanks to Rhys's untimely arrival.

'I see.'

She gave his hand a squeeze. 'I can explain everything, but not now, OK?'

'Let's get you inside,' Patsy said. 'You've had a dreadful fright.' She looked at Zac and gritted her teeth for a moment. 'You've no idea what my girl has gone through with that man.'

Mortified, Melody hugged her grandmother, desperate to calm her. 'It's fine, Gran,' she insisted.

Melody noticed the expression on Zac's tanned face and could tell he thought it was anything but fine. He nodded.

Wanting to show the others how grateful she was for their support, Melody turned to them. 'Thank you both for being there for me. I'm so sorry he came here like that. I've no idea how he knew where to find me.'

Lettie took her hand. 'It's fine. He's the problem, not you. I'm just worried that he threatened to return.'

'This is all my fault.' Melody sniffed, barely able to contain her tears of frustration.

'No it isn't. I only worry in case he does come back and you're by yourself. I think we need to make sure there's always one of us with you. Bullies like him are usually less inclined to pick on someone if they have company.'

Melody knew he would be, but only slightly. Rhys had just shown how unbothered he was about how people perceived him and that had been with an audience, but the thought of having witnesses was a comfort. 'That would make me feel a bit better.'

Desperate to divert the attention from herself, she added, 'Can we forget he ever came here and try to enjoy the rest of our evening? We have a few busy days ahead and I don't want anything to distract from that.'

'Yes,' Lettie said. 'Let's do that.'

25

ZAC

Zac helped Melody, Patsy and several of The Book Club Girls to fill three hundred tote bags with all the promotion merchandise they had been sent by the businesses taking part in the wellness festival, while Lettie worked on the farm. When all the bags had been packed, the ladies went back to the barns to put up posters and make final touches while he went to help his mother make some drinks in the kitchen.

'Mum, stop worrying,' he repeated for the third time, still shaken to discover that Melody was married. That changed everything despite what he had said to that revolting husband of hers.

Since his relationship with Jazz had ended and she had moved on so quickly after losing the baby, Zac had been anxious about taking a chance and becoming too involved with someone else. Surely if Melody was still married to Rhys, regardless of whether they were separated, then she wasn't in a position to take things further with him, Zac thought miserably. Clearly there were too many obstacles between himself and Melody for them to move forward.

'I'll never forgive myself for letting that dear girl face that man without any forewarning,' Lindy grumbled.

'How were you and Lettie to know he was a nasty piece of work when you let him wait for Melody? He came across as perfectly charming when we arrived. If it hadn't been for Melody's reaction,' he said, pained to recall her obvious fear of the man, 'then I wouldn't have picked up anything either. Anyway, we soon sent him packing and with all the people we hope will come to the festival I think there'll be little chance of him causing any aggro.'

Lindy wiped the kitchen worktop despite having only done so a few minutes before. 'That poor girl. I hate to think what she's been through with that ex of hers. Such a shame.' She narrowed her eyes. 'He'd better not come back here and give her a hard time when I'm around.'

Zac relaxed slightly, happier now his mother's usual fighting spirit had returned. He hated to see her upset and believing she was the cause of something unsavoury. He knew that Rhys would get more than he bargained for if he did come across his mother again. It would serve him right too. The bully. He pictured Patsy's expression and knew his mother wasn't the only person Rhys needed to be on the lookout for. And he would also give him what for if he came across the narcissistic bully again. How dare he bully a woman, Zac thought angrily. No, Rhys really needed to stay well away.

He finished refilling the ice trays and placed them back into the freezer compartment at the top of his mother's large fridge. 'I'd better go and join the others. They'll be wondering where I've got to and will probably assume I'm skiving.'

'No, they won't,' she said, smiling and looking as if she assumed that's exactly what they would do. 'Do you need me to come and give you a hand with anything?'

He looked at the racks of cooling cupcakes and others holding biscuits and shook his head. 'I think you've got more than enough to do decorating that lot for tomorrow. Anyway, we've only got the final bits to sort out now.' He noticed the oven light on and then more mixture sitting in the mixing bowl waiting to be baked. 'How many of these things are you planning on making?'

'Enough,' she said. 'Don't look at me like that. You'll be the first one to scoff any leftovers.'

She was right – he would. He gave his mother a hug. 'Promise me you'll stop worrying. Melody seems much more like her old self again today. I'm hopeful she's managed to put the whole incident behind her now.' He didn't really believe that to be the case at all but needed to say something to try and assuage his mother's concerns.

'Fine, if you're sure.'

'I am.' He picked up the tray of drinks.

'Zac,' Lindy said, slipping her hands into oven gloves and standing next to the cooker. 'You will make sure you keep an eye on that girl, won't you? I don't want anything happening to her, especially while she's under our roof.'

He stared at her, a weary expression on his face as he wondered why he wasted time trying to pacify her. 'Will do, Mum.'

He walked back to the barn and stopped. The six-foot posters they had ordered were standing just inside the door, one on each side displaying the logo, which he had to admit looked impressive.

'What do you think of our first impression?' Lettie asked, entering the room behind him. 'They look amazing, don't they?'

'They do.' He looked at the tray in his hands. He hadn't

realised Lettie had finished work yet but saw there were enough glasses for her to have a drink and save him having to go back to the kitchen. 'You finished outside then?'

'For now,' she said. 'I thought I'd come and help with sorting any last-minute bits.'

He sighed. 'I was beginning to think we'd never manage to pull this together in time,' he said, relieved that everything seemed to now be in place and looked even better than he had expected.

'Well, don't just stand there,' Lettie grumbled. 'What do you think?'

He beamed at the expectant faces next to his sister, waiting for his response. 'For a first impression it's an excellent one.'

'Really?' Melody asked, walking over to join them. He noticed her biting the skin on the side of her finger and knew it was because she was troubled about Rhys being on the island. He hated to see her anxious like this. 'You honestly think so?'

'I love the lighting and the bunting. It all looks incredible and well thought out. We're a great team.' He walked over to the first stall and went to place the tray onto it.

'Not there,' Lettie snapped.

'Why not?'

'You shouldn't mess it up.'

It was on the tip of his tongue to tell his sister that they had all worked perfectly well together that morning without her fretting. He wasn't sure if it was the stress of the past few weeks, or tiredness from running the farm and the run-up to the event, but he thought his sister might be spiralling. 'Er, Letts, this is a stand. If it can't take my tray of glasses of water then it's not going to be much use to someone loading their products on top of it.'

Patsy, Melody, Kathleen, Phyllis, and Bethan looked at Lettie waiting for her to react.

He spotted Joe, a firefighter friend who Lettie had briefly dated before getting together with Brodie. He hadn't realised he was there.

'I haven't seen you for a couple of months,' Zac said, surprised to see him again. 'Where have you been hiding?' Zac asked, unsure why he was there. Zac spotted Lettie pull a face at him but couldn't fathom what she was trying to tell him. Then it dawned on Zac that his sister had probably called on Joe to come to the farm to help out with the festival.

'Lettie called me this morning saying she could do with another pair of hands helping to set this lot up,' Joe explained. 'I had a few days owing to me so took them off to come along.' He looked pointedly at the tray of drinks in Zac's hands. 'Is one of those for me?'

Zac nodded. 'You can have mine. I'll fetch more from the house in a minute.'

So he had been right then. How clever of Lettie to call on a few friends to make up the numbers and keep everything in order. He wondered if his sister had called on Callum and asked him to pop round if he had any free time.

'Have they been giving you all the heavy things to lift?'

Joe laughed. 'No, but I think you had already done most of that.'

They each took a glass of water and when Zac offered his to Joe, he thanked him but refused.

Melody held out her glass to Joe. 'It's fine. Zac and I can share this one,' she said, gazing up at him.

'I think tomorrow and the next day are going to be good fun, don't you?' Lettie said.

'I do,' Melody agreed.

Zac knew they were all going to have to keep alert just in case Rhys decided to make good his promise and return. Fun was probably going to be the last thing Zac was bothered about.

26

MELODY

Before everyone had arrived, Melody had checked all the tote bags were neatly stacked discreetly behind the small desk they had set up just inside the large barn door. They were ready for Phyllis to hand out to each attendee after they had paid their entry fee to Kathleen.

Melody was relieved to have a lot to keep her mind off her situation and was looking forward to giving her first yoga class in the lower paddock near the meadow. It was such a beautiful day and the stunning views across the fields would add atmosphere to the lesson.

Everything seemed to have started off well and she hoped they had thought of everything. The stallholders and all business owners or vendors taking part had signed an agreement to pay five per cent of their takings over the two days to the farm at the end of the second day. So far everything was going very well and Melody hoped it stayed that way. They had all been nervous that morning over an early breakfast in the kitchen with only a little bit of chatter from Lettie and Zac, who were doing their best to encourage the rest of them to be enthusiastic and enjoy the festival rather than worry too much about it.

Melody hadn't missed the siblings' nervousness though and knew both were putting on a brave face, as was she. They all knew this festival had to make money. The roof needed to be repaired and she thought of the blue tarpaulin Zac had helped Gareth and his brother Leonard fix up there a few weeks before. Hopefully none of the attendees would notice it, but even if they did, she reasoned, it might spark their sympathy for the lovely Torel family and encourage them to spend just that little bit more than they otherwise might have done.

She glanced at her watch. She had just under an hour before her first yoga class would begin and she was nervous. Melody wasn't sure why she would be. It wasn't as if she hadn't done this sort of thing many times before. She waved at Lindy when she spotted her looking in her direction from the other side of the barn. Then, looking to her right, saw Phyllis and Kathleen watching her and speaking about something.

For a second she couldn't work out if she might have forgotten something. Did she still have slippers on, or something? She glanced down at her feet and saw with relief that she was wearing her trainers. Zac came out of the storeroom carrying several yoga mats and gave her a nod. She hurried over, wanting to help him set up for her demonstration with the class she was soon to take.

'Let me help you with those,' she said, taking them from him.

He rested an arm on her shoulder and peered into her eyes. 'Everything OK, Melody?'

'Yes, of course.'

She turned and took the mats to the wall at the back of the area set aside for her class, unsure why everyone was behaving oddly towards her. Then it dawned on her. The rest of them were all concerned about her and no doubt worried about how she would cope if Rhys turned up again.

She thought back to how she had needed to clear up their trashed living room on a couple of occasions and was only too aware he didn't bother to hold back when he lost his temper. She had seen the fury on his face when he realised there was a connection between her and Zac. Rhys wasn't stupid though and would definitely notice that she wasn't the only one to see his reaction.

But would he be stupid enough to risk causing any drama during the festival, especially knowing the others would suspect he might reappear? The realisation calmed her slightly. She was going to have to trust that nothing would happen while the event was taking place and focus on the jobs allotted to her. She, Lettie and the rest of the volunteers had spent far too much time and effort bringing the event to life to waste any of it fretting about Rhys.

She thought about the others keeping an eye on her and felt comforted to know they were around, even if the chances of Rhys turning up were small. What a lovely community this was, she mused, and how lucky she was that they had taken her so quickly under their collective wing.

She saw Zac returning with more mats and went to fetch the final few.

'Zac,' she heard Lindy calling as their paths crossed. 'Come and see who I've just been talking to.'

'On my way, Mum,' Zac said, pulling a weary face at Melody, making her laugh.

She fetched the final few mats and as she carried them back to stack on the other ones, she thought back to Zac's comment about them still being married and felt her mood dip. Legally they were still tied together and it was her own fault. However, she had been too desperate to get away from him to spend time booking an appointment with a lawyer and getting separation papers drafted up. Not that Rhys would have signed them anyway. He seemed to specialise in doing the opposite of what she needed him to do.

She took a calming breath and closed her eyes for a few seconds. She could do this. She had got away from him once before and now she had people other than her grandmother to support her. New friends only too willing to back her up. And Zac was one of them.

She pictured the fury on Rhys's face when he had noticed Zac's arm around her. Maybe part of Rhys's fury had been because Zac wasn't only with her but that he was clearly fit and strong. Well, she thought, hopefully that would be enough of a deterrent to stop the weasel coming to Hollyhock Farm again.

Melody noticed one of the stallholders giving her a wave and walked over to her. 'Is something the matter?' she asked the girl selling organic vitamins and vegan facial cleansers and creams.

'I was wondering if you might watch my stall while I go to my car and fetch another box of these,' she said, pointing to the body lotions. 'It never occurred to me I could sell so many.' She laughed. 'I only hope I'll have enough for tomorrow.'

Melody smiled. 'I'd be happy to. You'd better explain to me what I need to know before you go. I don't want to lose you any customers.'

The woman began explaining about her products and what they were used for and Melody quickly realised there was far too much information to take in. She grimaced. 'Sorry, but I think it might be better if you give me your car keys and let me know the make and colour, and number plate of your car.'

The woman nodded. 'Yes, I suppose you're right. As long as you don't mind going for me?'

'Not at all. I'll have to get a move on though because I need to go and change for a class I'm giving in half an hour.'

The woman took a deep breath. 'If you wouldn't mind fetching the box for me. There's only the one in the boot of the car. It'll be quite heavy and I wouldn't want you to strain yourself.'

Melody smiled. 'I'm stronger than I probably look.' Two young women walked up to the stall and looked at the produce. 'Better give me those car keys.'

Once she had them in her hand and the number plate for the woman's car, Melody left the barn. She could hear a lot of chatter and laughter coming from the smaller building next door. She noticed there was already a queue to the door for the pop-up café area where Lettie's friend Tina was selling healthy snacks and drinks alongside Bethan, a girl she had been introduced to a few days before who also worked at Brodie's veterinary practice.

It was good to see people having a fun time and it also meant more money for the repairs, she thought cheerfully as she turned down the pathway between the two barns that led to one of the fields Gareth had kept free for parking. They had decided that people would need to park as close to the venue as possible, in case they had difficulties walking, or if it did rain after all, and now that Melody was in a rush to find one of the cars she was relieved she didn't have to walk too far to get there.

She was stunned to see so many vehicles and wished she had thought to ask whereabouts in the field the car had been left. Not wanting to take too long and risk the woman running out of the few bottles she had left, Melody quickly walked up and down the rows of cars, trying to find the right one.

She welcomed people and thanked others as they left, happy that so far at least the event was a success. Lettie would be enormously relieved and the rest of them justly proud for all their hard work setting everything up.

Soon there was no one apart from her in the car park.

She eventually came across the woman's car and hurried over to it, vaguely aware that another couple of vehicles had arrived. Pressing the fob, she watched with satisfaction as the car lights flickered, then went to the boot and opened it, surprised when she lifted one side of the box how heavy it was. The stallholder hadn't been kidding, she thought.

'So, this is where you've been hiding?'

Melody stilled, her breath catching in her throat. She didn't need to turn around to know Rhys was standing behind her. Even if he hadn't spoken, she was sure that his closeness would have caused her nerve endings to jangle. She looked from side to side, hoping to see other people around, but unsurprised that he had waited until they were alone. Bracing herself for what she was about to face, she turned around.

'I'm not hiding anywhere,' she snapped, determined not to show him how petrified she was of him still. 'I'm fetching something for someone. You're the one who is out of place here, Rhys.' She almost spat his name, hoping her aggressive reaction to him made him realise she wasn't the woman he'd spent those years bullying. 'Why don't you do yourself a favour and leave. You've no business being here, and you know it.' She turned her back on him and focused on the box in the boot of the car, hoping he wouldn't notice how much her hands were shaking as she reached to pick it up.

Before she knew what had hit her, his fingers grabbed hold of her neck from behind, squeezing tightly as he pushed her head lower towards the box. He bent over her, his body pressed against hers, making her cringe. She could feel the tension in his body as she clung to the sides of the box desperately hoping not to fall in.

'Don't you ever, ever, speak to me like that again, do you hear me?' he hissed in her ear.

She didn't have a chance to reply before his fingers let go and he moved back from her. Confused, she didn't dare turn around straight away, hoping he had spotted someone coming and was about to leave.

'And don't let me ever see you touching her like that again,' she heard Zac say. His voice was cold, reminding her of razor-sharp steel. Surprised and relieved, she turned to see him push Rhys backwards onto the grass. 'In fact, I'd better not ever see you speaking to her again. Now, get the hell out of here and if I see you here or anywhere near Melody again, I promise you'll regret it.'

She was stunned to see Rhys on the ground scrambling backwards as he tried to get to his feet. He glared up at Melody and opened his mouth to say something, but she turned away from him, unable to find the words to convey how much he disgusted her.

They watched Rhys stumble away from them, get in a hire car and speed out of the field.

Zac shook his head. 'Thank heavens there isn't anyone coming in the opposite direction,' he said.

'And that all the animals are up in the top fields.'

Zac turned to her. 'Are you all right, Melody?' he asked, his voice gentle as he placed his hands on her shoulders and turned her slowly to face him. 'He didn't hurt you, did he?' He checked her neck. 'I think you're going to have a bit of bruising there.'

She saw the muscles in his jaw working and noticed he had

clenched his teeth. She suspected Zac would have loved to punch Rhys, hard, and a part of her wished that he had. She was glad he hadn't though. She loved Zac for his gentleness and just because Rhys was a thug who picked on people physically weaker than himself, Zac had no reason to do the same thing by hitting him.

'Hey, you OK down there?' a deep voice shouted and Melody looked over to see Joe.

'Thanks, Joe,' Zac replied. 'We're fine. Thanks though.'

After watching for a couple of seconds, Joe walked away seemingly satisfied that his help wasn't needed. Zac gazed at her, his expression troubled, and she realised he needed her to comfort him as much as she needed to feel his arms around her.

'I'm so glad you arrived when you did,' she said, slipping her arms around his waist and resting her head against his chest. His heart was racing and she wasn't sure if it was fear or suppressed rage. 'I can't believe he dared to come back when he knew people would be looking out for him.'

She realised that even if she had hoped Rhys wouldn't return, she had never really believed it. He had always been self-assured and certain that he was right about most things, so why not believe he had every right to come back to Hollyhock Farm to confront her when he wanted to?

'He's a vicious bully,' Zac said partly to himself. He leant back and peered into her eyes. 'You can't have had an easy life with him and that saddens me. You deserve so much more than him.' He shook his head. 'No one deserves to be with someone who treats them like that.'

'I know. I promise you he wasn't always like that. I never would have knowingly become involved with someone who behaved like he did today.' She recalled the version of Rhys she had fallen in love with. 'He used to be charming and kind.' She gave a shuddering sigh. 'I'm not sure what happened to make him change so drastically and I won't make excuses for him because as far as I'm concerned no one has the right to behave like he does.'

'And if I have anything to do with it, he won't get another chance to take you by surprise like that.'

Melody rested her head against him again. 'And I love that you feel so protective of me,' she admitted. 'But realistically there's nothing much anyone can do.' She felt him stiffen and looked up at him. 'You have to work, Zac, and there are times when I will be out in the fields by myself or at the farm.' She thought of all the people that seemed to be drawn to Hollyhock Farm and smiled. 'And what happens when I return to Edinburgh?' It was something she wasn't ready to think about. Not yet.

He went to say something, but Melody gasped.

'What's the matter?' He looked over his shoulder then back at her.

'Sorry. I've just remembered one of the stallholders is waiting for me to take a box of her products to her, but I'm going to be late for my class if I don't hurry. Would you take them to her for me?'

'Of course.' His shoulders relaxed and he smiled. 'You nearly gave me a heart attack just then. Right, where's this box then?'

27

ZAC

It had been a long and tiring day, Zac thought as he and Melody helped tidy the larger barn, making it ready for the following morning. He was still seething about Rhys and what he had done to Melody, but she had insisted several times that she was fine and Zac didn't want to keep going on at her. He thought how relieved he was that the first day had gone so well. Lettie still had to wait for Kathleen to calculate the takings but even he had seen how many cars had come and gone over the course of the day.

'I know you were busy,' he said to Melody as she stood on a stepladder straightening one of the banners by the door. 'And I could tell how much others enjoyed your yoga demonstration and then the class you took.'

'I'm glad you think so,' she said, retying the corner of the banner. 'Quite a few of them took the time to speak to me about classes and were sad that I wasn't staying on the island to set up my own yoga studio.'

Hope coursed through him. 'You could do, you know.'

She didn't turn around and he wondered if he had said something he shouldn't.

'Did you manage to enjoy any part of the day?' he asked.

She stopped what she was doing and turned to him, smiling. 'I loved it.' She sighed, looking happy, which was a huge relief after her nasty encounter with Rhys earlier. 'Although my debit card did more work than I had intended it to.'

Confused, Zac frowned. 'What do you mean?'

'I gave myself a daily budget for this trip but today I spent over three times what I had promised myself I would.'

He helped her down from the stepladder. 'But do you like everything you bought?'

'What an odd question. Of course I do.'

He shrugged. 'Then don't worry about what you've spent. I mean, you don't have to cover bed and board here and you've been working hard so can't have been anywhere much to spend any money recently.'

She gave what he said some thought and slowly smiled. 'I hadn't thought of it that way.'

Zac folded the metal ladder. 'Come on. I think we've finished in here. Let's go and chill somewhere while we can. We'll have another early start in the morning but we can still go and do something for the next couple of hours.'

'Sounds good. Can we go and see the huge willow puffins at...? Where are they?'

'Plemont. Yes, we can go there, it's not far away from here and,' he said, realising that it was later than he had expected and that it would soon be sunset, 'if we hurry we'll be able to watch the sun setting. The light is beautiful there at sunset and you should get some great photos.'

She beamed at him. 'That's a perfect idea. I've only seen

them from a distance one day as Lettie drove us somewhere near the racecourse. I've been dying to see them up close.'

He took her by the hand and went to shout out to his sister to let her know they were leaving.

After a brief exchange, he watched Patsy wink at Melody before giving her a hug and whispering something in her ear leaving Melody with a smile on her face. He wondered what had been said but didn't like to pry about something private.

Patsy waved at Zac. 'Thank you for the invitation, Zac,' she called. 'But I think the two of you deserve a lovely evening by yourself for once.'

Realising Patsy was conspiring for him and Melody to spend time alone, he was glad for her encouragement and struggled to hide his delight. 'Thanks, Patsy. You must come with us another time though. It's well worth visiting Plemont and I think you'll like it. Lots of photo opportunities.'

'We'll make a plan to do it another time then.' She shooed them away. 'Go on then, you two, before I change my mind and decide I do want to come with you.'

Zac took Melody's hand and they quickly left, laughing as they hurried to his mother's car. 'Wait there,' he said. 'I won't be a sec. I need to ask if it's OK for me to take it and get the keys.' As he hurried into the kitchen to find the keys and Lindy, he decided that now he was back on the island full-time it really would be a good idea to buy a car of his own. It was one thing using his mother's when he was over for the weekend or a longer holiday but how bad must it look to someone, Melody particularly, that a man in his mid-twenties had to ask to borrow his mother's car?

A few minutes after they set off they neared Plemont and Zac saw the sculpture of the two puffins, beak to beak in the distance. He pointed at them for Melody to see.

She leant forward and peered past him out of the window. 'They look big.'

He laughed. They were. 'I seem to recall they're about four metres high.'

She gasped. 'I can't wait to see them up close.'

As much as he would have liked to go faster, Zac didn't dare. The road to the headland where the puffins stood was narrow with room for one car and drivers coming across each other having to pull over and wait in one of the few passing areas along the way. He was eager to be there too, he realised as he drove carefully along the walled road.

Concerned that Melody hadn't spoken about Rhys and what he had done to her, Zac decided to check she was all right. 'Melody,' he began.

'Yes?'

She sounded so happy but he needed to check she was fine and not dwelling on what had happened. 'About earlier.'

'Earlier?'

'In the car park.' He had to pull to the side of the narrow road to let another car go past and looked at her to try and gauge her thoughts.

'Oh, that.' Her smile disappeared and she turned to look back out of her window. 'Please don't ruin our evening talking about him, Zac.' Looking back at him, she reached out and rested her hand on his. 'I just want this evening to be about you and me,' she added softly. 'Nothing else.'

Happy to do as she had asked, he nodded. 'Whatever you want.'

'Thank you.'

Shortly after, they arrived and parked the car. 'Look at that sunset,' he said, taking her hand.

Melody was too busy staring at the enormous steel and

willow puffin instalments and didn't seem to hear him. Deciding they needed to go and walk up to the puffins first, he led her there, not wishing them to miss the spectacular sunset either.

Leaving her there, he retraced his steps.

'Where are you going?' she shouted, starting to walk after him.

Zac raised his hand, wanting her to stop. 'I'm only going back far enough to be able to take photos of you standing with them,' he explained. 'I presume you'll want some.'

'I do, thanks. I'll take some of you afterwards.'

He nodded, loving how easy it felt to be with her. 'We can take some selfies when we're further away.' He noticed the sun was going down quicky, but turned back to face her again. Seeing how the golden light glowed on her and the statues, he sighed. 'These are going to be amazing photos,' he insisted. 'You're going to love them.'

His assurances made her laugh and he quickly took more photos of her, enjoying seeing her so happy. 'There,' he said, checking he had enough good photos for her to choose from. 'I think that'll do.'

She ran towards him and checked the screen. 'Brilliant work. Right, your turn now. We need to hurry if we're not going to miss the sun setting.'

He ran to stand in front of the puffins and smiled for a few seconds, then hurried back to her, taking her hand closer to the cliffside. 'Look at that,' he said, slipping his arm around her shoulders, then remembered he hadn't yet taken their selfies. He quickly took a few photos, struck by the golden hue on Melody's beautiful face as she stared in awe at the spectacular sunset.

Then, pushing his phone into his back pocket, he stared in

silence at the scene in front of them. It didn't matter how many times he watched a sunset on the island or how many places he had visited, nothing ever compared to a sunset over the Channel from the coastline in St Ouen as far as he was concerned.

He felt her arm slip around his waist and wished he could capture this moment and never have it end. Standing here with the woman he was falling in love with in his arms, enjoying one of his favourite things meant an enormous amount to him.

'There,' she said quietly as the sun disappeared behind the horizon in the distance. She turned to him.

Zac smiled down at her. 'What did you think? As good as I said it would be?'

'Perfect,' she said quietly, slipping her arms around his neck and pulling his head down so that their lips met in a kiss.

Zac held her tightly, kissing her and relishing every second. He couldn't imagine ever experiencing another evening as perfect as this one.

28

MELODY

Melody sat in the kitchen nursing a cooling cup of tea. She gazed out of the window, loving how the different-coloured hollyhocks framed either side, and thought back to seeing Rhys earlier.

He would not have been happy to see her and Zac together and she couldn't blame him. If he had fallen out of love with her and then met a beautiful girl who seemed to suit him in all the ways that she didn't, she probably would have been upset too. But it wasn't her fault Rhys refused to accept that their relationship was over. She also wasn't sure what else it would take for him to grasp that she was not going back to him.

'Are you all right, Melody?'

Hearing Zac's concerned voice, she forced a smile. 'I'm fine now. Honestly,' she said, aware that he would still be concerned about the after-effects of her being grabbed by Rhys. When he didn't seem convinced, she admitted, 'I was thinking about Rhys though.'

'What about him?'

Zac seemed so caring and she could tell he wanted to help

her, so she decided to be open with him about how things stood. 'We were only married for just over two years, but we had been friends at school when we were in our early teens. We drifted off into different friendship groups and then his family moved away from the area when I was about sixteen. When we met up again in our early twenties, we began seeing each other and got engaged after only five months and married a couple of months after that.'

She saw the look of surprise on his face. 'I know it seems quick but because we had known each other as youngsters I wrongly presumed I knew him well.' She sighed heavily, still troubled by her error of not taking more time to get to know how he was as a partner. 'I now realise how silly that was of me.' She raised her hand to touch where he had hit her most recently. 'I left him a couple of months ago.'

Zac's eyebrows shot up. 'A couple of months? I hadn't realised it was that recent.'

'Things between us got steadily worse and we began to argue and then he finally went too far, smashed up the living room in our flat and...' She hesitated, not wanting to say it out loud but needing Zac to understand that she hadn't left Rhys without good reason. 'And then he hit me.'

She saw him clench his teeth and suspected he was trying not to say what he was thinking. 'Go on,' Zac said finally.

'I had been unhappy for quite a while by then, but he always made me feel as if him losing his temper was instigated by something I had done. When he hit me, I realised that was a choice he made.' Aware her mouth had gone dry, she took a sip of her cool tea. 'I knew that was it for me. I didn't deserve to be treated that way and I had no intention of standing for it.'

'Good, I'm relieved,' he said, leaning forward and resting his elbows on his knees.

She thought for a moment before continuing, wanting to be honest but trying not to think about how things had been bad for so long. She was more used to avoiding any thoughts of their disastrous marriage now and not focusing on it or how it descended into viciousness by the end.

'I still sometimes try to work out what happened to make him this way, but then I remind myself that I'm no psychologist. I think the worst thing for me is understanding myself through all of this.'

Zac shook his head. 'In what way?'

'I consider myself strong, happy to stand on my own two feet. If you'd have told me before this happened to me that I would end up being treated this way I would have thought you didn't know me at all, but it did happen to me.'

'It happens to many strong people,' Zac said, making her wonder what experience he might have endured. 'I don't think there's a type of person who finds themselves in an abusive relationship.'

'Thank you. I've always thought of myself as able to deal with things and I think this has knocked my self-belief rather a lot.'

She could see Zac was struggling to hide his anger. 'That saddens me but I'm sure it's only natural for people to react that way.' He reached out and took her hand, comforting her. 'I think the most important thing, apart from getting away from him, which you've done to a certain extent, is to go easy on yourself and allow your self-belief to return.'

She tried to think what she might say to a friend going through what she was now and realised it was the same as Zac's advice.

'To be honest, I don't have any experience of this sort of thing.'

'It's fine. I know you mean well and I'm grateful to you for giving me a safe space to open up about this.' She sighed heavily. 'Rhys is clever. The change happened very slowly as he become more and more abusive over the last few months of our marriage.' She swallowed a lump in her throat as she thought back to that first time he had pushed her, causing her to slam her shoulder into their living room wall and bruising it badly. 'He always had a reason for it being my fault, and at the time I believed him.'

'That's coercive behaviour.' He scowled.

She barely heard him, recalling the things Rhys kept accusing her of – seeing other people, belittling him in front of their friends, none of which she thought she had done. 'In the end I began to think I didn't know what I was doing, or whether or not what I did was insulting for him. I began to lose trust in my judgement and...' She sighed deeply, wanting the conversation to end. 'Then he hit me.' She looked into his eyes, wanting to see how disgusted he would be with her next words.

They sat in silence for a little while, both lost in their own thoughts.

'How do you think he knew where to find you?' Zac asked. 'I presume you weren't the one to tell him.'

She shook her head. 'No, of course not. I suppose it must have been my mum. She and Rhys's mum are best friends.'

'I don't see what that's got to do with anything though.' He stared at her for a moment then something dawned on him. 'You haven't told her about him hitting you, have you?'

'I didn't have the heart to.'

'But why not?'

Melody pictured her mother, sweet and kind and always wanting to focus on the best in people. 'She would have only blamed herself and then I would have needed to deal with her guilt.' She closed her eyes at the thought of the countless times she had spent listening to her mother's concerns about something she had done that might be perceived as not being right. 'I just told her we were struggling a bit, weren't getting along any more, and I needed time out from the relationship.'

'What did she say to that?'

'I'm not sure if she believed me or not, but I don't think for a second that she had a clue how our relationship really was.' She gave him a wry grin, grateful for his understanding and kindness.

'And you don't think your mum would have put you before her own feelings?'

Conflicted by her loyalty to her mother but wanting to be honest, Melody shrugged. 'I would like to think so, but there's a part of me that didn't have the energy to cope with anyone else's angst.'

Zac stood and pulled her into his arms. 'Thank you for sharing this with me, Melody,' he said quietly, kissing the top of her head and holding her tightly against him, her head resting on his chest comforting her in a way she couldn't recall ever feeling before. 'You deserve love. Everyone does, but you are such a wonderful person and it upsets me to think you didn't feel you could turn to your own mother about this.'

'I did have Gran, don't forget.' She sniffed, clinging to him, unable to halt the tears coming to the surface. Within seconds she was sobbing as if her heart was breaking, which she thought it possibly might be. She heard him making soothing sounds and felt his hand stroke her hair lightly and knew she was safe to give in to her sorrow.

She had no idea how long it had been – only that she felt wrung out. She realised she was sitting back on the chair with a light blanket around her shoulders and a fresh mug of tea on the table in front of her. There were several tissues in her hands and Zac had sat down opposite her again, his eyes not leaving hers.

'Better?' he asked gently.

She sniffed then blew her nose. 'Yes. Thanks, Zac.'

'No need to thank me. I'm just relieved you're feeling a little better.' His face clouded over. 'And that you were brave enough to get away from that man.'

It was good to hear someone remind her that she had been brave. At least she still could muster up some strength. 'That's kind of you to say.'

'I'm only speaking the truth, Melody. Having met him, twice now, and seen him in action, I can only imagine how terrified you must have been leaving your home, then your mother's to come here.'

He stared at her without speaking for a moment and she sensed he had something he wanted to say but was wary about doing so.

'What is it, Zac?'

He hesitated. Trusting that he had her best interests at heart, she urged him to tell her what was on his mind.

'I know you're concerned about your mother's friendship with Rhys's mother and about how she might react to your situation, but I'm sure she would be more upset if you kept this from her. I really believe she deserves to know.' He shrugged. 'And who knows, she might even surprise you.'

She didn't have to think about what he had said. Melody nodded. 'You're probably right.' A thought occurred to her. 'And having been here for the last few weeks, I do feel much stronger mentally again,' she admitted.

'Good – that makes me happy.'

'My mother is going to be upset about unwittingly leading Rhys to me though.'

'Just remind her that she had little reason not to give him your contact details. Now I've seen him in action I believe she needs to be made aware of everything you've been dealing with, for both your sakes.'

'I know you're right.' She sighed. 'It's going to be a difficult conversation though.'

'But a worthwhile one.' He leant forward slightly. 'I also think everyone else at Hollyhock Farm needs to know what he did to you in the car park.' She went to argue but he shook his head. 'You don't have to give details. That's your business, but I do think they need to be aware of what he's capable of doing.'

Melody picked up the mug and took a sip, swallowing. 'I understand what you're saying,' she said, 'but I can't bear the thought of anyone feeling sorry for me.'

He seemed confused. 'Melody, I'm sure no one will do that.' When she gave him a doubtful frown, he stared at her. 'You're among friends and they will want to support you. Surely your safety is what matters most?' He reached out and took her hand. 'You don't have to do anything you don't want to though. These are only suggestions.'

She groaned and pulled the blanket further over her shoulder, aware it had slipped down. 'No. You're right – I know you are. I'll call my mum after the festival and speak to everyone else over supper in a little while.'

'I'll be there with you. All any of us want is to look out for you.'

She smiled at him. 'You are a special man, Zac Torel. I hope you know that.'

29

MELODY

Melody and Lettie were crossing the yard when she heard a car. Tensing, Melody stopped and waited with Lettie to see who was arriving that early.

'Callum?' she said, surprised to see him there and relaxing instantly at his smiling face as he stepped out of his car. He walked over to Melody, giving her a kiss on the cheek before doing the same to Lettie. 'What are you doing here?'

'Hi, ladies. I've come to offer my services, like I said I would. I gather from Brodie, who I bumped into last night when he was on his way home from supper here, that Day One was successful.' He gave an impressed nod. 'Congratulations. I knew you'd make this work.'

Lettie laughed. 'I'm glad you were confident in our efforts.' She looked at Melody. 'I'm not so sure we were.'

'No, we weren't. Maybe if we had been a little more confident,' Melody said with a grin, 'all of us would have been able to sleep better these past couple of weeks.'

'I mentioned the festival again on my show yesterday,'

Callum said. 'I also said I'd be available for selfies for those wanting to give a donation to the festival.'

Lettie laughed. 'You didn't!'

He pretended to be shocked. 'What, you don't think people will pay to have a selfie with me?'

Melody giggled. 'Crikey, if I'd known I was having a drink with a celebrity that time, I would have taken a few selfies of us together to post on my social media accounts.'

He narrowed his eyes. 'You lot are bad for my ego – do you know that?'

Zac came out of the barn. 'I might have guessed you're the reason these two are keeping me waiting,' he teased.

'Don't blame me,' Callum said, pointing at Lettie and Melody. 'They're the ones distracting me and keeping me from helping.' He began walking to the barn. 'Well, come on then, you lot, what are you waiting for? Point me in the right direction and let me know what you need me to do.'

Melody stood with Lettie, both watching the two friends disappear into the barn. Melody was relieved to see that her evening out with Callum and then her closeness with Zac hadn't seemed to put a dampener on the men's friendship. She had enough conflict in her life with Rhys and didn't need to be involved in another drama, especially between two men that she liked.

'Those two have always been great friends,' Lettie said quietly. Melody wasn't sure if she was making a point to her, or simply stating a fact, and chose to go with the latter.

She wondered if Zac had confided in Callum about Rhys, immediately deciding that she didn't mind and trusted whatever Zac had decided to do, aware that he was acting in her best interests.

Lettie tilted her head to one side and then to the other and for the first time Melody noticed she was nervous. They needed to be busy, she decided.

'Come along,' Melody said. 'Let's get in there and slay today.'

Lettie linked arms with her. 'Yes, let's do that.'

* * *

Just like the previous day, crowds of people arrived at the farm. The queue to the café area in the small barn was continually out of the door and Melody wondered if she had made an error persuading Lettie to reduce the duration of the festival to only two days.

Zac walked up to her as she stood at the back of the barn watching people, trying to see if there was anything she might need to do.

He took her hand, his face serious. 'Would you mind coming with me for a moment?'

Wondering what he might need to speak privately to her about, she agreed. 'We'll have to be quick,' she said. 'It's so busy here that I'd hate to not be here if I'm needed for something.'

'This will only take a minute.'

He opened the storeroom door and led her inside, closing the door quietly behind them before leaning against it.

Seeing the twinkle in Zac's eye, Melody instinctively knew why he had taken her there. She didn't say anything but waited for him to act.

Melody slipped her arms around his waist, holding him tightly against her, smiling to herself when his arms wrapped around her and held her close against him. She felt him kiss the top of her head and for a moment neither spoke as they stood there. She wondered what he was thinking then decided she didn't care. All that mattered right now was that he was in this room with her.

She raised her head to kiss him, but his expression changed and he looked down at her neck. He let go of her and, lifting her chin gently, turned her head one way and then the other, checking her neck. 'You've got bruises,' he said, his eyes steely. 'Does it hurt much?'

She shook her head, realising that the make-up she had used to try and cover up the purple patches Rhys's fingertips had caused on her neck hadn't been enough to hide them completely.

'No. Not really.' Not wanting him to focus on her injuries, she took hold of his hand. 'I'm fine. I promise.' Wanting to kiss him, she added, 'We'd better go and help Lettie, so if you want to kiss me you'd better get on with it.'

'You don't need to tell me twice.'

He lowered his head and their lips met. Pushing aside all thoughts of Rhys, Melody held Zac tightly and lost herself in the sensation of being with him.

* * *

Melody was grateful to have been kept busy all day, running from helping one person to clearing up from a class and setting up for another. She was glad they had set up ice baths near the small barn with the noisy café area nearby. All the chatting and laughter from people sitting and eating was proving to be a great distraction for those brave enough to try the extreme cold, with lots of encouragement being called out to them. But it was something to note down should Lettie decide to continue with the wellness festival the following year.

With all that she had to do, the one constant thought on her mind was Rhys and whether he would appear from around a corner, from a car, or follow someone inside and get past her friends and colleagues looking out for him. Zac barely left her line of vision – whenever she looked over to find him he was either nearby or glancing at her to keep an eye on her.

She thought about what Gareth and Lindy had said and was relieved to know she was welcome to stay at the farm for as long as she wanted. She realised she had become very fond of the whole family and, she thought, their friends too. The whole community seemed to take people under their wing, and she wasn't sure if it was an island thing, or because those around the Torel family liked and respected them so much that they also wanted to take care of their friends. She was glad to be considered one of them now and was in no rush to leave.

It dawned on her that she would not be ready to leave even if she didn't have this issue with Rhys and the need to broach the difficult subject of her situation with her mother. She was glad she had decided to wait for the time being before phoning. Perhaps it would be better speaking to her about this face to face anyway, Melody thought. At least then she would have the time to go over what she told her mother as many times as her mother needed to hear it.

'You're looking thoughtful,' Zac said quietly.

Melody jumped. 'Oh, I didn't see you there.'

He frowned. 'Sorry, I didn't mean to give you a fright.'

She rested a hand on his arm. 'It's fine – you didn't. I was miles away,' she said, not wanting to admit she had been thinking about the call to her mother and what she would say.

He stepped back to let a group of people pass by on their way to the sound bath class that was about to begin in the meadow by the stream.

She realised she hadn't told him about staying on the farm.

The teacher welcomed the class and, not wishing to interrupt everyone, Melody motioned for Zac to follow her outside. 'We'd better talk somewhere where we won't be bothering anyone.'

They walked outside and sat on the low wall to one side of the yard.

'Is everything all right?' he asked, looking concerned.

She explained about the offer for her to stay as long as she wanted at the farm. 'It's so kind of them. I never imagined they would do something like that. I mean, they've only known me a few weeks.'

Zac smiled. 'Maybe so, but they know you well enough to be comfortable offering you a room here at the farm. I know without doubt that you've made a very good impression on my parents.' He nudged her with his shoulder. 'And they're not the only ones.'

She went to say something but noticed his expression change slightly. 'What is it?'

He stared at her for a few seconds, then shrugged. 'I can't help wondering how long it's going to take for you to be divorced.'

She hadn't expected him to say that. 'I've no idea,' she said. 'But I intend getting straight on to it as soon as I'm back in Edinburgh.' She thought how she would feel if she had discovered the same thing about Zac and sighed. 'I understand how much of a shock this must have been for you and I wouldn't be happy to discover you had a wife, if things were the other way round.'

'It is what it is, though,' he said, his voice filled with resignation. 'Now I'm mostly concerned Rhys doesn't come across you while you're by yourself again.' He frowned. 'Your time here is coming to an end though, and I'm dreading you leaving.' The sadness in his voice reaffirmed his feelings for her.

'I'm not ready to leave this beautiful place either.' She rested her hand on his. 'Or ready to leave you.'

He kissed her. 'That makes me happy.'

She noticed Lettie rush out of the larger barn and look around for someone. Presuming she might be wondering where Melody was, she jumped off the wall to her feet.

'I'd better go. We're so busy today and I really shouldn't be sitting around chatting with you.'

He stood. 'You were due a break. You're right though – we should be getting back.'

'There you are,' Lettie said, hurrying over to them, her attention going to Zac. 'I need you in the smaller barn, now,' she added when he didn't move.

'What for?' His eyebrows lowered. 'Is something the matter?'

Melody tensed, hoping it wasn't anything to do with Rhys. She was still mortified by what he had done the previous day and couldn't bear to think he might have somehow found a way to sabotage the event. She would never forgive herself if he had caused trouble.

'The volunteers for the ice bath can't do it,' Lettie said frantically. 'Joe had agreed to be one of those demonstrating but he's been called in to work, so can't do it, and the demonstration is in two minutes. I need you to get undressed and get in the barn ready to help out.'

Zac cringed. 'If the volunteers have changed their minds then I can understand why, but I don't see why I have to be the one to take their place. Who the hell voluntarily sits in ice?'

Melody watched as a steely glint appeared in Lettie's eyes. 'Zachary, I don't care whether you want to do this or not. I can't let the owner down.'

He winced. 'Please don't call me that. Anyway, why can't she do it herself?' he asked, and Melody had to wonder the same thing. 'She must think they're a good idea.'

Lettie took one step closer to him. 'Because, Zac,' she said through gritted teeth, her voice low, 'she has a cast on her foot. Now, will you do this to help raise money for our roof, or not?'

She had never seen the siblings at odds like this before and Melody wanted to quash their quarrel before it escalated. She hadn't ever tried out this particular therapy, but aware that there was little time to persuade anyone else and wanting to pay back all the support the Torel family had given to her, she took a deep breath.

'You'll need two people to do it,' Melody said, recalling there were two ice baths set up near the front of the barn. 'Zac can do it with me.'

She saw Zac's look of shock, although it only lasted an instant before he gathered himself. He groaned. 'Fine, I'll do it.'

'Great. Follow me.' Lettie led the way.

'I only have shorts on though,' he said half to himself.

'Just get in with those then,' Lettie said over her shoulder. 'Melody, you'd probably be best going to quickly change into a swimming costume though. I'll help with the introductions and delay everything for a minute or so.'

Melody hadn't thought about the mismatched underwear she was wearing. 'Good idea.' She ran into the house and up the stairs to her bedroom, quickly locating her cerise costume. She hurriedly stripped off her clothes, pulled on her costume, then pulled her shorts and T-shirt back over it. Grabbing two towels from the airing cupboard on the next floor just in case Lettie hadn't thought to supply any, she slipped her feet into her trainers and ran to the smaller barn.

She caught Zac's eye as he stood behind one of the barrels that looked as if they were made from PVC or nylon, both filled three-quarters of the way to the top with almost freezing water. Ice cubes floated in the water and she hoped she wouldn't have to sit in it for any longer than was necessary.

She stood next to Zac and both listened as the woman spoke about the benefits of this therapy. 'As well as helping reduce inflammation and stress, other benefits include helping with relaxation. It therefore has benefits for improving sleep. It also helps with mindfulness. Now, I'll go through some breathing techniques and then our two volunteers, Melody and Zac, will demonstrate for us.'

Having listened to instructions from the woman, Melody took a calming breath and stepped into the freezing water. What the hell? Her heart raced and her breathing sped up.

'Get control of your breathing, lovey,' a woman in the audience suggested. 'It works.'

Melody gave her a disbelieving look, wondering how much time the clever clogs in the audience had spent time in one of these things.

The woman laughed. 'It's true,' she insisted, somehow sensing what Melody had been thinking. 'I had to do it when I was in labour with my three. Whenever I had my breathing under control the labour pains weren't nearly so bad.'

Melody forced a smile in her direction, wishing the woman would be quiet and let her focus on trying to take her mind off the shock to her entire body.

She listened as the woman who ran the business moved to stand closer to her and Zac. 'She is right, you know. If you can calm your breathing and do the exercises I told you about, this will be a far more pleasant experience.'

Closing her eyes to help her focus, Melody listened as the woman repeated the instructions. She lowered herself and although every part of her screamed to get out, she knew Lettie needed as many businesses as possible to succeed at the festival and was relying on her right now. She slowly began to get control of her breathing and although she doubted she would ever want to try something like this again, had to admit to herself that the sense of achievement it was giving her helped her to get a sense of why people might want to practise something like this.

Hearing movement next to her, she opened her eyes to see Zac wincing and stepping out of the tub. 'I'm afraid that's enough for me for today,' he said apologetically. The woman handed him a thick bathrobe Melody hadn't noticed earlier.

She was about to get out too when someone laughed. 'Haven't I always said, Ginny, it's the women who have the strength to deal with discomfort far more than these blokes.' Melody realised it was the same woman who had told her about being in labour.

Unable to help smiling, Melody decided she had also had enough, and rose to her feet, grateful when Zac reached out his hand for her to take as she stepped out. Within seconds she had wrapped herself in a thick towelling robe and was drying her feet.

'He might have got out before me,' she said to the woman. 'But only just.'

'Thank you, Zac and Melody,' the business owner said. 'You're both free to go if you want to dress now.'

They left the barn without speaking.

'Thank heavens that's over,' Zac said. 'I can't see how doing that could calm anyone.'

Melody took his hand in hers and gave it a soothing pat. 'I actually didn't mind it all that much.' He gave her a look of astonishment, making her laugh. 'It's true.'

'Well done, you two,' Lettie said, running to catch up with them. 'You did well.'

'Yes,' Zac said. 'But don't expect me to do that again next year if you do decide to repeat this festival. Once is enough for me.'

Lettie seemed baffled. 'You surf, Zac. Our sea isn't exactly warm most of the year round.'

'No,' he said. 'But it doesn't have ice floating around in it either. And I wear a wet suit most of the time.'

30

ZAC

Zac followed Brodie and Callum, each of them carrying the last of the trestle tables to the storeroom at the back of the large barn. It had been another long and exhausting day but at least it was over.

They still had to tally up the takings but from the number of people who had come through the festival and everything he had been told when he had stopped to speak to attendees, it appeared to have been a great success. He hoped so.

He was glad Brodie had been able to pop by several times and that Callum was there for most of the day. Each time Zac had seen Callum he was keeping an eye out for Melody and it had been a huge relief to know that there were people other than him who were looking out for that nasty sod she was married to. He thought back to the previous evening when she had told them about her relationship with this Rhys character and he couldn't help feeling angry that anyone had to live with such an abusive partner. Especially someone as kind and decent as Melody. Maybe it was her gentleness that had given

Rhys the confidence to treat her so badly and assume he would get away with it.

'You look as if you could punch someone, or something,' Callum said, moving out of the way to give Zac space to place the table down next to the others the three of them had already brought through.

'I'm raging about that ex of Melody's.' Zac gritted his teeth, trying to calm his temper.

'I know how you feel,' Callum said, making Zac feel guilty again for getting close to Melody. 'Don't look so guilty. We can't help how we feel and even though I like Melody and took her out that one night, I think I realised when the pair of you arrived together that there was little chance of me having anything romantic with her.'

'What do you mean?' Zac asked. confused by what his friend was trying to tell him.

Brodie raised his hands. 'Look, maybe I should leave you two to speak privately about this.'

Callum shook his head. 'No, it's fine. I admit I like Melody. I mean, who wouldn't? She's funny and beautiful, but there's no point having unrealistic expectations when she is clearly into your best friend.'

'Callum, I—'

'It's fine,' Callum repeated, shaking his head. 'Anyway you were saying about that revolting husband of hers.'

Brodie groaned. 'He really is a piece of work. I can't believe he had the gall to come to the farm when he could see how many cars there were in the car park. Surely he must have known someone would see him there when he went for her?'

Zac had initially thought the same thing. 'Maybe one of us might think that way, if we were that way inclined, but I think he was probably too enraged that she had left him and was too focused on getting to her to consider anything else.'

'You're probably right,' Callum agreed.

Zac glanced in the direction of the farmhouse. 'I can't get it out of my mind. I'm only in here now because she's in the farmhouse with my mum sorting out the takings and I know she's safe.'

'Lettie and I were talking about what he had done,' Brodie said. 'Disgusting way for anyone to treat someone they supposedly love.'

Zac agreed and gave a nod to Callum. 'I was glad you were here today. I know Melody was more relaxed having extra friends around.' He noticed his comment appeared to make Callum happy. His friend was a decent chap, honest, hardworking and willing to help anyone, but it was clear for anyone to see how much Melody had meant to him, and the familiar sense of guilt ran through Zac.

'I didn't see him anywhere,' Callum said. 'I'm not sure how calm I would have been if I had caught him giving her a hard time again.'

'You're not the only one,' Brodie said thoughtfully. He smiled and Zac wondered what he might be about to say. 'I think that Rhys chap would be better off if the three of us caught him, rather than the women. I daren't imagine what Patsy might do to him with Lettie, Lindy and Melody's help.'

'I think you could be right.' Zac liked being reminded that the women around him were tough and even if they were frightened by something, once they recovered from that shock then they would come out fighting. His sister and mother certainly wouldn't stand back and let Rhys pick on Melody again and he knew without doubt that Patsy would give him what for should he ever corner her granddaughter again. The thought made him calm slightly. He heard footsteps.

'Zac, are you in here?'

Zac smiled at the sound of Melody's lovely voice and immediately walked to the door leading to the main part of the barn. 'We're through here,' he called back.

Zac wasn't sure but thought he spotted a momentary look of disappointment cross her face. 'Did you want me for something?' he asked, wishing he was alone with her. Talking to the guys about Melody reminded him that her time on the island was drawing to a close and she would soon be leaving to return to her life back in Scotland.

'Your mum was looking for you,' she said. 'She's set up drinks and nibbles on the terrace out the back of the farmhouse and wants us all to go and join the rest of them when we're finished tidying things away.'

'Have they tallied up the takings then?' Zac asked.

'I believe so. She seemed happy, so I'm hoping it's good news.'

Zac held back to let Joe and Brodie leave the barn. As soon as they had gone, he took Melody's hand in his. 'Have you had a good day?' he asked. Then, laughing, added, 'A knackering one, but hopefully fun all the same.'

She held his hand tightly. 'It's been an experience, I'll admit that.' She giggled. 'Especially seeing you in the ice bath.' She kissed his cheek to show she was only teasing. 'Seriously though, I've learnt a lot. It's been fun seeing Gran in her element chatting to people and giving them advice about some of the stuff she's spent her life learning, like nutrition, crystals and that sort of thing. She's had a ball.' She walked next to him to the farmhouse. 'I've had a brilliant time too. But I think I could sleep for a week if I was given the chance.' She stopped walking and raised her left foot. 'And I have a blister on that heel that's the size of a small mandarin.'

He winced. 'Would you like me to give you a piggyback then?'

'What, you have enough energy to carry me?'

Zac laughed. 'I'd always find it from somewhere if I needed to.' He turned his back to her. 'Hop on. I'm thirsty and I could do with getting one of those drinks before they disappear.'

'I hadn't thought of that.' She leapt onto his back and wrapped her legs around his waist.

Zac took her ankles in his hands and pretended to canter into the house, making Melody squeal with excitement. He went into the hall and almost collided into his mother as she came out of the kitchen carrying a tray of nibbles.

'For pity's sake, Zac,' she shouted, swerving to stop from banging into him. 'Why can't you act your age occasionally?'

'Sorry, Mum,' he said, pulling a face and pressing his lips together to stop from laughing.

'Sorry, Lindy,' Melody said, trying to climb down.

Zac let go of her legs and saw she was blushing. 'Don't worry. Mum wasn't really cross.'

'No,' Lindy said from down the hallway. 'But I would have been if this lot had crashed to the floor.' She turned to them. 'While you're there, you can fetch the rest of them and bring them outside. Everyone is starving.'

As they passed the living room Zac heard voices. Unable to hear what was being said but seeing a serious expression on his father's face, he stepped into the room to check his father was all right.

'Everything OK, Dad?' The words were just out of his mouth when he noticed Brodie standing behind one of the chairs looking awkward. When his father didn't immediately reply, Zac turned his attention to his friend. 'Brodie? Anything the matter?'

Brodie shook his head at the same time Gareth said, 'All fine in here, thanks. If you'll give us a moment, Zac, then we'll join the rest of you outside.'

Confused, Zac did as he was asked, leaving the room and closing the door behind him.

'I wonder what that was about?' Melody said quietly.

Zac shrugged. 'No idea. Come on, let's get those trays for Mum.'

They went into the kitchen and each picked up two trays. Studying the blinis with smoked salmon, others with cream cheese and another tray of rolled pieces of Parma ham, slices of melon and strawberries, Zac breathed in the smell of the delicious food he couldn't wait to eat. 'These smell as good as they look.'

'As do these,' Melody said, holding her two trays in front of him so he could see the array of cheeses, meats and crackers. 'Let's get a move on.'

He wondered what had been going on between his father and Brodie. Maybe it was something to do with one of the animals and his father was simply asking for Brodie's advice. He had no idea but hoped there wasn't anything for him to worry about.

As soon as they stepped outside, Lettie hurried over and took a tray from each of them. 'Thank heavens – I thought you'd never get here,' she teased. 'Get yourselves drinks and take a seat,' she said. 'You must both be exhausted and I want to thank everyone for all you've done during the run-up and over the past two days.'

Zac took the other tray from Melody. 'Go and sit down – that blister must be smarting badly.'

'It is a bit.' She went to sit at one of the tables where there were two seats left.

'Shall I get your usual?' he asked, liking that he knew what her usual was.

'Please.'

A few minutes later with a bottle of lager in one hand and a glass of white wine spritzer for Melody, Zac went to sit down next to her. 'There you go.' He took a sip from his bottle. 'I hope my sister doesn't speak to us for too long. I hadn't realised how hungry I was until I smelt that food.'

His mother placed one of the trays of blinis in front of him and Melody. 'There you go,' she said, her eyes twinkling in amusement. 'Try not to eat them all.'

When his mother had gone, he turned to Melody and keeping his voice low whispered, 'She's always had amazing hearing. It's scary sometimes.'

Melody laughed. 'Stop being dramatic.'

'There's nothing dramatic about it. She heard what I'd said and I was only speaking to you.'

'You have a loud voice, Zac.' Melody grinned. 'Maybe her hearing is perfectly normal and she just happened to overhear you moaning about being hungry.'

He had to admit that probably was the case. 'You go first.' He indicated the food and as soon as Melody had taken one for herself, picked up a blini and popped it into his mouth. 'Mmm, they really are tasty.'

31

MELODY

After the excitement of the previous two days, Melody felt much better. It was a massive relief that everything had gone to plan, or at least had ended up working out. She thought of Zac and how different he would have been as a husband than Rhys. Not that she knew for certain but having spent more time with Zac and seeing him interact with people of all ages, as well as knowing how he behaved towards her both in front of company and alone, she was already certain that he was a much better man than Rhys could ever hope to be.

He was so unlike Rhys, who only seemed to feel confident by putting others down or picking fault in something they had done. She thought back to the times Rhys had waited until they were about to leave the house to go to a party and had chosen then to question her fashion sense.

She didn't used to have pink hair; that was something she had felt compelled to do once she had left him and moved in with her mother. She supposed it was some sort of act of defiance. She realised he must have been watching her for a little time before accosting her by the car. She would have liked to see the shock register on his face when he saw what she had done to her hair, cutting off six inches and dying it pink. He would have known it was a reaction to him and a nod to her own new-found independence.

She was excited to hear how well they had done with the takings and stood next to Zac and Callum while Lettie and Lindy spoke about the workings-out Lettie was holding in her hand.

'We won't keep you long,' Lindy said. 'Because we're all tired after the running around we've done for the festival.' She indicated her feet. 'If yours are as tender as mine are right now, then you definitely won't want to be hanging around.'

'Get on with it, love,' Gareth grumbled.

'Sorry, yes. Lettie, this was your brainchild, so I think you should be the one to share how well we've done.'

'I am excited to let you all know that with the cash and card takings, plus the five per cent fee paid by each of the stallholders, we've managed to raise four-fifths of the repair costs.'

Melody was delighted. 'That's a splendid outcome,' she said, hoping the Torels and especially Lettie were as happy as she felt.

'It is,' Lettie agreed. 'We will still need to raise the balance, but I'm sure we'll find a way.'

Melody noticed someone move forward and saw Zac and Lettie's Uncle Leonard. He raised his glass of red wine. 'I'm very proud of my niece and nephew for all the hard work they've put in to keep this place going over the past few months. Especially you, Lettie, as you've been the main stalwart here.' He turned to the rest of them. 'For those of you who didn't know, Lettie is not only my niece but also my goddaughter and I'm using that as my excuse to gift the outstanding balance to cover the cost of the repairs.'

'Leonard!' Lindy covered her mouth with her hands. 'That's incredibly generous.'

He shook his head. 'I'm more than happy to do it.'

Melody was tired but relieved that all their hard work had paid off and enough money had been raised to fix the damaged roof. Her throat restricted with unshed tears as Lettie ran forward and hugged her uncle tightly.

'That is very kind of you, Uncle Leonard. You've been such a support to me and I will want to pay you back for this.'

'All I want you to do is continue enjoying running this place.' He kissed her cheek. 'It makes me happy to see youngsters enjoying farming and taking over the reins from us older ones.'

'Who are you calling old?' Gareth laughed, chinking his bottle of lager lightly against his brother's glass. 'I am grateful to you for your offer, but Lindy and I have already decided to cancel one of our trips away to cover the difference.'

'Dad, no,' Lettie argued.

'We want to,' Lindy said, linking her arm with Gareth's.

Melody saw Zac looking thoughtful and sensed he was about to speak. 'Tell you what, why don't you split the cost between you?'

Leonard nodded. 'Yes, good idea. Why don't we do that?'

Relieved that an agreement had been reached, Melody took a drink from her glass. This really was a wonderful family and she was going to hate leaving them.

* * *

The following morning, Melody stretched and stepped out of her bed, wincing when the soles of her feet touched the floor. She hadn't realised until now how much time she must have spent on them during the lead-up to the festival and the event itself. She sat back down and rubbed them. Then feeling a bit better, walked over to the window and sat on the window seat to gaze at the peaceful view across the fields, wanting to make the most of every minute she had left.

She loved this place so much already and had every intention of staying here for as long as she could but needed to return home to start divorce proceedings against Rhys.

She might even be able to come back to the island at some point. Melody was happy to work for nothing just to cover her bed and board. What else could she need money for living in a beautiful farmhouse and being fed better food than she had ever enjoyed before especially now that Lettie had insisted on paying her and Patsy a weekly wage for all their hard work? She didn't go out anywhere that cost money and she had a little in her account for emergencies that she could always dip into if necessary.

She sighed happily, then remembered Rhys might still be on the island somewhere. Talk about tainting paradise. Then again, if anyone was well practised at spoiling things, Rhys was that person. If only she hadn't been charmed by him love-bombing her when they had first met in sixth form. How naive she had been to believe that him telling her everything she wanted to hear made her assume he was the perfect man for her. This situation was her fault. The being caught in the marriage part, she mused, not the violence. That was Rhys's doing. Maybe if she had been a bit more worldly, or simply questioned some of what he told her, even thinking at the time that he seemed too good to be true, then she wouldn't now be having to deal with the repercussions of his most recent behaviour.

A knock on her door snapped her out of her thoughts. 'Come in.'

The door opened and Lettie walked in. 'You OK?'

Melody was about to assure her friend that she was fine, but decided that hiding her feelings about what was going on in her life had helped lead her to this point. It was time to change things.

'I was thinking about how much I love this place and how the only thing tainting my life is Rhys.'

Lettie walked over to the window and sat down next to her. 'And do you think he's still here somewhere?'

'I'd love to say no, but that would be a lie. Rhys doesn't know when to give up on something,' she said miserably.

'He's a bad loser then?' Lettie gave her a knowing look.

Melody sensed a kindred spirit. 'I get the feeling that you know how it feels to have a partner like that.'

Lettie nodded slowly. 'Not one as nasty as Rhys, I'm relieved to say, but I do have some experience in the controlling partner situation.' She stroked Melody's arm. 'Have you been berating yourself for getting involved with him in the first place?'

'Is it that obvious?' Melody asked, embarrassed.

'Only to someone who has punished herself about doing the same thing. My ex – Scott – and I parted ways because I found his controlling behaviour too much to deal with. It was more obvious somehow when he began working at the same firm as me and in the end I couldn't ignore it. I think sometimes you need to experience this sort of quiet, coercive behaviour to understand it.'

Melody sighed, relieved she wasn't the only one, although hating that her friend had also experienced an unhappy relationship. 'Thanks, Lettie. I was beginning to feel very frustrated with my lack of ability to judge someone's character.'

'These people who say all the right things do it to cover up for their shortcomings,' Lettie said quietly. 'You weren't supposed to see his true personality.'

The thought troubled her. 'So how will I know whether to trust my instincts in the future?'

Lettie nudged her. 'I have to admit I suspected there might be something between you and Callum and I was a little surprised when I saw that you and Zac had become close.' She rested her hand on her heart. 'Not that my brother isn't a great guy, because he is and I can see he has feelings for you, too...'

Melody couldn't help smiling. Zac was wonderful, she mused, a warm feeling flowing through her. 'Callum is very good-looking and good company.'

Lettie laughed. 'If he's so perfect, why did you two only go out on a couple of occasions? If you don't mind me asking.'

'Of course I don't. I did like him, but I think I knew within the first five minutes of our first, and only,' she added with emphasis, 'date, that although he's an amazing man, and a kind one...' Melody suspected a dreamy look had crossed her face '... he's not Zac.'

'He's not,' Lettie agreed. 'I'm happy for you both. My brother hasn't had an easy time of it either,' she said half to herself.

Melody decided that now might be the perfect time to ask about that. 'Lettie, I've been wondering about something.'

'Go on, what is it?' Lettie tilted her head slightly to one side, looking at her curiously.

Feeling a little unnerved for a moment, Melody almost changed her mind. She should be asking Zac about anything personal to him, but worried that if she did he might be concerned about telling her. Deciding that if she was hoping for some kind of relationship with Zac, she needed to know more about him regardless of how upsetting it would be to hear it. She had had enough of hearing others who knew him well, like his sister and Kathleen, refer to things in his past in vague terms, and needed to know more.

'I was thinking about something Kathleen mentioned the first time I met her,' Melody began. 'About Zac. He's such a good man and always seems to want to make everyone happy, but I can't help thinking there's something...' She struggled to find the exact word to describe what she wanted to say.

'Sad about him, do you mean?' Lettie suggested, looking unhappy herself at the thought.

Melody nodded. 'Yes, sad.'

Lettie gazed ahead of her and thought before speaking. 'Zac hasn't been in a relationship for a couple of years,' she said. 'Oh, I'm sure he's seen the odd girl, but nothing serious in that time.' She looked at Melody. 'Are you sure you want to hear this?'

Melody wasn't sure how she was supposed to decide when she had no idea what she was about to be told but reasoned that if she was to continue getting closer to Zac, especially after her dreadful relationship with Rhys, then she needed to know as much as possible about him. 'Yes. Go on.'

Lettie pushed her hands through her hair and folded her arms. Melody could see she was uncomfortable and struggled between telling Lettie not to worry about telling her and wanting to know more about Zac.

'It's fine, if you'd rather not tell me,' she said, her conscience getting the better of her.

'No. I think you should know. I'd want to know this if it had happened to Brodie, and I can see that my brother seems happier than I've seen him look for a long time. Although...'

Melody knew where this was leading. 'You're not sure how it will work long-term because I have to return home shortly.'

Lettie sighed heavily. 'He's going to be devastated when you do leave.'

Melody hated to think of Zac being upset, but what could she do? She would also stay here if things were different but they weren't and that was all there was to it. At least until she had sorted out her divorce.

'The situation isn't ideal,' Melody said quietly. 'But it's early days yet and who knows what might happen.' Aware they would soon have to get to work, Melody said, 'You were telling me about Zac's previous relationship.'

'Yes, right. Well, Zac was on tour. It was his biggest tour yet and he was incredibly excited about it. At the time he was seeing a girl called Jazz. They met each other on their first day at university and just clicked. They were really cute together,' Lettie said wistfully.

Melody's stomach dipped and it hurt to think of Zac with someone else, especially someone he had clearly been very close to.

Then seeming to recall who she was talking to, Lettie apologised. 'Sorry, that was insensitive of me.'

'It's fine,' Melody fibbed. 'Please carry on.' She wasn't sure why she was torturing herself this way, but knew that if she was going to find a way to be with Zac even if long distance, then she had to know all there was to know about him. There was no way Melody intended on getting into a serious relationship again and getting caught out like she had done with Rhys.

Lettie took a deep breath. 'As I said, Zac was away on tour. One day Jazz called Mum in floods of tears.'

'Oh no, why? What had happened,' Melody asked, shocked.

Lettie stared at her for a moment. 'You're sure you want to know this?'

Hating to think that Lettie was about to change her mind about confiding in her, Melody smiled at her sympathetically. 'I do.'

'OK then. Well, she broke the news to Mum that she was pregnant.'

Shocked, Melody bit her lower lip to stop from making a sound. Then asked, 'Did Zac know?'

'He did. They had discovered she was pregnant a couple of weeks before the tour. She hadn't wanted him to go, but Zac felt it was too late for him to realistically let the tour management down, so insisted he had to.' Lettie shrugged one shoulder. 'The tour was for three months and he flew home a few times during that period. Apparently each time he came back, she pleaded with him not to return, but it would have ruined his reputation if he let them down, so he insisted he had to keep going.'

'I suppose his reasoning about the pregnancy,' Melody said, speaking as the thoughts entered her head, trying to under-stand what it was like for both parties, 'was that it was still early days and it wasn't as if he would miss the birth of the baby.'

'That's it, I imagine. Also, Jazz was close to her family and had a good support network of friends around her.' Lettie sighed. 'I met Jazz many times, and liked her. To a point.'

Surprised, Melody asked, 'What do you mean?'

'I don't want to be unfair, but I always felt that she was the dominant one in their relationship.' She stared silently at Melody as if deciding whether or not to say what she was think-ing. 'That Zac loved her more than she did him.' She winced. 'Sorry, but you wanted the truth.'

'I do.' Melody could have done without that particular nugget though, she decided.

'Well, I suspect part of her being so angry about him going on the tour was Zac doing what he wanted for a change rather than agreeing to do what Jazz insisted he did. She did mean a lot to him but so did the tour and...' Lettie frowned '...Zac knew that if they were to have a future together, and the baby, then he needed to earn a living. Letting everyone down on the tour by backing out could ruin that for him. For them. But Jazz couldn't seem to understand that.'

Melody wondered why Zac had never mentioned having a child, and then it dawned on her. 'What happened?'

Lettie swallowed. 'It was heartbreaking. When Jazz phoned my mum it was to tell her she had lost the baby. That would be devastating enough for Zac, but then Jazz turned nasty and insisted that him refusing to stay behind with her had been the cause of her miscarriage.'

'How?'

'The stress it had caused her.' Lettie puffed out her cheeks. 'He came back days later, devastated and shocked that his choices could have led to Jazz losing the baby. He insisted he go with Jazz to speak to her doctor, desperate to understand what could have gone wrong. The doctor explained that they shouldn't blame themselves, and that these things can happen, especially in early pregnancy.'

'So it wasn't his fault then?' Melody asked, relieved.

'No. It wasn't anyone's fault. But it did lead to the end of their relationship. Jazz couldn't forgive him for going away when she needed him with her and Zac couldn't shake off his guilt for a very long time.'

'Poor things,' Melody said, hating to think that anyone should go through something so sad. It made sense to her why Zac put on a happy-go-lucky exterior.

'Yes. I don't know if it was the trauma of losing the baby that made Jazz decide to move on only weeks later but Zac was devastated. It took him the best part of a year to get over what had happened and their break-up, and as far as I'm aware they've had no contact since then. Zac had to grow up pretty quickly after that but there was always a sadness about him that was upsetting to see. Not that he ever admitted it, as I'm sure you can imagine.'

Melody wasn't surprised to hear that. 'I can.' She wondered why Lettie was smiling at her all of a sudden.

'It's only been since you came here that I've seen that sadness slowly vanish.' She sighed. 'My brother likes you, Melody. A lot. And whatever happens between you, I'm grateful that you came here and have shown him that he can fall in love again.'

Melody's breath caught in her throat. It was the loveliest thing anyone had ever said to her.

Lettie cleared her throat and looked at her watch. 'Oops, I've been longer than I expected. We should be getting a move on. I was sent up here by Mum to let you know breakfast is ready.'

Melody got to her feet. 'We'd better hurry up and get to the kitchen then, especially if Zac is up, otherwise there might not be any left for us.'

32

ZAC

Zac was on his way to the car to pick up some shopping for his mother when his mobile vibrated. Groaning, he took it from his back pocket and looked at the screen. Brodie was calling. He wondered what it could be about.

'How's things?' Zac asked, interested to see what Brodie wanted. They got along well but neither phoned the other very often and he presumed something important had happened.

'I'm glad I caught you,' Brodie said, his voice filled with concern.

'What's the matter?' Zac hoped it wasn't anything to do with his sister but couldn't miss the urgency in his friend's voice. His mood dipped.

'Only that I've just popped out of the surgery to check on a patient and while I was talking to the dog's owner, I thought I spotted Melody's ex, Rhys.'

Angry to hear Rhys was still hanging around the village, Zac clenched his teeth together as he tried to calm himself. 'Did you speak to him?'

'No, I didn't get the chance. Sorry. It was a bit of an emergency and I'm sure you understand that the welfare of my patients must come first.'

'As it should.' He thought quickly. 'When did you see him? Recently?'

There was a momentary silence and Zac presumed Brodie was trying to work out the timing. 'It was probably around thirty-five minutes ago. He was near the store. I'm sorry, I didn't get a chance to speak to him.'

'That's fine. Thanks for letting me know. I'll give Callum a call and we'll see if we can track him down. We need to have a word with him and warn him to stay away.'

'I would have thought he got the message when he saw how angry you were after what he did to Melody, but I suppose someone as arrogant as him is used to ignoring other people's feelings.'

'You're not kidding.'

'Let me know how it goes if you do track him down, won't you?'

'I will. Thanks again for the tip-off, Brodie.'

Zac ended the call, fury raging in him that Melody wasn't free to be able to get on with her life simply because this bully wouldn't leave her alone. It wasn't acceptable. He scrolled through his contacts until he found Callum's number and called him, unsure whether he would be working and able to answer.

'Zac? Is something wrong?'

Callum's friendly tone calmed Zac slightly. He regretted that he was about to interrupt his friend's day but knew he would want to help. 'I've just heard from Brodie that Rhys was seen in the village about thirty-five minutes ago. I have to go there to collect some shopping for Mum so I'm going that way already, but I thought if you were in the area, you might join me. I think he's the sort of chap who only backs down when he's outnumbered. I wasn't sure if you were working or not.'

'No. I'm not doing anything right now. I'll make my way there and see if that bastard is still hanging around.'

'Good. I'll be there in a couple of minutes and will look out for you.'

Zac raced to the village but, having spent ten minutes searching for Rhys in every shop and the pubs without success, collected his mother's shopping and hurriedly put it in the cool bag she kept in the boot of the car.

Spotting someone leaning down and chatting by the open window of a taxi, he recognised Callum's T-shirt and walked over to join them.

'Hi,' Zac said, realising he also knew the taxi driver. 'Good to see you, Bill. How's things going?'

'Busy, thankfully. Then again, if they weren't at this time of year I'd be panicking.'

Callum straightened up. 'Bill's been telling me he dropped someone off who fits Rhys's description at the Premier Inn at Charing Cross.'

'That's good to know,' Zac replied, thinking that at least they knew what part of the island he was staying in. 'He would be easy to lose in town with all those back streets.'

Callum nodded, then frowned. 'Don't forget he doesn't know this place like we do, but I do think we should get there as soon as we can to try and see if he's still around.'

'I agree.' He smiled at Bill. 'See you soon, Bill, and thanks for the tip-off about Rhys.' As they walked away from the taxi, Zac patted Callum on the back. 'Good idea asking Bill.'

'Thanks. I thought it was worth a try.' Callum laughed. 'Glad I was right in this case. My uncle is a taxi driver and I know there isn't much that gets past them over here.'

'I need to drop this shopping off at the farm,' Zac said, 'but if you want to come with me, we can head straight to town afterwards.'

'Suits me. I just want to catch that bloke and give him a piece of my mind. I'm sick of poor Melody having to worry about him. It's not right.'

'It isn't.'

'Tell you what,' Callum said as they reached the parking area. 'My car is faster than yours. You take the shopping to the farm, and I'll follow you, then we can take my car to St Helier.'

'Good idea.'

33

MELODY

Melody heard Zac's and Callum's voices coming from the yard. They sounded excitable and she wondered what had happened. She hurried downstairs to see them, shocked when she reached the front door just as they sped off out of the yard, dust billowing from the wheels of Callum's Golf. Where were they going in such a rush? She hoped nothing was wrong.

She decided to go and find Lettie and see what she could do to help her. Unsure where Lettie might be, Melody made for the barn, shocked when she heard Lettie calling her name. She sounded upset, or maybe angry. Melody wasn't sure.

* * *

She turned to see Lettie running towards her from the lower field and hurried to join her and find out what was the matter.

'Has something happened to one of the animals?' Melody asked, assuming that's what might upset her friend the most.

Lettie reached her and bent over to catch her breath,

shaking her head and raising a hand. 'No, they're fine. It's Rhys,' she panted.

Melody's stomach dropped. 'Oh, hell. What's he done now?'

'Brodie's just called me and told me he's seen him in the village. Apparently he was dropped off in town a while ago.'

Zac's speeding out of the yard made sense now. 'Oh no.'

Lettie stood and stared at her. 'What is it?'

Melody explained about Zac. 'I think he had someone else in the car and I'm presuming it's Callum.'

Lettie looked as anxious as Melody felt. 'They'll be racing off to track him down,' she said, wincing. 'Brodie mentioned he had already spoken to Zac about seeing Rhys in the village.'

Aware how vicious Rhys could be, especially when in one of his rages, Melody grimaced. 'We have to go after them. I couldn't bear it if Zac or Callum were hurt.'

'I agree,' Lettie said. 'Come on, let's take Mum's car. We'll try to catch them up. The last thing I need is my brother losing his temper and doing something he'll regret.'

'Yes, I couldn't forgive myself if he got into trouble looking out for me,' Melody agreed as the car slowed at the roundabout at the bottom of Beaumont Hill.

Lettie slapped the steering wheel in exasperation. 'This damn traffic. Typical that it's this bad when we need to get somewhere urgently.'

'It's bad for everyone though, don't forget,' Melody reasoned, feeling guilty that everyone's angst was due to her ex-husband being a complete pain.

'Good point.'

It only took them a further fifteen minutes to reach Charing Cross.

'This one-way system drives me nuts,' Lettie moaned. 'It was much easier driving through town before all these changes were made.'

'It is frustrating.' Melody's stomach was in knots. She scanned the area, desperately trying to spot Zac or Callum, or even better, Rhys. If only she could reach him before the two men managed to.

'Oh no,' Lettie shrieked.

'What is it?' Melody glanced at Lettie to see the direction she was looking in and spotted Zac and Callum running down the street. 'Oh no, there's Rhys. They've seen him. Quick,' she said, going to open the car door to get out and follow them. Rhys was sauntering along without a care in the world. How typical of him.

'What are you doing?' Lettie asked.

'Going after them, of course,' Melody said.

'Wait, I need to come with you,' Lettie insisted.

'But you have to park the car somewhere. I'm fine.' She gave Lettie an apologetic look. 'Sorry, I can't wait. I have to get to them and stop Zac and Callum from confronting him before something dreadful happens.'

Lettie groaned. 'Fine. I'll catch you up. We can't lose Rhys, not now we've seen him.'

Melody got out of the car and slammed the door, immediately setting off at a run. She had no intention of losing Rhys again. She'd had enough. She was going to put a stop to this nonsense once and for all, and she had no intention of letting the men do her dirty work for her.

'Melody!' Lettie called.

Ignoring her friend, Melody gritted her teeth. She could find out what Lettie wanted soon enough. She saw Rhys stop and turn to look in her direction. Damn, Melody thought, guessing he had heard Lettie calling out to her. Callum's step faltered but Zac kept running. Seeing Zac, Rhys looked stunned for a split second before taking off again. He turned and ran down one of the back streets.

'Damn.' She had no idea where he was going and if she lost him now, she doubted she would find him again. Melody kept running, ignoring a couple of surprised looks from holiday-makers out shopping.

He ran down another street and unable to keep him in her sight, she was relieved Zac and Callum were following. She lost them for a moment, then saw a sign saying Hue Street. She was unsure where it would lead them. Assuring herself that Rhys couldn't have expected to see them coming after him or have any of this planned, she doubted he was taking her down a dead end. Even if he was, she decided, she was too furious to care.

She lost him again, then hearing Zac's enraged voice followed by a commotion, turned left down another street and saw he had cornered Rhys by some large wheelie bins. He must have taken one of the small lanes and bypassed the pair of them. She was relieved to see he had caught Rhys.

'You OK?' Callum asked her when she reached him.

'A little out of breath,' Melody said, spotting Lettie bringing up the rear. 'You could have stayed with the car,' she said, hating that her three friends were getting so deeply involved in her drama.

Melody saw Rhys's eyes narrow dangerously. She recognised that look, it came before he lashed out. Zac's fists clenched and he moved forward. Determined not to let Zac get into trouble on her account, she ran forward and pushed her way in between them.

'I can deal with this now, Zac,' she said, turning her back to him as she glared into Rhys's steely eyes.

'No chance. I'm not leaving you to deal with this creature.'

'It's fine. I've got this,' Melody said. 'But thank you for tracking him down, guys.'

Rhys laughed. She ignored his mocking.

'Are you sure?' Zac said after a moment's hesitation. She looked at him and saw his concern and loved him even more for wanting to protect her.

'One hundred per cent certain.'

Melody folded her arms so Rhys couldn't see how badly her hands were shaking, although she wasn't quite sure whether it was through nerves or having needed to run after him. Her legs were a bit shaky too, she realised.

'Why are you still here, Rhys?' she snapped, turning her full attention back onto his contemptuous smirk.

'Why shouldn't I be?'

She noticed Zac's hands were closing into fists then opening again out of the corner of her eye but was glad that he left her to deal with Rhys when she had insisted on doing so. He was clearly struggling to keep control of his temper. But she needed to do this for herself.

'Because there's nothing here for you,' Melody said as calmly as she could manage through gritted teeth. 'Surely even you must understand that by now, Rhys? Our marriage is over. Well and truly finished. Let's be honest, neither of us have been happy for months now.' He went to argue, but she shook her head slowly. 'It's true and, what's more, it's about time you took responsibility for the way you've treated me. Your behaviour was disgusting, but hitting me, well, surely even you must have known that was going way too far. Maybe you even subconsciously knew that by doing so I would leave you, so that you didn't have to make that decision for us.'

It was the first time the thought had occurred to her but

now it had she suspected that's exactly what he had done. He was a coward; it was as simple as that.

He glared at her for sharing their private moments, but she didn't care, aware that doing so took away some of the power he felt he had over her.

Melody held up her hands and pointed over her shoulders to Zac and Callum who she knew were still behind her. Lettie joined them, out of breath for the second time that afternoon. 'I've told my friends everything,' Melody said, aware how much he would hate to think others had been made aware of the way he had treated her. 'I'm not embarrassed to tell them how the man I married ended up treating me.'

'Friends.' He spat the word. 'Don't tell me you and farmer boy here haven't got something going on.'

'We have.' She was taking a chance that her admission might push him too far but was past caring. 'You no longer have any say about the choices I make, Rhys.'

She felt less afraid of him with every word. Her shoulders felt lighter and she wanted to be open about her and Zac, but more than anything had every intention of letting Rhys know exactly where he stood.

His mouth opened to say something but nothing came out.

After a few seconds of staring at her Rhys looked down at his feet and she wondered if he was giving himself time to think of a reaction, or whether he had finally got the message that their relationship was over. Melody's hopes that she had got the better of Rhys rose briefly before she saw a smug expression form on his face and he looked up and smiled at her.

'Who do you think you are to tell me how to behave?' He sneered at Zac. 'And you. You've known her, what? Five minutes?'

She turned to see the muscle in Zac's jaw moving frantically and Melody knew she needed to speak quickly if she wasn't going to lose control of the situation.

'I think we all know you lost your right to have any opinion on what I do when you acted like a thug towards me. Whether you choose to acknowledge it or not, Rhys, you gave me no choice but to leave you. And, what's more, you can be certain that whatever you say or think you're going to do, I will never be coming back.'

'Exactly,' Lettie agreed.

'Now, it really is time for you to leave,' Melody said, desperate to see the back of him but not wanting to give him the satisfaction of knowing how frustrated she was with him.

'It certainly is,' Zac said. 'There's a ferry returning to the mainland in three hours and I'm sure you should be able to embark as a foot passenger.'

'And if I refuse?'

Melody wasn't ready to step back from this fight. 'Then I'll report you to the Jersey Police for assaulting me in the car park.' She glanced at Zac. 'You know I have a witness and I'm sure Zac won't have any reluctance about backing up my story.'

'I'd be only too happy to do that,' Zac said.

Rhys looked from one to the other of them. She could tell he was unsettled by her threat. The last thing he would want is to be arrested, especially in a place where he didn't have his own lawyer; she knew that much.

'And how will you know if I've left?' he asked, a look of bravado on his face.

'Because, Rhys,' Callum explained, a weary tone to his voice. 'This is a small island, and we have friends everywhere. One of my closest friends is a customs officer at the harbour. Another two work in security at the airport. You can be certain we'll make sure all the ports are covered to keep an eye out for you from now on.'

'And I suppose you have photos of me to show them.' He jeered. 'No, of course you don't.'

'Don't be ridiculous, Rhys,' Melody said, losing her temper with him. 'I have photos of you and won't hesitate to share them.'

'We're not kidding, Rhys,' Zac said calmly. 'If you want to be anonymous anywhere, this really isn't the place to choose. Not if you're intending stalking someone who is a friend of the locals.'

Encouraged by the look of defeat on Rhys's face, Melody began to relax.

'Fine, but I want to see to you alone before I leave.'

'What do you think, Melody?' Zac asked, clearly not happy at the thought.

Rhys laughed. 'You two are pathetic.'

Melody waited for Zac to reply and when he did his voice was low and he spoke very slowly. 'Whether Melody is or is not interested in me is irrelevant as far as you're concerned. Your opinion on our relationship is of no consequence to me, and I imagine to her. You are separated, don't forget.'

'Not legally,' Rhys snapped triumphantly.

'Either way,' Lettie said. 'Melody has made it clear she doesn't want you in her life any more. She is finished with you, and I can guarantee you that none of us will stand by and allow you to bully her again.'

'Allow me?' Rhys snapped, spittle flying from his mouth. 'How dare you? You want to watch what you're saying.'

Lettie wiped the spittle from her cheek without diverting her gaze.

Melody was impressed with her friend's calm reaction.

Furious with Rhys, Melody stepped closer to him. 'Be quiet, Rhys. Your threats no longer bother me. Now, why don't you do the sensible thing and leave? Return to the mainland and get on with your life. I'll be starting divorce proceedings soon and have every intention of getting on with my life. I suggest you do too and stop wasting your time hounding me.'

She stared deep into his eyes, determined not to look away first. She needed him to understand she meant what she was telling him. Seconds later Rhys averted his gaze. She had finally got her message across to him. For now.

'Fine. Do what you like. I don't care.'

Not trusting that he meant what he was saying and aware that she still probably had a long battle on her hands while their divorce went ahead, Melody decided to enjoy her triumph while it lasted.

'Now,' Zac said. 'If it's OK with Melody, I suggest Callum and I accompany you back to your hotel, help you pack and give you a lift to the harbour. It's not far, but I have a car parked nearby so there's no need to walk.' He looked at her. 'Melody? Is that all right with you?'

'It is. Thank you.'

Without another look in Rhys's direction she turned and walked away.

34

ZAC

Zac watched Melody speaking with her grandmother while Lettie stood at the sink near Callum, washing her hands, and explained to Lindy all about their encounter with Rhys. Melody looked exhausted.

'How are you holding up after everything that's happened?'

'I feel emotionally drained.'

'I'm not surprised,' Lindy said, opening her arms and pulling Melody into a hug. 'I'm very proud of you for standing up to that beastly man. And proud of the rest of you for forcing him to get on that ferry.' She rested a hand on Melody's shoulder. 'You must feel better knowing he's definitely left the island now.'

Melody didn't react immediately and Zac suspected she was unsure about how long it might be before Rhys took another chance and came back to the island.

Wanting to reassure Melody, he said, 'I think Callum telling Rhys about his friends at both ports should make him think twice before he gets any stupid notion about coming back here again.'

Her shoulders relaxed slightly and he was glad to see his reminder seemed to have helped calm her.

'That's true,' Melody said. 'Hopefully even Rhys won't be that silly. I have to admit, it is a huge relief to have stood up to him and then see the back of him.'

No one spoke for a few seconds.

'Enough of this seriousness,' Lindy said. 'It's a beautiful evening and I've decided we're going to make the most of it and eat outside. You can all help take out crockery, cutlery and everything we need.'

Ten minutes later they were all seated on the terrace and everyone seemed much happier, Zac noticed.

'This is fun,' Melody said.

'Mum likes to make the most of the late summer weather and we tend to have a lot of meals outside.'

'I don't blame her,' Melody said. She looked around her. 'This is the perfect summer scene.'

Zac had grown up eating outside on this terrace with various groups of his parents' friends joining them for evenings such as this one. He tried to look at it through her eyes. There were neatly set-up tables and as always, on occasions like this, his father was standing in front of his barbecue, wearing his favourite 'Cooks Are In Charge' apron he had bought himself years before, concentrating on turning over steaks and sausages with a huge pair of metal tongs. The smell of cooking made Zac's stomach rumble and mouth water. 'I can see what you mean.'

'Barbecues weren't really something my family ever tended to do.' She pointed to the oak posts cemented into the ground on either side of the terrace. 'I mean, someone has taken the time to string lights across each one.' She sighed. 'I'm looking forward to when it's dark and I can see the full effect. And that,' she added. 'Over there.'

Zac gazed across the vast lawn, neatly mowed with huge pine trees that must be hundreds of years old growing in several places, giving much-needed shade. One of them had a huge branch with a swing hanging from it.

'No doubt that was set up for you and Lettie?'

He thought back to their childhoods – they had been idyllic, he now realised. 'The original rope has been replaced, but yes, that was for me and Lettie.'

Brodie brought round a tray of drinks and Zac took one for Melody.

'Fancy a Pimm's?'

She nodded, taking the glass and thanking Brodie.

'It's Mum's favourite. You can take out the mint and cucumber, if you'd rather not have them in there. You'll also find slices of lemon, orange—' Zac thought for a second '—and probably a strawberry.' Zac grinned. 'It's more like a fruit salad than a drink when you think about it.'

She laughed. 'It's not far off it.' She took a sip and groaned in delight. 'Now that is delicious.'

He drank from his glass. She was right – it was delicious.

'I've had quite a few of these over the years but this is the tastiest by far.'

Seeing a shadow cross her face, Zac moved closer to her. 'How are you feeling after the dramas with Rhys in town the other day?'

She shrugged. 'I'm fine really. Still a bit stunned by his nerve coming here and behaving like he did, but relieved he's gone.'

Zac checked no one was looking in their direction and gave her a quick kiss.

'What's that for?' Melody smiled.

'Does there have to be a reason?' he asked, wishing they had some time alone together without the chance of anyone interrupting them. He had an idea. 'If I arranged something, just for you and me, overnight, would you mind?'

She stared at him thoughtfully for a few seconds, and he wished he could tell what she was thinking. Then Zac felt Melody's hand slip into his. 'I'd like that very much,' she whispered.

His heart raced at the thought of the two of them with time on their hands, alone. 'You seem very certain about that,' he teased.

'That's because I am.' She kissed him. 'So, where were you thinking of taking me for this rendezvous then?'

He tapped the side of his nose. 'That's for me to know and you to wait and find out.'

Melody looked deep into his eyes. 'You don't know yet, do you?'

He laughed. 'Fine, no, I don't. To be honest, the idea only just occurred to me.'

'Because we never have time by ourselves and we'll be parting ways soon, you mean?'

He saw the sadness in her face at the mention of them having to say their goodbyes in a week. 'Exactly that.'

She took a sip from her drink. 'I'm taking so many amazing memories home with me and to have a night together alone with you will, I'm sure, be perfect.'

He felt his mood deflate slightly. 'You don't think that maybe it'll make things even harder than they're already going to be after we do this?'

She nodded. 'Most probably, but I wouldn't let that put me off, and I imagine you won't either.'

He shook his head. 'Hell, no.'

Lindy banged a tray with a serving spoon, making Melody jump and Zac roll his eyes in irritation. 'Why she can't just call out to us, I don't know.'

Melody went to go to the table, just as it dawned on Zac exactly where he would take her. He only hoped there was availability. It was still not quite autumn and there were a lot of holidaymakers on the island. He walked next to her to the tables. 'I know exactly where I'm going to take you,' he whispered.

Melody stopped walking and looked up at him. 'Where?' she asked, an excited look on her tanned face.

'You'll have to wait and see.'

After supper, when Lettie had left to spend the rest of her evening at Brodie's cottage, Patsy had retired to her room to continue working on her next book and his parents were in the sitting room watching something on the television, Zac suggested he and Melody go for a drink at the pub.

'It's a beautiful evening and if this winter is anything like that last one, we should make the most of the warm weather while we have it.'

Half an hour later Zac left Melody to get comfortable at the last table outside the pub, nestled among tubs of colourful trailing geraniums and ivy, while he went inside to buy their drinks. When he came outside, he stopped on the doorstep and watched the girl he loved for a few seconds. She was gentle and kind to everyone and there was something refreshing in the way she never seemed to try to fit in with current fashions, or the usual social-media-influenced women he usually dated.

Melody seemed to sense his arrival and looked up, smiling at him and causing Zac's stomach to flip over. She really was the perfect woman for him in every way. 'You were quick.'

He placed their drinks on the circular metal table and sat opposite her. 'I think my timing was spot on. There's a large group of people in there being served just after me and they'll probably want to come outside like the rest of us.' He raised his glass to her. 'To a happy last week of your visit.'

'It's all going far too quickly,' Melody said. Zac listened as she told him how much she and Patsy had enjoyed their time on the island. 'It's been wonderful getting to know your family and friends. And we've loved living on the farm. It's such a peaceful, pretty place.'

'I'm glad you've enjoyed your time there.'

She took a sip of her drink then set it down and rested her elbows on the table and her chin into the palm of one hand. 'We've loved every moment. I know we're both sad that our time here is almost over.' She looked around while he watched her wistfully, wishing he could persuade her to stay. 'Even this village is like something from a picture book.' She sighed.

'You don't have to go.' He said the words without meaning to. He knew she was close to her grandmother and couldn't imagine Patsy wanting to stay long term when she had a home and family back in Scotland to return to.

'I don't want to,' she said, gazing into his eyes. 'I've been happier here than I have been for a very long time. And most of that is due to meeting you and spending time with you. You've made this trip very memorable for lots of reasons, Zac.' She smiled. 'I'll miss the farm and your family but most of all I'll miss you, very much.'

He reached out and took her hands in his, happy they had found each other. 'You know my mum has offered for you to stay on at the farm and I know she meant what she said.' He watched her expression change and before she even told him her answer he knew what it would be.

'I can't think of anything nicer, I really can't, but I came with Gran and need to go back with her. And then there's my divorce. I want to get that sorted as soon as I can. I still need to have a talk with my mother about this and explain more about what's gone on between Rhys and I, and I won't feel free of him until the divorce has been finalised.'

He understood and said so. 'There's no reason you can't come back again though once Patsy's settled back at home and everything with Rhys has been sorted out, is there?' he asked hopefully.

'It might not be that easy though.' She looked as if she was struggling to contain her emotions. 'The thing is that Gran is used to me helping with her podcasts.' He wasn't sure what that had to do with Melody not coming back but didn't like to question her.

'She's always been there for me and I feel obliged to be there for her whenever she needs me. I've also got the sketches for her next book to finish. I'm sorry,' she said miserably. 'I know that's not the answer you were hoping for, but I can't let her down now, especially not when she's always been there for me.' She took his hands in hers and looked down at them. 'Anyway, I enjoy spending time with her and want to make the most of having her around.' She reached up and rested her hand on his right cheek. 'I'm so sorry.'

Zac tried to hide his disappointment but could tell by the guilty look on her face that she realised how he was feeling. 'There's no need to apologise. We can't always have what we want.' He thought back to his previous relationship and why it had ended too abruptly.

She drank some of her lager. 'Maybe if you get any gigs near our home, then you could come and visit us. We could spend some time together, maybe, and go out together?'

He loved that she was trying to find ways to make sure their relationship, for what it was, didn't have to end with her leaving Jersey. It wasn't a perfect solution, but it wasn't an ending either. Not really. He would find a way to make things work somehow. Maybe he could only agree to tours around the United Kingdom, so they could see each other regularly. He told her his thoughts.

'I like that idea,' Melody said happily.

'Good. It's a start.' He smiled at her. 'I might have spent the summer here on the island, but as you know I have a tour coming up. I can't afford to refuse too many jobs or I'll lose out on some of my more lucrative gigs, but hopefully it won't be too long until I'll be on the mainland again.'

She beamed at him and he was relieved to see that she had truly meant what she said about hoping to see him again. 'That makes me very happy,' she said, raising her glass to say cheers.

'Me too.' He tapped his glass against hers, then stood and leant over the table to kiss her. Their tentative plans weren't perfect by any means, but what they had already proposed was better than nothing. A lot better.

It dawned on him that maybe this was the best way forward for now. After all, this way they would have the chance to spend more time together and get to know each other better. Then, maybe Melody would find a way to come back and give island life another go.

35

MELODY

A couple of days later, Melody had just finished replenishing the honesty box with Lettie and returned to the house. She was thinking about the story Lettie had told her about Zac's past relationship and wondered whether she now knew him well enough to broach the subject. Would it be too nosy of her to do that though? She wasn't sure. But as her gran had often told her, there was no harm in speaking to someone as long as you accepted that the person you asked the question of might not wish to tell you.

She heard Zac call her name and went over to the window and looked down at him. 'Do you want me for something?'

'I do.' He waved for her to join him out in the yard.

'What is it?' she asked, excited to see him as she always was now. He had a look of satisfaction on his face and she was fascinated to know why.

'I've booked us a night's stay somewhere special. I'm afraid I could only get one night, but it's at least at the place I was hoping to book for us.'

She flung her arms around his neck. 'That's so exciting. Where?'

'Nope. It's a surprise.'

She pursed her lips. 'Right then. When?'

'Tonight?'

'That soon?' She was astonished, although she wasn't sure why. She knew that Zac could be impulsive and loved him for his enthusiasm. And, she reminded herself, it wasn't as if they had all that long before she had to leave again. She pushed away the thought and flung her arms around him. 'I'm so excited. I'd better let Gran know.'

'I've already mentioned it to her, and to my family. They all know we're going out together for the night and that we'll see them at some point tomorrow evening.'

She bit her lower lip, planning what she needed to pack before going. 'Do I need something smart to wear?'

He looked a little thrown by the question and then concerned.

'What is it?' She hoped she hadn't said the wrong thing.

He winced. 'It's not a posh sort of place, Melody. It is somewhere special though that I think you'll like.'

She kissed him. 'Zachary Torel,' she said, laughing when he winced at her use of his full name. 'You could have planned to pitch a tent up at Les Landes and I would be happy.'

'Damn,' he said, frowning. 'If I'd known I could get away with that I wouldn't have booked the place we're going to.'

'Very funny.' She pushed him lightly on his shoulder. 'When do we leave then?'

'In a couple of hours.'

* * *

It took a while before Melody realised someone was calling for her and Zac, interrupting their stroll around the garden. Zac groaned.

'Is that your mum's voice?' Melody asked, intrigued to understand the urgency she could hear in Lindy's voice. Excitement too, she realised.

'We're going to have to see what this is all about.' He gave Melody's hand a squeeze as they made their way across the lawn together. 'I'm sorry, sweetheart. I don't know how she does it but my mum always manages to find a way to interrupt our time together somehow.'

'It's fine,' she said. He had called her sweetheart, Melody mused dreamily. Even Lindy interrupting them couldn't dampen Melody's mood to hear him say that to her.

They entered the house and found his parents, sister, Brodie and her grandmother congregated in the living room. 'What are you all doing here?' Zac asked.

Patsy immediately hurried over to Melody's side. 'I'm sorry about this but there's been some exciting news.'

'Mum, what's this all about?' Zac asked. 'Is everything all right?'

'Sorry, son,' Gareth said, slapping Zac on his back. 'Your mother insisted this couldn't wait.'

'Of course it couldn't, Gareth, we have a plane to catch first thing in the morning.'

Zac went to stand next to Melody again, took her hand and mouthed sorry. 'Since when are you going away so soon?'

Gareth gave them a weary look. 'Since she booked a last-minute cruise this morning.'

'Yes,' Lindy said, glaring at her husband as if it was his fault. 'Only I didn't know then that my daughter would be getting engaged and now we can't cancel without losing our money.'

Had she heard right?

Lindy turned her attention to Melody. 'We had to pay the entire cost of the trip, you see.'

'Sorry,' Zac said. 'Did you say Lettie's engaged?'

Lindy held her hands up in exasperation. 'Yes.'

Melody struggled not to laugh at the altering expressions on Zac's face. Wanting to divert attention from his confusion with his mother, Melody sought out Lettie, seeing her and Brodie over by the dining table, setting up two bottles of champagne and several glasses.

'Congratulations, you two,' Melody said, delighted for them. She ran to hug first Lettie, then Brodie. 'This is amazing news.' She looked down for Lettie's left hand in case she was already wearing an engagement ring, and there it was. Melody gasped. 'Oh, Lettie, what a stunning ring.'

Lettie lifted her hand, the widest smile on her face. 'Brodie chose it, too. My fiancé has wonderful taste.'

'Fiancé,' Brodie said to himself as if trying out the word. He beamed at Lettie, the look on his face one of such happiness that it took all Melody's efforts not to cry. 'I'm just relieved she said yes.'

Lettie nudged him. 'But what if I hadn't liked the ring?' she teased.

'I'd have changed it but taken you with me to choose the replacement, of course.'

'Right,' Lindy said, handing one bottle to Zac and the other to Gareth. 'I think we should open these and toast the happy couple.' She gave Zac a sideways smile before patting him lightly on his cheek. 'This is so exciting, don't you think?'

'It is, Mum.' He smiled at Melody, clearly happier now, then looked across the room at his sister and Brodie. 'Congratulations to the pair of you. I don't think I've ever seen you this happy, Letts.'

'That's because I've never been this happy.' She clutched Brodie's arm and beamed up at him.

Melody listened as Lindy tried to persuade her daughter and Brodie to decide on a date for the wedding.

'Give them a break, love,' Gareth said. 'She's only just said yes. There'll be plenty of time for a wedding.'

Melody could see Lindy was having none of it. 'I'm going to need to start planning everything soon though,' she argued. Lindy grabbed Lettie's wrist to get her attention. 'Do you think you'll want to have the reception at Hollyhock Farm?'

'Mum, seriously.' Lettie scowled at her. 'I know you're excited, but Brodie and I haven't had a moment to think about any of these things yet.'

'Don't worry, Lindy,' Brodie said, giving his soon-to-be mother-in-law a peck on the cheek. 'We won't leave you out of any of the planning.'

Melody caught Lettie's eye and could tell she had other ideas. It was going to be an interesting few months in the Torel household.

Melody felt Zac's arm slip around her waist and she looked up at him. 'I'm so happy for them,' she whispered.

'Me too, but would you think I was selfish if I said I hope they won't mind if we decide to go soon?'

'No. I was thinking the same thing.'

He bent to kiss her. 'I like that we're on the same wavelength.'

Melody did too. She noticed Lettie place her hand against Brodie's cheek and kiss him.

'I agree,' Gareth said, cocking his head in his wife's direction. 'Come along, Lindy. Time we were off to do that packing.'

Melody couldn't miss Lindy's surprise.

'Since when do you pack a suitcase?'

He rolled his eyes. 'I think Lettie and Brodie need a bit of time alone together.'

Lettie rushed forward and hugged Melody. 'Sorry to interrupt your evening, but Mum did insist.'

'Don't be silly,' Melody said, hugging her back. 'I'm over the moon for you both. I'm sure you'll be very happy. I wouldn't have wanted to miss celebrating with you all.' She meant what she said. Lettie had been a good friend to her, and Melody couldn't be happier to see Lettie and Brodie this content. 'I'll see you tomorrow when I get back and you can tell me all about Brodie's proposal.'

'I will, don't you worry about that.' Lettie laughed, grabbing hold of Brodie's hand.

'See you tomorrow, lovey,' Patsy said, kissing Lettie, then waving at Melody and Zac. 'Enjoy your evening.'

'I'm sure they will,' Gareth said. 'Let's leave the pair of them alone.'

'Yes,' Zac said, congratulating his sister and Brodie again before taking Melody by the hand. 'We'd better get a move on too.'

Melody could barely contain her excitement when Zac parked at the car park above the slipway leading to the beach at Les Laveurs.

'Are we taking a walk on the beach?' she asked, confused about why they were there. 'Or are we visiting the Military Museum?' She doubted they would be doing the second option.

However impressive the museum was, it wasn't a romantic place to visit.

Zac took her bag from her and then her hand in his and led her along the path with long Marram grass either side but didn't answer her. All he did was smile and give her a wink. 'You'll soon find out,' he said, continuing to walk.

They passed the museum and a set of steps leading to the beach but kept going. Just when she was thinking that maybe he had planned to camp somewhere for the night, Zac stopped.

She turned and looked up the pathway leading to the boat-shaped Art Deco folly, thinking how it should look out of place standing proudly above the beach but seemed to fit in perfectly well to the landscape somehow.

She waited for Zac to walk on again, or say something and when he didn't do either, she looked at him, wondering if she was missing something. He turned to her and smiled but still didn't speak.

Then it dawned on her and she gasped. 'You haven't booked us to stay here. Have you?' She could barely breathe; the anticipation that he might confirm her suspicions was too intense.

'I have.'

Melody's mouth dropped open and she quickly covered it with her free hand. 'Honestly?'

He laughed. 'Yes. You told me how much you loved it that first time you saw it, and as luck would have it they have one night free, but it had to be tonight.'

She squealed in excitement and grabbed hold of him around his waist, kissing him. 'You are perfect, Zac Torel. Do you know that?'

'Er, I wouldn't go that far, but I'm relieved you're happy.'

'Happy! I'm ecstatic.' She let her arms fall from around his waist. 'Well, are you going to show me inside, or are we spending the night out here?'

'You're so impatient,' he said, leading her up to the door.

She waited for him to take the key from his pocket and unlock the door, not caring that she had a beaming smile on her face that probably made her look a little odd to the dog walker who was passing. She was trying not to show how intrigued she was to have a peek inside the property.

He stepped back to let her go inside first. Melody stood trying to absorb every detail inside the barge-shaped property. It was incredible. She listened as Zac explained how the building had been requisitioned by the Germans during the occupation, how it had also been used as everything from a clinic by a doctor who specialised in dealing with stutters to a scout hut.

'But it's now owned by Jersey Heritage, isn't it?' she said, recalling the information she already knew. Everything was perfect, from the lounge diner that took up most of the building with its perfectly polished walnut herringbone flooring, to the 1930s furniture.

'There's even a kitchen,' she said, excited to see it seemed to have everything anyone might need. Finding the bathroom, Melody was relieved to see a pristine loo, basin and even a shower. 'There are two portholes in here, too, just like in the kitchen,' she shouted excitedly, hearing Zac laugh with amusement at her excitement. She spotted a wide ladder fitted in an alcove and read the plaque. 'We go up here to the roof,' she said. 'I hadn't noticed there was an area up there too.' She gasped as an idea occurred to her. 'We could go up there later when it's dark, drink cocktails and take a blanket to lie down and watch the stars together.'

'We could. Although I'm not sure we have any ingredients for cocktails right now.'

'I don't mind.'

She caught Zac watching her, aware he was enjoying her delight at all the discoveries she was making in this incredibly special place. Determined to see everything, Melody went in through the next door and found two tiny bedrooms. She tried to hide her surprise that both only contained bunk beds. She couldn't have hidden her disappointment very well as she returned to the living room, because Zac pointed at another doorway.

'There's a sofa through there, which I gather opens out to a very comfortable sofa bed.'

'A double?' she asked, before thinking.

He nodded, looking happy that they seemed to be on the same wavelength.

Melody gazed out of the bedroom window at the view of turquoise waves rolling onto pale golden sand on the beach below the folly. She smiled, feeling Zac's hands slip around her waist as he came up behind her.

He kissed her neck. 'Happy?'

'Very,' she admitted. 'This is the most romantic thing anyone has ever done for me.'

He slowly turned her to face him. 'I'm hoping we'll have many more romantic occasions.'

She liked the thought. It occurred to her that this was the first time any man had ever made her feel like they were meant to be together, and it made her question whether what she had initially felt for Rhys was anything other than naive infatuation.

She slipped her arms around him and held him tightly. 'It's the oddest feeling,' she said almost to herself. 'But I feel as if I've come home.' Then, wondering if she was getting carried away by how special he made her feel, looked up at Zac, embarrassed. 'I know that probably sounds a bit strange but it really is how I feel right now.'

Zac kissed her. 'It's exactly how I feel when I'm with you.' He smiled and she relaxed, glad that sharing such feelings hadn't unnerved him. Like it would have done Rhys, she thought before pushing his memory from her mind.

'I wish we had more than one night here,' he said. 'There's so much I want to say to you, although I also just want to be here quietly with you. Just the two of us.'

'I know exactly how you feel,' she said, happy that they were so in sync with their feelings.

He pulled her against him and Melody was only vaguely aware of one hand in her hair and the other holding her tightly against him. She wrapped her arms around him, feeling the taut muscles in his back, and kissed him. Finally they were alone and for a whole night.

36

ZAC

'Isn't it exciting news about Lettie and Brodie?' Melody sighed.

'I am delighted for my sister. And Brodie – he clearly loves her very much.' Just as I love you, he thought, taking Melody's hand and leading her to the table. He knew she had feelings for him and presumed they were fairly deep ones, but after all Melody had dealt with and was still going through, he couldn't expect her to be as open to falling in love as he seemed to be.

'I've got us a bottle of champagne?' he said, holding it up. 'I thought we could toast each other and talk about what happens next.'

Melody laughed with delight at his thoughtfulness. She didn't say anything but waited for him to fill her glass, then went with him to sit on the sofa. Zac turned towards her, his left arm resting on the back of the sofa, and raised his glass.

'To us, whatever that means.'

Melody grinned. 'I like that.' She raised hers to chink with his. 'To us, whatever that means,' she repeated, before taking a sip of the bubbly liquid. 'We do have a lot to work out, don't we?'

'Unfortunately, it seems that way, but I'm sure we can sort something that suits us both.' He saw her expression change and wasn't sure what it meant, then it occurred to him that she had found out about him and Jazz. 'You know, don't you?'

'If you mean about you, Jazz and her losing the baby, then yes.'

Zac tensed. Was their relationship about to come to an abrupt end just when he thought things were really starting to go somewhere? He studied her face and watched as she took another sip of her drink, deep in thought. 'It wasn't my finest hour.' He cringed at his words. 'That is...'

She reached out and rested her hand on his knee. 'I'm not judging you, Zac. You couldn't help what happened just like Jazz couldn't. Horrible things happen sometimes and it's up to each of us to find a way to deal with it,' she said quietly. 'I only meant that I understand you've also had difficult things to cope with relationship wise.'

Relieved to hear her comforting words, Zac relaxed back into the sofa. 'It was a heartbreaking time, especially for poor Jazz. I still feel guilty for not being there for her.' He thought about the last time he had seen his ex, pregnant again, newly married and looking the picture of happiness. 'We knew each other vaguely from Jersey. We were the same age but at different schools and I sometimes saw her in town or down by the beach but was often too shy to speak to her. It was only when we met that first day at uni that things really clicked between us.'

'I imagine you didn't have to part ways during holidays then, if you're both from here?'

It had worked out perfectly for most of the time, he realised. 'No. We travelled back to the island together, even got jobs during the summer holidays in the same place if we could.' He hoped Melody didn't mind him being this open. He tried to study her expression more deeply. 'I'd understand if you didn't want to know all this.'

She seemed shocked by his question. 'No, I do.' She smiled. 'I was wondering how long you were together?'

He thought about it. 'About four and a half years.'

She didn't say anything so he decided to share what had happened between them. He knew a lot about her troubles with Rhys and if he wanted a future with her then he needed to share parts of himself that he kept hidden. He told her about bumping into Jazz and her new husband. 'It was last year,' he explained. 'She had moved over to Australia to be with him. They married and came here on honeymoon. I had always dreaded seeing the pair of them together and until then I had presumed I would feel upset seeing her with someone else, especially someone serious, but it was not like that at all. There was a sereneness about her I'd never seen before, a confidence. She was with her husband and Jazz was the one to wave me over to chat when we spotted each other on opposite sides of the road.'

'That must have laid a lot of ghosts to rest for you?' Melody said, resting her head on his shoulder.

'It did. We chatted politely for a little while and I could tell she had moved on from what had happened. She even said that although our relationship had ended acrimoniously, she treasured the good times and hoped I was happy.'

'And were you?'

He thought for a moment. 'About her moving on and not holding any ill will against me, absolutely. With my work, yes. That's always made me happy because I love what I do.' He put his arm around her and snuggled closer to her, careful not to spill their drinks. 'But other than that, I knew something was missing.'

'Like what?'

She sounded as if she genuinely didn't know. Zac's heart filled with even more love for her. 'Like this. You. You're the first person my family have seen me with since that relationship ended. I hadn't dared risk becoming involved with anyone else, not seriously.'

'No?'

'Not after not being able to get to Jazz when she was miscarrying and letting her down so badly.'

'Zac, that's so sad.' She hesitated. 'You do know that although it didn't work out between you and Jazz that it can be different for us, don't you?'

'I suppose so.'

'It's true. At least you now know Jazz is fine after everything that happened between you.'

'More than fine. She's happier than she ever was with me.'

'I'm glad you're both OK.'

'I am, too.' He was silent for a few seconds but before she could speak, he continued, 'Do you know that before meeting you, I don't think I knew what it meant to properly fall in love with someone. I now know what I felt for Jazz was deep but it was a love between two inexperienced people. This feels...' He laughed, feeling awkward. 'It'll sound odd.'

'Go on.'

'Well, it's not the same thing at all. I feel like this is a grown-up love. An all-encompassing deep love, if you know what I mean.' She stilled and he worried he might have said the wrong thing. Just because he was ready for a serious relationship, Melody might not be, especially with all she had to contend with. He hoped he hadn't scared her off.

When she didn't say anything after a couple of minutes, he thought he should try to explain further. 'I'm sorry if that felt a bit too heavy.'

She moved slightly back from him and looked up into his eyes. 'You have nothing to feel sorry for, Zac, and you haven't said anything I don't want to hear.' She leant forward and kissed his cheek lightly. 'I was trying to work out how we could make this work between us going forward, that's all.'

'I see.' He tried to take in the implications of her words. 'You mean you feel there is a future for us both then?'

She turned in her seat towards him. 'I'm sure between the pair of us we'll work something out.' Her beautiful turquoise eyes seemed to stare deep into his soul. 'Right now, though, Zac Torel, I think we should forget about talking and start showing each other exactly how we feel.'

Zac watched silently as she took his drink from his hand and placed it along with hers on the nearby coffee table. He was barely able to think. Then moving to face him, Melody placed her knees either side of his thighs on the sofa, took his face in her hands and kissed him.

Zac's mind raced. Was she trying to tell him she loved him too? Could he possibly be that lucky? He wrapped his arms around her back and pulled her further onto his lap, feeling the heat of her body against his, and he kissed her right back.

37

MELODY

Six weeks later

Melody gritted her teeth. For some reason, she couldn't get the shading right on her drawing and it was driving her nuts. She heard a passer-by laugh and thought of Zac and how incredible their night had been together at Seagull, or Barge Aground as Zac insisted it was actually called. She thought back to entering the property that evening and her delight at finding the stairs up to the roof space. So much for drinking cocktails up there and watching the stars together. Then again, she mused, she and Zac would soon be able to watch the stars, drink cocktails together and do many other things whenever they chose to do so.

She smiled to herself as she reminisced about that blissful night and the following morning. Making love with Zac had been exciting, dreamy and more perfect than she could have ever imagined. Was this what it was like to find your soulmate? she wondered, because that's what she was certain they were to each other.

She sighed, recalling how she and Zac hadn't left the bedroom until it was time for them to pack up and depart from the beautiful deco building. It had been the start of their future together even though she had needed to leave the island days later and Zac had flown out to join the tour. Since then, they had only been able to spend time together on a couple of occasions when Zac had been given enough of a break from the tour to catch a flight to London. Melody had flown from Edinburgh and they had made the most of every second. Even with the unusual start to their relationship she believed that their future was turning out to look brighter each day.

'Melody?' Patsy called from the kitchen.

Realising she hadn't had a drink for a few hours, Melody stood and went to see what her grandmother wanted. 'Yes, Gran?'

Patsy was wearing a thick coat and was wrapping a scarf around her neck. She pointed to a sandwich and a cup of steaming tea. 'That's for you. I'm off out for a bit. Glen is coming to fetch me and take me to meet a couple of friends of his for afternoon tea. They're involved in festivals and want to chat to me about taking part in a few of them.'

Melody picked up Patsy's woollen hat and gloves and held them out to her, kissing her grandmother on the cheek after she had put them on. 'That sounds like fun,' she said, then pointed to her late lunch. 'Thanks for looking after me so well. I know I'm a bit lax when I get caught up with my work.'

'It's no problem at all.' Patsy patted Melody's cheek with her woollen glove. 'Don't forget about it and let it go cold, will you? I won't be pleased if I get back later and see you've not had anything.'

'I won't, I promise.'

Hearing a car pull up outside, Patsy cocked her head towards the front door. 'That'll be Glen now. I mustn't keep him waiting. I won't be too late back, love.'

'Take all the time you want, Gran. I've got enough here to keep me busy,' Melody said, following her grandmother to the door and standing on the doorstep to wave at Patsy's new boyfriend, before going back inside and closing the door against the bitter November wind.

She walked back to the kitchen and pulled out a stool at her grandmother's breakfast bar. Wrapping her hands around the hot mug, Melody thought how different her and her grandmother's lives were since hurriedly leaving Edinburgh that summer and setting off to Jersey. Both of them were in love with wonderful men, and both of them had so much more to look forward to now than they had done only a few months before. Life really had a way of throwing in a couple of unexpected twists, which was fine, Melody mused, when they were the type to change things for the better.

Smelling the tasty sandwich on the counter next to her, she picked up the top slice of bread to check what was inside. Her favourite: tuna and mayonnaise with a sprinkling of black pepper. Her gran knew her well.

Her stomach gave a noisy grumble and Melody sat quietly trying to work out how to make her sketch work as she took the first bite. She had put too many hours into it to want to scrap it and start again, but she was beginning to think she might have to do that when she heard her phone vibrate. Putting down her sketch pad, she picked up the phone to see Zac's name.

She quickly answered the video call, her heart leaping to see his beautiful mouth smiling back at her.

'You look tired,' she said, wishing she didn't have to wait

another week until they were able to spend a couple of days together again. All she wanted to do was step into his arms and be next to him. He was halfway through his tour now, and although she hadn't seen him for two weeks, she looked forward to him spending a little time with her in Edinburgh.

'You look beautiful,' he said, gazing at her and making her feel slightly guilty for being so honest.

'Zac.' She laughed, pushing her dark hair away from her forehead. 'I look a complete mess. I haven't left Gran's house for two days because she needs these latest sketches finished by Monday, and I need to do something with this mop.'

'I miss the pink,' he teased.

She laughed, doubting it. 'We both know you don't.'

'I'm not going to argue about it, but I really did think you looked cute with your hair that way.'

Her hand went to her hair. 'You don't like it now?'

'I don't mind what colour you have your hair, Melody – you'll always look gorgeous.'

'How's everything going with the tour?'

Zac pulled a face. 'The same as it was when we spoke at midnight last night.' He grinned. 'I'm just counting down the hours until I can take you in my arms and kiss you again.'

'So am I,' she said, impatient to hold him and breathe him in. 'At least this is the last time we'll have to go through this long separation.'

'I agree.'

She realised she hadn't thought to tell him her exciting news. 'I was going to message you earlier,' she said, excited. 'But I wanted to tell you face to face.'

'What is it?'

'No need to look worried, it's good news. My solicitor called me this morning and said that because Rhys didn't contest our divorce proceedings that it should only be a few more weeks, probably five or six, before it's granted through the court.' Just in case he hadn't worked it out, she added, 'So I should be a single woman again by the time your tour is over.'

The look of pure joy on his face cheered her immensely. 'That's brilliant news, Melody. I'm so happy.'

'I can see that,' she said, smiling back at him. 'I think it was Gran threatening to tell his mother that did it.'

'And how's your mother been?'

Melody thought of her mother's sadness that Melody hadn't felt comfortable enough to confide in her. 'We're slowly working through our issues, but we're better than we have ever been,' she said, relieved. 'Anyway, never mind all that. I'm just excited that I'll soon be returning to Jersey full-time.'

'You're not the only one.' He laughed. 'I still can't believe how quickly things change. Good for Patsy, though. I like her spirit.'

'Me too,' Melody said, thinking about Patsy's new relationship with a man she had dated in her twenties but had lost contact with for four decades until meeting at a party soon after they returned to Edinburgh. It was exciting seeing her grandmother happy again four years after losing Grandad. 'I agree with Gran when she insists life is too short to waste time not having fun, and she's seventy-seven. I'm just relieved they're both into their alternative therapies and planning to take part in festivals together. It means I can work on my sketches for her books from Jersey while Gran is having a ball rekindling her romance with Glen.'

'Your gran is a legend,' Zac said. Melody was delighted he thought so and could see he meant it.

'I agree,' she said, picturing her Gran, certain she would be entertaining her new friends round about now with anecdotes about her life. 'I hope I'm like her at her age.'

'I'm sure you will be.' Zac laughed. 'Although I hope I'll be the one you're having fun with.'

'I hope so, too,' Melody said, picturing how perfect their future was going to be.

ACKNOWLEDGEMENTS

Thank you to my wonderful editor, Rachel Faulkner-Willcocks for her patience and help. Also my copy editor, Helena Newton for picking up any continuity errors and suggestions and to Anna Paterson for proofreading this second book in the series.

I can't forget the rest of the brilliant team at Boldwood Books, for their constant support, expertise and for another beautiful cover. Thank you.

My thanks also to Rachel Gilbey from Rachel's Random Resources and her excellent team for reviewing my books on the blog tour and for all their brilliant quotes. I read and am grateful for every one of them.

The inspiration behind the wellness festival in *Second Chances at Hollyhock Farm* comes in part from my sister Kathryn Troy Goddard, a complementary health practitioner, and my lovely relative, Roxanna Le Lievre, a yoga instructor who teaches in various locations on the island including on the beach and at Mont Orgueil Castle.

Finally, I'd like to thank you for choosing *Second Chances at Hollyhock Farm*. I hope you enjoyed this second book in the series and can't wait to bring you the next one.

AUTHOR LETTER

Dear Reader,

I'm enormously grateful for all the love, support and amazing reviews for *Welcome to Hollyhock Farm*. I hope you love *Second Chances at Hollyhock Farm* just as much.

As I mentioned in my author letter for *Welcome to Hollyhock Farm*, I grew up next door to a farm where my sister Kate and I spent much of our time playing with Carlton and Helen-Claire, the children who lived there. They are similar ages to Kate and I and the four of us enjoyed having adventures around the farm. Kate and I called their parents Uncle Alan and Aunty Mon, and some of my favourite memories are enjoying Aunty Mon's delicious rock cakes. She was an amazing lady and sadly passed earlier this year at almost ninety, but my whole family has many fond memories of her. It's magical times like these that make childhood enchanting and I'm grateful I have these incredible memories to look back on.

Second Chances at Hollyhock Farm is Zac and Melody's story and I hope you enjoy spending time with them as their feelings for each other grow and they attempt to overcome the difficulties standing in the way of their future together. I've introduced another new character, Melody's grandmother, Patsy – who is rather like my own mother – as well as revisiting Lettie, Brodie and the rest of the family at Hollyhock Farm, including Spud and his best friend, Derek.

I should mention that although there are rescue alpacas at Hollyhock Farm, these beautiful animals aren't allowed onto the island unless under special licence and as far as I'm aware none of these have been granted.

Until next time, I wish you happy reading and warm wishes from sunny Jersey.

Georgina x

ABOUT THE AUTHOR

Georgina Troy writes bestselling uplifting romantic escapes and sets her novels on the island of Jersey where she was born and has lived for most of her life. She lives close to the beach with her husband and three rescue dogs. When she's not writing she can be found walking with the dogs or chatting to her friends over coffee at one of the many beachside cafés on the island.

Sign up to Georgina Troy's mailing list for news, competitions and updates on future books.

Visit Georgina's website: www.deborahcarr.org/my-books/georgina-troy-books/

Follow Georgina on social media here:

facebook.com/GeorginaTroyAuthor

x.com/GeorginaTroy

bookbub.com/authors/georgina-troy

ALSO BY GEORGINA TROY

The Sunshine Island Series

Finding Love on Sunshine Island

A Secret Escape to Sunshine Island

Chasing Dreams on Sunshine Island

The Golden Sands Bay Series

Summer Sundaes at Golden Sands Bay

Love Begins at Golden Sands Bay

Winter Whimsy at Golden Sands Bay

Sunny Days at Golden Sands Bay

Snow Angels at Golden Sands Bay

Sunflower Cliffs Series

New Beginnings by the Sunflower Cliffs

Secrets and Sunshine by the Sunflower Cliffs

Wedding Bells by the Sunflower Cliffs

Coming Home to the Sunflower Cliffs

Hollyhock Farm Series

Welcome to Hollyhock Farm

Second Chances at Hollyhock Farm

BECOME A MEMBER OF

THE SHELF CARE CLUB

The home of Boldwood's book club reads.

Find uplifting reads, sunny escapes, cosy romances, family dramas and more!

Sign up to the newsletter
https://bit.ly/theshelfcareclub

Boldwood

Boldwood Books is an award-winning fiction publishing company seeking out the best stories from around the world.

Find out more at www.boldwoodbooks.com

Join our reader community for brilliant books, competitions and offers!

Follow us
@BoldwoodBooks
@TheBoldBookClub

Sign up to our weekly deals newsletter

https://bit.ly/BoldwoodBNewsletter

Printed in Great Britain
by Amazon

56132979R00165